FOR THE INTENDED: JOURNAL ONE

Haven Berg

For the Intended: Journal One © 2018 by Haven Berg. All Rights Reserved.

All rights reserved. No part of this book may be reproduced in any form or by any electronic or mechanical means including information storage and retrieval systems, without permission in writing from the author. The only exception is by a reviewer, who may quote short excerpts in a review.

Cover designed by Haven Berg

This book is a work of fiction. Names, characters, places, and incidents either are products of the author's imagination or are used fictitiously. Any resemblance to actual persons, living or dead, events, or locales is entirely coincidental.

Visit Haven Berg's websites:

fortheintended.com
havenillustrates.com

Follow @havenillustrates

Printed in the United States of America

FTI Publishing

ISBN-13: 978-1-948720-01-4

For the Intended is a trilogy comprised of three journals that were discovered on a park bench. The journals belonged to an author who could not publish the story directly. We thought the best way to honor her would be to take it upon ourselves to spread her message. Every effort was made to leave the story as she wrote it. Some minor edits were made, but the tale remains the same.

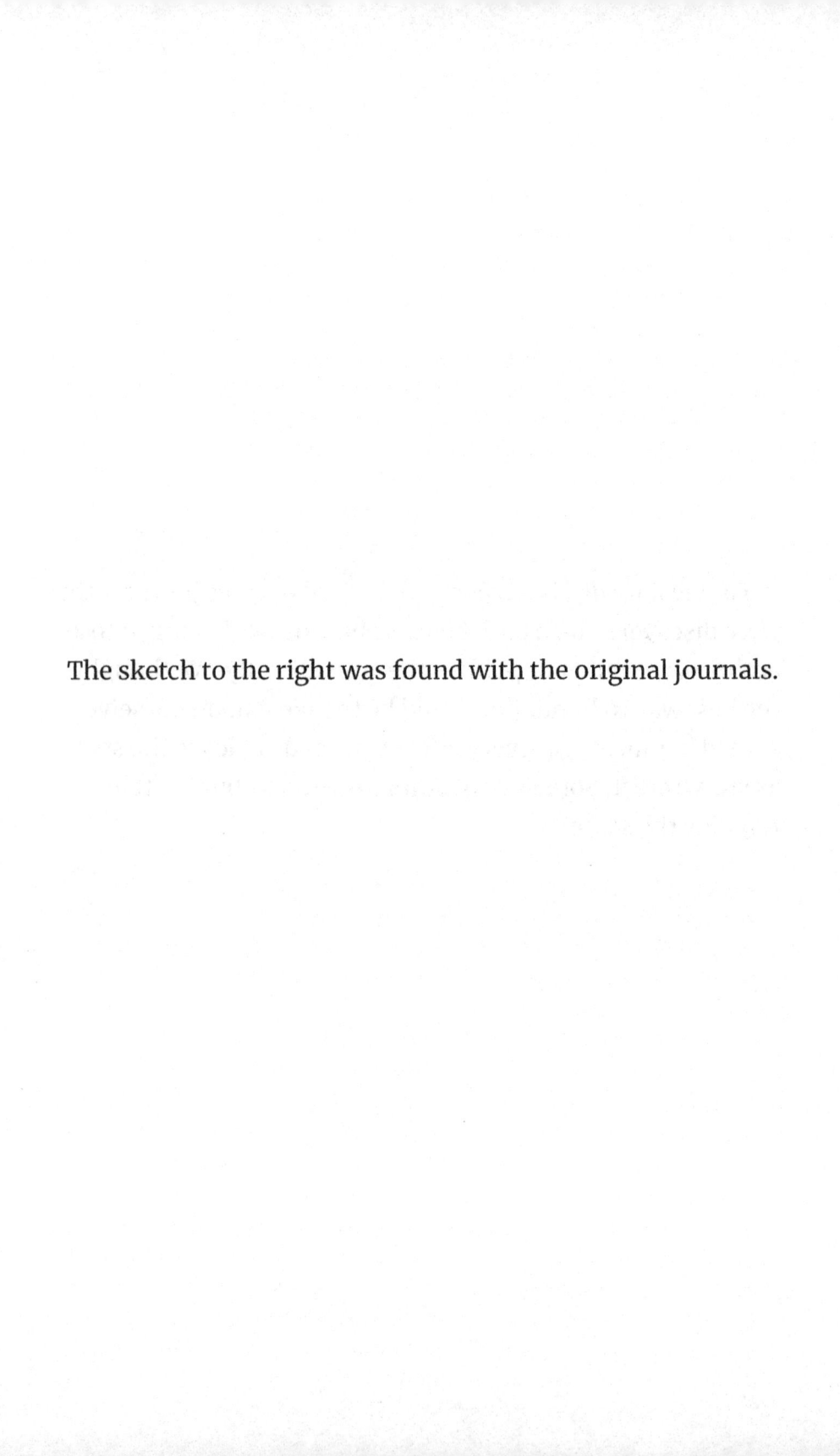

The sketch to the right was found with the original journals.

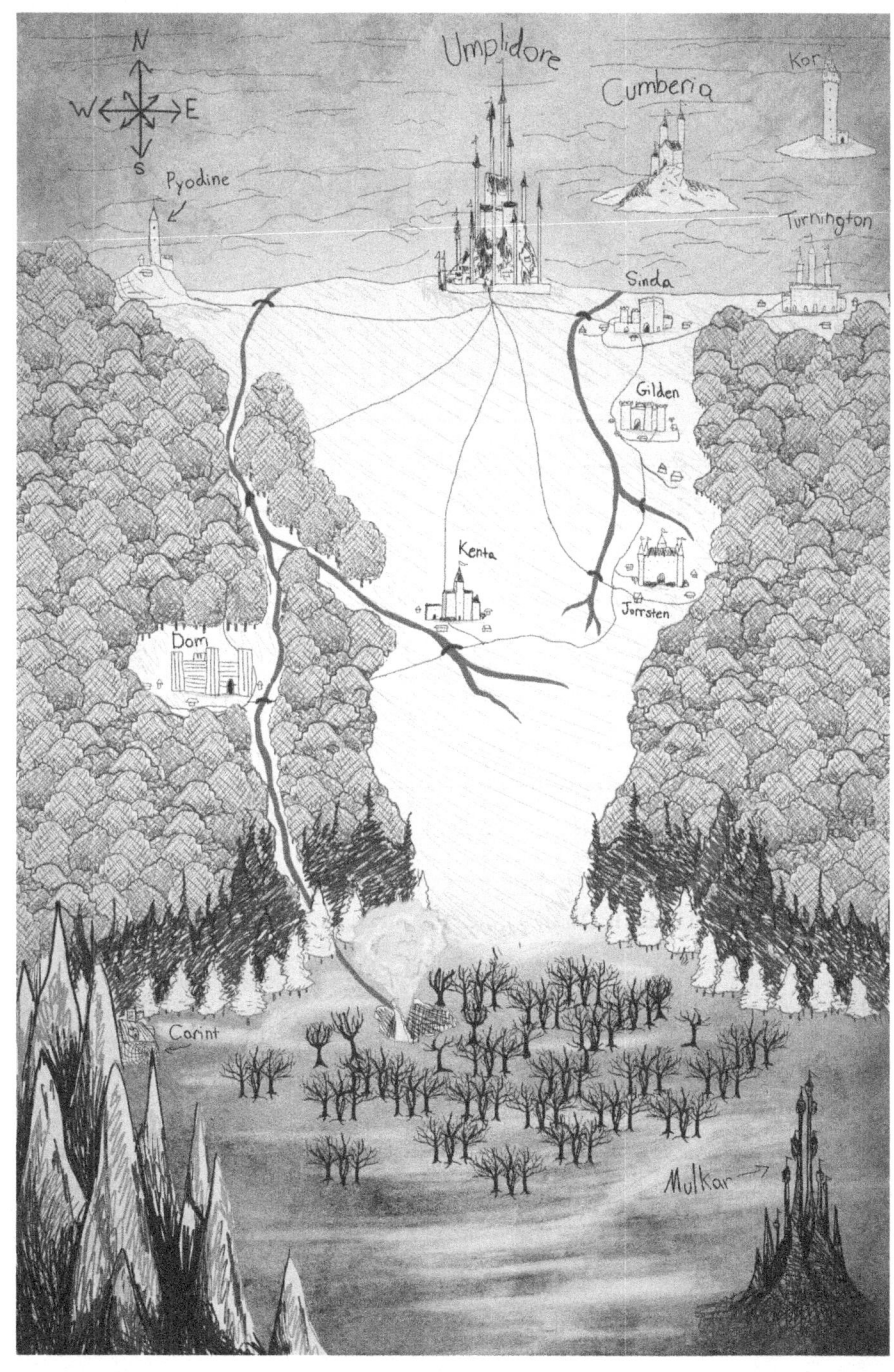

CONTENTS

Prologue 8
Going Home 24
Sunset 33
Royal Privileges 37
Friends 44
Occupational Hazard 52
Sisters 57
Responsibilities 60
Dress Fitting 67
Social Customs 72
In Hot Water 80
Raptor Captor 90
Solitary Confinement 102
Secrets 110
Ham Sandwich 118
"Mud" 126
Lost and Found 131
Drayla 139
Caspian 143
Spontaneous Combustion 164
Naetera 174
Happy Birthday 182

Blue 191
Assertive Assassin 211
Unconventional 224
Family 234
Misunderstanding 240
Shattered 251
Going Home 257

PROLOGUE

Just like that, I found myself in the middle of the woods. I was only seven and knew nothing and no one. My only company was the chilling, starving eyes that silently followed me from the brush.

I wandered aimlessly for days, eating what berries and nuts I could scavenge, sleeping in the hollows of trees, and fleeing from the monsters who made my life so much more difficult than it already was. It was the only life I knew, and even that I didn't understand. Often cold, hungry, and lonely, I desperately longed for a friend.

I grew weaker and weaker each day. Not only from the lack of adequate food or shelter, but from anger and confusion. From not knowing why I existed or how I came to be. Why was I there? Where did I come from? Why was I alone? My head would spin in swirling thoughts as I tried to make sense of my existence. I had no answers . . . just a vague, determined notion that there had to be more to my story.

After a few weeks of barely surviving, something happened that turned fortune in my favor. Though it didn't answer any of the questions about my past, it did give me some hope for the future.

The sun began to set as I dug through a large blueberry bush. I hurried to get them, so I could get out of the vulnerable open, but I heard something rustling on the other side. I cautiously rose up from my knees, trying not to make any noise. I grabbed a broken branch from the ground at my feet and held it ready just in case I saw one of the beasts I had become so used to encountering. Standing on my tiptoes, barely breathing, I peered over the top leaves.

After being alone so long with nothing but monsters for company, I was shocked to discover a boy about my size crouched down by the base of the bush, ravenously snatching up berries. He had the darkest hair I'd ever seen—short and shaggy, but long enough to hang in front of his eyes. He wore all black, which made him appear more like a shadow than a living creature.

He didn't notice me at all as he continued to gulp down berries as fast as he could get them into his mouth. I stepped a bit closer to the bush, trying to get a better look. I gasped as I crunched down on a dead branch.

His head shot upwards as he yelled.

I didn't know why, but I fell backwards into the dirt screaming as well. When I stopped, I realized that he had become quiet too. I watched as a pair of curious eyes peered over the bush.

I wasn't prepared for the intensity of the gaze that met mine. His eyes were a shocking shade of light electric blue. We just stared at each other in stunned silence until he finally demanded with a skeptical glare, "Who are you?"

Instead of answering, I blinked my green eyes and asked him the same question.

A bewildered expression crossed his face. "I don't know," he answered hesitantly.

But his story matched mine, which we soon found out. We were both alone in the woods—having no idea where we came from, outwitting the monsters, and trying to survive. But we realized we weren't alone anymore. Together we could survive, and so our partnership began.

We gave each other the names "Blue" and "Green" based on our eye colors since that was the first thing each of us had noticed about the other. We shared what we had and kept each other safe. Months passed as we watched each other's backs and fought off the monsters that chased us. We made an odd little family out of the two of us, but the companionship brought light with it in that dark forest.

But as time passed and winter approached, food and water became scarce. The winds were harsh, the temperatures deadly, and we had a harder time competing with the monsters for the last sources of food. I remember one day in particular...

It had been several days since we had eaten, and there was nothing to be found. The ground had frozen over, and the last rain had hardened to thick clusters of ice in the trees. It was beautiful, but I couldn't enjoy it. I just huddled closer to Blue in our hollow. But that day was different—that morning the snow started. Blue noticed the look of despair on my face when I saw the first snowflake, and he snapped. He leaped out of our makeshift home with a holler and started dancing around, his hair attracting the thickening clumps. I couldn't even help but laugh as he stuck out his tongue to catch one. He grinned, holding his hand out for me, "Come on!"

I beamed, taking it.

We ran everywhere—all over the forest. It was incredibly freeing as we both momentarily forgot our troubles. Yes, the cold bit at my toes, but I was running too fast to care. Yes, I was still starved, but I swallowed deep breaths of exhilarating air. Yes, I still feared the monsters, but they couldn't catch us. Not at that moment. The notion was so compelling, I believed it whether or not it was true.

Blue suddenly tapped me before bolting away, "Tag, you're it!"

I laughed, "Hey!" I raced after him. I followed him through a few glens before I spotted something to my right. It was a couple of little white rabbits... eating carrots! I turned from Blue's trail and clawed at the dirt to reveal dozens of bright, crisp carrots while the rabbits bolted away.

FOR THE INTENDED

I cried excitedly, "Blue! Blue, come quick! Carrots!" I knelt in the thin layer of snow and continued to add to the pile of vegetables in front of me, including the half-eaten ones with tiny teeth marks. I giggled to myself—as best I could remember, it was the greatest day of my life.

I had only collected half of them when I heard Blue sprinting up behind me. I opened my mouth to share in his joyful exclamation, but I ended up crying out in horror as rough hands latched onto me. They had charged me too quickly, so we both ended up toppling over and rolling away. I shrieked, chucking rocks and sticks one after the other at the attacker while I tried to find a good escape route. I hadn't seen a monster like her before. She was only a little bigger than me, and kind of resembled a human. But she had bat-like wings, grimy, gray skin, patches of dark grey fur, a distinct pointed nose, sharp fingernails and teeth, pale eyes, and cat-like ears. I learned later that she was a gretzan, but it wouldn't have mattered to my seven-year-old self anyway. Knowing what she was called wouldn't help me beat her.

She didn't like all the sharp things heading her way, so she retreated behind a wall of ice. I panted, wanting to make a run for it, but her malicious gaze made me freeze in fear. She showed her teeth, and the ice made her smile contort in a dreadful way. The brief interlude made me realize running away wouldn't work anyway. We were in a fortress of ice. Between the downpour we had experienced the past few weeks and the indecisive temperatures, the icicles on the trees were almost to the forest floor—all around us. Playing tag with Blue had worked because we both had to slow down for the tight turns and strategic openings, but I couldn't play that game with a creature with wings. She could just fly over the ice, so I wasn't going to risk turning my back to her. I had to defeat her somehow.

She started pacing around me like a predator circling its prey, careful to stay behind the ice. I swallowed, following her lead, keeping her in front of me as we turned in circles. I searched our surroundings for anything, any idea at all. Then I saw it. There was an opening that was smaller than the others that I thought I could still fit through. When she came back from behind the ice wall, I dashed for it.

    She screeched, coming after me. I slipped through, avoiding the sharp tips that were centimeters from my back. Even though she couldn't fit under it, I saw her grin cruelly as she approached slowly. She put her hands on the thick icicles, intending to snap through them to get to me, but she had barely touched them when a dozen tiny icicles rained on her head from above, some of them managing to draw a little blood. Apparently, all the ice in the glen was connected like a spider web. The slightest disturbance or the littlest vibration could have had some unfortunate consequences. She hissed, but her smirk returned as she realized her advantage. She unfurled her wings and carefully dodged the icicles above as she quickly approached my side.

    I was ready for that though, so I slipped back through the opening to the other side. She landed where I had been only a moment before and snarled before launching herself into the air for a second attempt. I slid to the other side again. She was enraged. We did our dance one more time before she screamed with fury. I didn't know what else to do—I guess I was just hoping that she would get bored and find breakfast somewhere else. But she had had enough. Faster than I would've thought, she clawed at the dirt underneath the opening. Then, she lowered herself and began to struggle through, ignoring the spear-like spikes as they scratched her back.

    I yelped and scooted away. I was about to dash when I heard a great cracking sound and watched as all the ice in the glen came crashing down. It sounded like a thousand glasses shattering. It was overwhelming and unexpected, so I fell into the fetal position and shielded my head, refusing to open my eyes as ice struck the ground all around me. Finally, all the tinkling and clinking stopped as the pieces settled, and I could only hear my gasps. I didn't want to look up, afraid to find my numb self impaled with ice, or a hungry monster reaching for its meal. But I did eventually open my eyes.

Since I was in the middle of the glen with no branches hanging over me, the ice had missed me. The gretzan had been beneath a large bough . . . I gasped at the sight of her lifeless body and turned away, but I spotted the cause of all the destruction. Blue perched on the limb above her, a resolute look on his face. I had thought she just bumped the ice while trying to get to me, but that cracking sound had been too abrupt, as if someone had kicked the ice. It had been timed perfectly as well. I don't know how he managed to climb that tree without affecting the network of frozen water, but I didn't care at the moment. I was just glad he had my back.

He climbed down and wrapped his arms around me, pulling me close.

I shivered. The day had turned bleak, and I suddenly felt cold and hungry and scared all over again.

His positive attitude had left him too, and reality hit us both hard. He smiled though, handing me a carrot which I practically swallowed whole, as he said, "We should get back to the hollow."

We didn't have any more fun snow days.

Winter dragged on, but Blue didn't mind. His eyes gleamed with newfound perseverance when a snowstorm reflected in them. He gathered food swifter when the wind went with him. He laughed when a thunderstorm made the icicles chatter on the limbs of our tree. He took it all in stride.

I, however, became ill. I had to stay in our tree at all times, sheltered from the gales. Blue never argued with me about that fact unless it was to convince me to heed it. I hated not helping, but I was constantly sick and only made our daily chores more difficult to complete.

Blue tried to brighten every day for me and gave me almost all of the food he could find without me knowing. But it wasn't enough. Over time I grew weaker and weaker. After weeks of giving up his portions and continuously losing hope every time he looked at me, Blue wasn't doing much better.

One night—a night we felt might be our last—we were lying side by side on the forest floor. We were being tracked down by gargles and had become too weak to do anything about it. We heard the horrifying screeches getting closer and we just lay there in that dark glade waiting for them.

Just as we thought the monsters were upon us, a light broke through the thick brush and a kind voice came through the misty cold air. With the light of a lantern, I could just make out the outline of two men and their horses. One of them stepped closer and bent down next to me, the other in a dark blue vest went to Blue.

The man next to me smiled and it seemed to warm the cold right from me. He looked a bit older than the other man, perhaps in his forties, but very healthy and fit. In the lantern's light I made out his shoulder-length light brown hair and eyes. He took my head in his hands and lifted it gently. Normally I would've been terrified and fought back, but I was limp with fatigue. I couldn't do anything as he reassured me with such certainty that everything would be okay.

The strong palm of his hand cupped my forehead and, realizing that I had a fever, said, "This one is very ill, she won't last long."

He put a flask to my lips. Eager for water, I didn't question. I barely managed to open my mouth, but when I did, a refreshing fluid rushed down my throat. I guzzled it down, barely noticing the sickening sweetness of it.

He went over to his horse and pulled some bandages from his saddlebags. I had various wounds from monster attacks, and he began to dress them, talking to me with a calm, friendly voice. As the next few minutes passed, I felt some of my energy come back to me. I figured it must have been the flask of liquid he gave me.

FOR THE INTENDED

When he finished with the bandages, he said to the man in the blue vest, "I must take her to Umplidore now, can you manage?"

When the other man nodded, he gently lifted me up to his horse's saddle. As he raised me up, I noticed that the other man was taking care of Blue. It comforted me to know that my only friend would be alright.

The man held firmly onto me, made promises once again, and spurred his horse into a full gallop.

After that I pretty much gave up. I must have fainted because I couldn't recall the ride; I only remember waking in the arms of someone. I couldn't force my eyes open, but I could feel the up and down jolts of the person running. I also noticed that it became warm and dim, meaning we were probably inside a building of some sort. Every step echoed off the walls, so it must've been someplace large and open.

I sensed the person holding me slow down to a halt, then urge, "Hurry, let me in! I must speak with Her Majesty!" I recognized the voice of the man who rescued me in the woods.

"The queen is reading and has requested privacy. No one, not even you sire, is permitted to—"

"Now!" the person holding me demanded furiously.

A moment of pained silence passed before I heard a pair of huge doors creak open. The person holding me burst into the other room.

"Why, it's you!" exclaimed a cheerful voice farther in the room. "I thought you wouldn't be back until—" started a voice, but she saw that she had more than one guest. "Who is that?" She asked with grave concern.

The man caught his breath while I listened to the swishing of a skirt as the woman ran towards us.

I felt a hand brush against my skin. It felt soft, delicate, and deliciously cool against my hot face. I managed to open my eyes a slit. The lady was gorgeous, and somehow familiar. She seemed young but had an aura of authority and wisdom. She had light skin with a rosy complexion. She wore the most beautiful light green dress that perfectly matched her pale green eyes. It seemed as if there were stars embedded in them, always twinkling. Finally, a lovely silver crown rested upon her strawberry blonde curls.

I also noticed our extraordinary surroundings. We were alone in an enormous, open room with a ceiling that extended thirty feet upwards. The magnificent chair on the raised podium allowed me to conclude that we were in some type of throne room. The silver throne, with its graceful curves, shined brightly; shimmering blue sapphires were embedded in the head of it. Torches lit the entire place. Normally that might seem dark and dismal, but just enough light came from them to make it glorious.

Light blue tapestries with brilliant silver embroideries lined each wall. I noticed that stars were the constant theme for the designs. Several stunning marble statues of warriors stood along the walls. There were occasional tables with various trinkets of silver that sparkled beautifully in the torchlight. Two plush sofas rested on either side of the room; both were pale blue with silver frames, giving them a majestic look. A towering fireplace warmed the entire room, making it all the more comfortable. One wall—the wall directly behind the throne—had been constructed entirely of glass, meaning that the room was probably even more enchanting in the day time.

I saw all of this in a haze, but the effect of the winsome environment broke through my clouded senses nevertheless.

The man hesitated, "I-I think... She's the one."

The lady started, "Really?" I felt her hand on my face again. "What makes you think so? Here, lay her down there."

He walked over to the side of the room and laid me down on one of the sofas. I just about passed out again, engulfed in the comfort of the cushion, but was too interested in "She's the one."

"Droll! Come at once!" the queen called.

A servant shuffled into the room, "Yes, milady?"

FOR THE INTENDED

"No one is allowed in this room. Is that understood?" She gestured to her guest, "I must speak with him alone."

"Yes, milady."

"Very well. Care to this girl. Do everything you can for her!"

"Yes, milady."

Droll went to carry me away when the man who brought me said, "My lady, you do not fully understand her condition. I . . ." a long pause, "I think she needs . . ." he couldn't finish.

The lady gasped as she realized. "Are you mad?"

The man sighed.

"We don't even know if it will work! If it's not her, she'll die instantly!"

With a serious tone, "And if it is her, and we don't do it, we'll all die."

The room froze in tense silence. Droll stood there, waiting to be dismissed—quite relieved when he was.

After the door closed behind him, my carrier tried to speak up again, but didn't get the chance.

"But it's not supposed to happen so fast!" The queen seemed as if she were about to have a meltdown. She welled with fear, but I couldn't figure out why. She seemed as if she were about to break into some hysterical state as she said, "We were supposed to prepare her for this . . . *we* were supposed to prepare for this!" Her eyes pooled, "We—"

"Aurora," the man placed his hand on her shoulder, trying to get her to focus. He said her name calmly while trying to bring her back down, but he swallowed apprehensively as her eyes met his.

She breathed in deep before she asked in a slightly less crazed tone, "Well, what makes you so sure it's her?" She stared at me intently, as if dissecting every part of me with her mind.

The man began to explain but she interrupted. "Wait, no," she said suddenly, very calmly raising her hand and looking back at the man. "We can't do it. I do not doubt your wisdom," she paused and bit her cheek before forcing the word out, "*friend*, but we shan't try anything as dangerous as that."

"That is not for you to decide!" The man shouted angrily while the queen backed up in surprise.

Then the man looked regretful and started to say, "Aurora, look, I—", but didn't get the chance to finish.

"Guards!" The lady yelled. The man stood in shock as four guards came into the room. With a pained look, she said "I am truly sorry for this, old friend, but I can't risk you trying anything..."

His shock only lasted until two of the guards seized his arms, which unleashed the man's true self. He whipped his arms right from the guards' grips. Then, grabbing their arms, he bashed them into each other, leaving them lying disoriented on the stone floor. Before the other two were upon him he managed to draw his sword.

The queen called for reinforcements with a new look of power and control even though fear still shook her voice.

Both guards looked very uncertain, as if they knew they couldn't beat him. The first guard took a chance and thrust, only to find that the warrior parried with ease and sent his sword skittering across the floor. The warrior raised his sword to the first guard's chest. The first guard backed up slowly before running for help. I noticed then that the warrior held back, not letting loose his full skill. It became clear that he didn't want to hurt anyone; he just needed to do what he thought was necessary.

No one else had come yet. The second guard looked panicked as he yelled and charged blindly towards the warrior. The man brought his hilt down upon the guard's head, but only hard enough to knock him out.

The warrior took a second to look into the queen's wide eyes, "I'm sorry, Aurora." Before I noticed it, he had already snatched me up, shifted me to his left arm, and bolted through the large oaken doors, his sword raised high in his right hand.

FOR THE INTENDED

"Please, don't do this!" pleaded the queen as she ran after him, but in that long dress of hers, she would never catch up.

I remember just staring into the man's determined face as he charged down the castle's corridors. Normally I would have been terrified from being pinned in such powerful arms. But after looking into his face, I realized I trusted him.

The guards were coming out of nowhere, one or two of them occasionally appearing in the doorways that lined the halls, but my carrier fought them all off effortlessly. The trip took several minutes. Once we took our last turn, I looked over to see our destination and gave a little gasp. Two thirty-foot high doors that appeared to be made entirely out of intricately designed metal were at the end of a very long hall. A large bolt secured the doors and two stately guards were posted in front of them. They seemed to be wearing more armor than the earlier guards, and their stature intimidated me as they held ten-foot spears. I immediately knew that something behind those doors was incredibly important.

The warrior, still cradling me, fought off a few more guards as he made his way down the hallway. He slowed a bit as he approached the mammoth doors. He gently laid me down a ways away. He then approached the guards while letting out a deep breath.

To my surprise he tried diplomacy. "Farlen?" He seemed to be addressing the guard on the right.

The guard swallowed, his blank face faltering.

The warrior addressed the other one, a little too desperately, "Leon?"

The guard lowered his eyes. Even as a sick seven-year-old, I sensed an old friendship being put to the test. He looked back up, "I'm sorry, sir."

The warrior exhaled slowly, very disappointed in his answer, but a resolute expression filled his face. Apprehension overtook sadness in the warrior, as if those two guards would take all the skill he had.

Haven Berg

The guards took defensive stances, and the warrior pounced. I watched in weary awe as he staunchly fought both guards off. The guards were indeed more skilled than the others, and the man had a much more difficult time winning than with his earlier feats. The spears whirled, jabbed, and knocked together as they tried to overcome the man between them. They flashed in the light of the chandelier, and their noise clattered through all the surrounding hallways. Finally, after a grunt and a groan, silence filled the corridor again.

The man left both guards wounded on the floor, one unconscious. He sheathed his sword and ran over to the door. He heaved the heavy bolt and let it fall to the floor with a thud. He pulled the heavy doors open first before rushing back to me. He lifted my tiny body up while gasping for air. Then, seeming extremely worn out, he dashed into the next room.

I began fading quickly, but I could hear the many heavy footsteps pounding after us.

The room the warrior had brought me to was lit by torches and the moonbeams that poured through the only window. I looked up to see two small crystal-clear cases displayed on ornate oak stands on a raised podium. In between the two clear cases, on a much larger oak stand, lay a light blue velvet cushion. On that cushion rested the most magnificent thing I had ever seen—a sword shimmering brilliantly in the moonlight.

He pounded up the steps, giving me a closer look at the glass enclosures. In both cases were identical necklaces. Each pendant held a crystal in the center of the entwined silver. They seemed to glow with beauty, and I realized the gems themselves produced the white light.

He laid me down gently on the floor next to the stands. I gave a little yelp as he unexpectedly snatched the sword on the cushion and brought it down as hard as he could on the left case. The clanging sound must've been heard in every room in the castle. I would have expected it to have shattered with the littlest tap so I found it very confusing that it didn't even crack.

FOR THE INTENDED

He brought it down hard a second time, a small fissure appearing. "Come on!" he yelled. He bashed it again and a larger crack resulted. I saw him gather his remaining strength and go in for one more blow.

Exhaling triumphantly as it shattered, he snatched the necklace, ignoring the shards that cut his fingers. The guards were almost to the door when he knelt next to me. My eyes were fluttering, but I felt him lift my head and place the necklace around my neck as a bunch of guards burst into the room. Without a moment to lose, the warrior put one hand on my forehead and the other on the pendant. He mumbled something and then . . . it seemed as if time slowed down.

I saw the terrified expressions on the guards' faces as they ran in slow motion towards me. I saw the queen standing in the doorway, a look of horror on her face. Then time resumed its normal speed. Just as the guards were about to grab me, blinding light shot out from the necklace and filled the room with white.

In addition to the light, an unbearable amount of noise poured out, low and rumbling. The light and noise caused the guards to collapse to the ground on their knees, shielding their eyes and covering their ears. I thought I might go insane from it all when the best part happened. Searing, unspeakable pain shot through me. The pain became too much, so within a second of the bright, loud release . . .

I. Was. Gone.

I woke up in a way too comfortable bed. I had forgotten everything. It was a lovely morning: the birds chirping outside, the sunlight pouring into the room warming my face, and the occasional breeze finding its way through the window. I was about to doze off again when I realized something was wrong. When had I ever been comfortable and peaceful? I bolted up, my eyes darting back and forth frantically.

I found myself alone in a stone room—nicely decorated with expensive-looking furniture. I looked over at the door and found it closed but could hear people walking by it.

I vaguely remembered the two men helping me and Blue. My heart skipped anxiously when I thought of Blue. I hadn't seen him since then. Was he okay? Had he had as horrible of an experience as I had? I needed to find him. We had to get out of there.

I slipped as quietly as I could out of my bed, all the while watching the door. As I slid down I noticed my old ragged clothes had been replaced with a soft, white nightgown and my bandages were new.

After I had gotten out of bed without drawing any attention, I scanned the room for possible weapons. Over on the opposite wall from the door stood a dark dresser. Above the dresser hung a painting of a vase full of flowers, and on either side of the painting were silver candle stands. Next to the dresser sat a wooden chair with a red velvet cushion. I tiptoed over to it and tried to lift it as I figured I would put it in front of the door as a blockade. While I tried to lift the ridiculously heavy chair, someone had walked into the room without me noticing.

"Well," a hearty voice said, "you seem to be feeling better."

Because of all the monster fights I'd experienced, I reflexively snatched a candle and chucked it at the intruder.

"Whoa, hey there!" The man swatted the candle away just before it hit his face.

I raised the other candle when I recognized the light brown hair and gentle eyes. The warrior who had rescued me watched me from across the room. The previous night flooded back, and I lowered my hand, just staring at him.

He put his hands up in surrender and reassured, "You're safe here, no one is going to hurt you." He slowly made his way towards me, making sure I didn't throw anything else. I watched him skeptically. My fingers tightened around the candle the closer he got. When he stopped in front of me, he squatted down to meet my eyes. He held his hand out expectantly. Hesitating at first, I finally dropped the candle stand into his hand.

FOR THE INTENDED

He smiled, "Thank you." He very slowly moved his hand towards me, "How is Winlit Cordial this morning?"

I blinked, wondering what he was referring to until his hand met the pendant hanging around my neck. My heart leapt—it was the necklace that had caused so much pain.

He inspected it, "It's not glowing anymore." Relief flooded his eyes and his smile became even warmer.

I didn't know what that meant, but my fear of Winlit Cordial faded in his presence.

He stood up, grinning, and extending his right hand out for me said, "Now, how about some breakfast?"

I eyed him. I didn't understand the whole incident with the necklace, but in the end, I didn't think he had meant to hurt me. I wasn't sick anymore, and though I didn't know how, it seemed like the necklace had played a part in my recovery. Also, the nightgown and bandages proved that I had been well taken care of. The two final persuaders were my empty stomach and his convincing smile, so I slowly took his hand. He patted my hand with his left, "Let's see if we can find your friend and join him for breakfast, shall we? He'll be really glad to see you." He led me out of the room, and for the first time in too long, the corners of my little mouth curled upwards.

Haven Berg

GOING HOME

I woke from the same dream I had had on and off since I was seven. Seven years later, the memory remained just as vivid in my sleep. Every time I woke up just as my younger self smiled, but my older self held onto the expression. I lay in my hammock half-awake as it swung gently in the occasional breeze, which also brought a peaceful swishing of the leaves. A small creek trickled to my left, adding to the relaxing scene. I was carefree for the moment.

I was almost asleep again when a chirp pierced the silence twice. I sat up suddenly, my arrow already strung and ready to plunge into my foe.
"Easy! Easy, darling! It's only me," said a shaken little bird that sat on the edge of my rocking hammock.
I looked around, still drawing back the arrow. When I saw it was clear—meaning no bad guys, no monsters—I lay back down, staring at the tree tops. "Sorry, Elon," I said. I ran my hand through my hair, trying to relax.
He flew to a nearby oak tree, clearly used to it. His brown feathers matched the bark which caused his tiny figure to blend into the foliage. Just as he landed, a white wolf bounded into the clearing.
"Mornin'," the wolf said with a smile. His golden yellow eyes penetrated through my sleepy haze.

FOR THE INTENDED

I sat up, "Good morning, Caspian. Anything to report?" I asked while stretching so it sounded more like, "Good morni-huhh, Cahhspian, anythin tuhh reporrht?"

"Nothing at all, milady," he grinned, bowing low. Lately, he had insisted on calling me anything proper and annoying.

I turned, "What about you, Elon?"

"*Nothing at all, milady,*" the bird mimicked.

Caspian gave Elon his famous "if you don't cut that out I'll kill you" look, baring his fangs.

Elon gave a frightened chirp and quickly flew to a branch that hung close to my head.

I smirked, "Seriously, Elon, is there any news?"

He looked cautiously at Caspian who sat at the end of my hammock glaring at him, and then at me. "Nothing," he said in a normal voice.

I sat and reflected for a moment. As soon as my eyes weren't as blurry, I said, "Elon, fly ahead and tell them I'll be there by sunset."

Elon nodded, spread his wings, and took off.

As Elon disappeared through the top of the oak trees I looked at Caspian who seemed to be listening for the howl of a fellow scouting wolf, and asked, "Caspian?"

His concentration broke as he turned to look me in the eyes.

I nodded, "Scout about."

He nodded back, lifted his head, and howled. Another howl answered him. As he trotted out of the clearing, I slowly got up and began to walk across the open glade.

Flowers of Hartnia grew by the base of the oaks. Hartnias came in pretty much any color you could imagine, but these were just pink and white ones. I bent down and picked a white blossom. I looked around to make sure no one saw me, then took a whiff of the wonderful flowery fragrance.

Just then, an unnatural, strong-willed breeze blew from the south. Leaves were torn from their safe homes in the branches and thrown in the swirling wind traveling north. The birds were no longer singing, and I watched as one franticly made its way to its nest. I looked to the south, hoping to see the source of the wind. I didn't know what I expected to see, but knowing Edgeladine, it could've been anything.

The tops of the trees parted for a few seconds, so I could see a white, swirling mass coming towards me made of . . . what? I stepped closer, squinting and trying to make it out when I realized that I had just a second to duck. I turned and sheltered my face from . . . *snow*.

Shock invaded my thoughts, *What in the world? It's the beginning of summer, and it's snowing!* My breath got caught as I fell to my knees in the green grass. I couldn't get up as I gasped for air—I was shaking too bad to even try. The unexpected blast of cold had weakened me, and I had no idea why.

The snow lasted for several seconds before continuing its course north. After a while, I felt strength seeping back into my muscles. I staggered to a standing position. In a few more seconds, it was like nothing had happened.

The birds began to go about their business again—chirping, flying, finding food for their young. The warmth of an early morning in summer descended on the clearing, and the gentle breezes were the only disturbances about. I grabbed my head, shaking it. Was I crazy? Had I just imagined the whole thing? I decided not to stress over something I didn't understand. I would talk to Arnet about it later. I tossed the idea from my head, forcing a smile on.

I made my way over to my satchel. I reached inside and pulled out a small shiny whistle made of rarn (something a lot like silver, but a bit more common). I took a few seconds to admire the beautiful designs that my great friend Tucker had skillfully inlaid in the sides of the pipe. It felt like holding a piece of home. I put the instrument to my lips and made a shrill sound that rang out through the woods.

As I accounted for everything I had packed, I noticed I was subconsciously rubbing my hand. I looked down at the symbol that would always be stained on my right palm. It was white, curvy, graceful, and felt downright painful. Right then, it glowed slightly. I had recently noticed that the glowing seemed to occur at the same time as the pain. It didn't always hurt though, which was the only way I could tolerate it. It was a curse and a gift, but more on that later.

I peeked inside my bag one last time to make sure I had packed everything. *Check.* I had just placed my folded hammock on top, when I heard a whinny answer my whistle. I grinned as I snatched up my bag and ran towards the end of the forest.

I jogged out into the meadow and surveyed the waving plain. The tall, green grass bent and swished as I looked for my ride. Just then, a beautiful mix of black and white burst over the closest hill. Her mane streamed down her side and her tail billowed in the wind as she galloped to me. Her hooves were only visible when they struck the ground—the rest of the time they were cloaked in long silky hair. I smiled as the huge animal came to rest by my side. "Good morning, Drayla," I beamed.

She neighed in greeting to me, nudging me gently.

"I am so ready to be home," I mumbled.

She neighed again in reply and then turned sideways so that I could put her saddle on. Drayla could talk, though she rarely did. But I was familiar with the basics of Horse Speak, so I knew what she was thinking half the time anyway.

When I had just put her bridle on and slung my leg over her back, Caspian ran to Drayla's side, slightly out of breath from scouting.

Drayla glanced at him and snorted.

"Well, hello to you, too." Caspian responded sarcastically.

Their behavior wasn't terribly unusual, but I could feel Drayla's eagerness to be home. We were all weary of traveling and longed for our own beds.

I looked at Caspian as he tried to catch his breath. "Did you find anything?"

"No. Nothing," he said. It caught my attention that he didn't say anything like "milady" or "Your Highness." I realized he wanted to get home as much as Drayla did.

"Good," I said as I glanced across the open meadow. Even though I couldn't see it yet, I knew that somewhere to the north, on top of a hill, sat the glorious castle of Umplidore. Its white stones would be gleaming in the sun, the light blue flags waving in the wind with stars of silver etched into them, and the towers rising to the sky. It had been months since I had seen it, and it wasn't even my fault. The trip was expected of me. Honestly, I was thinking about having a talk with the elders about the whole dumb thing. I sat for a few more moments before prompting, "Ready?"

Drayla bobbed her head and Caspian barked. We were off.

Drayla's hooves pounded into the ground. I had been used to hearing that for weeks. As we traveled, Caspian would run right alongside Drayla, disappear into the forest, and an hour or so later he would be back after communicating with his wolves. We usually took breaks every three hours, but since we were all anxious to get home, we pushed a little harder. I would slow Drayla down to a small trot to recuperate. We would stay like that for a few minutes and then jump back to a gallop. At noon, we stopped for a break.

I pulled Drayla back into the forest where I knew there would be a river. The clear water of the river Narnstein sparkled as it ran over the shiny stones under the thick-leaved trees. It had round pebbles for a bank and made a great spot for lunch.

I dismounted and took Drayla's bridle off. After I loosened her girth, she went to the shore to drink alongside Caspian. He lapped up the refreshing water eagerly, his ears searching the surrounding forest constantly.

I peered into my pack for the hundredth time and confirmed that I had eaten the last of my food the morning before. I growled at my carelessness.

FOR THE INTENDED

I tossed Caspian a piece of meat from the pack. Normally he would hunt for himself, but I didn't want him to use any more energy. I looked over at Drayla to make sure she had found some nice grass and saw her munching on some very tasty-looking greens. She deserved it after being in the dark forests of the cold mountain, with barely anything to eat there but dead shrubs.

I took the map and made my way over to a damp boulder by the shore. I lounged on the cool rock while examining the crinkled paper, calculating how much time it would take to get back home. Suddenly my body tensed with premonition.

Caspian, who had been chomping away at his piece of meat, abruptly lifted his head. His ears pricked up in sudden alertness before he froze. I raised my head and, folding the map, asked, "What is it, do you hear something?"

"No," he said with a low growl, "I smell something." His tail swished from side to side.

I got my bow and arrow ready. I knew Caspian was never wrong when it came to these things. I went through the monsters I thought it could be in my head, *Matonda, gretzan . . . maybe varnants?* I opened my mouth to ask Caspian if he recognized the smell, but I didn't have to because I spotted the monster myself in the shady leaves above.

"Varnants!" I yelled. My body responded to years of training and quickly took a stance, aiming for the creature's heart.

We got into positions just in time as two hideous creatures whooshed down from the treetops. The creatures themselves were only slightly smaller than Drayla, but a whole lot lighter. They moved stealthily and were difficult to spot at night or in deep woods. A varnant had the body of a horse, but the wings, tail, and voice of a crow.

I aimed at the blur of black as the nasty creature rushed towards me, but I didn't get the chance to shoot. The beast moved way faster than I had first calculated. He charged me and knocked my bow out of my hands before I had even noticed. I had just enough time to draw my sword before the animal charged me again. I managed to barely slice some feathers off his right wing as he rushed past.

It squawked, clearly annoyed, its scarlet beady eyes looking for the best way to end my life. It quickly turned around for another plunge. I let out some adrenaline by yelling as hard as I could while scraping my sword along the area where his wings were attached to his body. He cried out in pain and skidded to a halt along the river, his wings tucked in. As he began to lick his wound, I had enough time to analyze the rest of the battle.

The other varnant—there seemed to be only two—attacked Drayla. She bucked, reared, bit, and kicked with all her might. The varnant hovered over her, mercilessly biting the top of her neck.

Caspian barked to her left to signal for her to stop moving.

She stopped abruptly, the varnant banging into her suddenly stationary neck.

The varnant was dazed long enough for Caspian to take action. He leaped over Drayla, grabbed the varnant by the top of his neck, and slammed the creature on the ground. Caspian growled viciously as the varnant got to his feet, threatening to do it again.

Despite the painful wound it had, the varnant started to go in for another beating. Before it could, its friend called to him in a language I didn't know. He looked furious, like he wanted to tear my guts out right then, but whatever his comrade said made him slowly back toward the river.

"We'll be back," he threatened with a raspy voice, glancing at me. "Yes, we will be back, and you better be ready!" With that, he galloped to his friend and took off. His companion struggled to raise his wings, but finally managed to follow him, heading south.

I watched them as they slowly disappeared over the tops of the trees, making sure they didn't come back. When we were safe, I turned, exclaiming, "Well, another point for us! We—"

That's when I saw the blood trickling down Drayla's neck, staining her beautiful white mane. I ran over, "Drayla! Are you alright?" Normally I wouldn't have asked. Drayla was a war horse, and I'd seen her much worse, but it was more blood than I would've expected.

She scoffed, swishing her tail, letting me know she was fine and I didn't need to be concerned. I figured she was probably just trying to be tough and not complain, but I knew better than to argue.

"Well, at least let me clean it up."

She sighed but let me rinse her mane and wash out the wound.

After I wrapped her neck in some clean strips of white cloth from my pack, I slumped back onto the rock and gazed at the river. Caspian had already gone back to his meat and Drayla sauntered over by him and distractedly finished off a clump of grass.

The time came for us to get back on the trail, and I felt starved. I reproached myself for not checking the rations the morning before. At least it wasn't as bad as the time I traveled to Pyodine leaving an entire pack at home. That was a journey to remember... *Well, there's nothing to do about it now*, I told myself. I rationalized that the entire castle would probably be holding a feast in honor of my return. It would taste a lot better if I attended it with an empty stomach. I pushed the hunger out of my mind and snapped the map open once more.

"We should be there in about six hours," I announced. I took my flask and went over and dipped it in the crystal-clear river. It reminded me of what Arnet, a great friend of mine, once told me.

I was several years younger and sitting on his lap, all of my friends gathered around us. With light reflecting in his warm brown eyes and his story voice deep, slow, and mysterious, Arnet promised, "The water of the Narnstein River is so reviving, it will magically restore all health and strength to anyone who drinks it."

The memory brought on a smile. I waited as the water rushed into the empty flask before taking a sip. The refreshing water instantly quenched my thirst. However, I didn't feel the tired aching of my legs or the nauseous hunger pangs leave me. I chuckled quietly as I knelt on the bank, turning the flask over in my hand. Although some of Arnet's tales were true and full of purpose, some were just for entertainment; the hard part was telling which was which.

I tightened Drayla's girth, readjusted her bridle, and mounted. Drayla noticed me rubbing my right hand. "Does it hurt badly?" she asked quietly. Her voice had a way of sounding regal and majestic.

I glanced anxiously towards the north. "Not too bad," I said, "but I don't think we should wait any longer."

I lied. It had never hurt so bad and I didn't know why it was flaring up. Also, Winlit Cordial only glowed when I used my powers, but that day it had glowed without my consent. I was never supposed to take it off, but sometimes I considered it, hoping that if I "lost it" all my problems would go away. But honestly, that could have made all my problems ten times worse. I wanted to get back to Arnet so he could explain the searing pain in the mark on my hand and hopefully stop it. He always seemed to have the answers when they mattered. He was the official Summer Born expert in the castle, and his only patient needed some assistance.

I took a deep breath. I just needed to get back. I called to Caspian, and as he came into sight, we continued our journey home.

FOR THE INTENDED

SUNSET

As Drayla trudged and Caspian slugged up the last hill before we saw the castle, I heard something I didn't expect to hear—silence.

It shouldn't have been quiet at that time of day. The city of Umplidore was on a major trade route that went to numerous other marketplaces and cities; you could always hear the ruckus in the fields surrounding the castle walls. Markets were set up in and out of the castle gate, spanning from the front doors of the castle to the hill of Garmt, which was what we were climbing up.

As I came to the crest of the hill, the usual uproarious cheer didn't come. In fact, nothing but the tall, green grass swishing in the wind could be heard. I sat there, confused. There were no people, no tents, and no markets. At first, I thought it was some sort of joke, but then an especially painful throb went through the mark on my right hand.

My left hand went up to my neck, clasping my necklace. I peered at my right hand, moaning at the pain that pounded through it. The silver symbol radiated light. I looked down at the precious jewel embedded in my necklace and saw that it glowed brighter than the moon.

Puzzled, my eyebrows came together. My heart began to pound. Then, I really got panicked. The Aedine Prophecy flashed through my mind like it did so often. But that time, the responsibility that came with it crushed me.

That was it. I had failed. The opportunity to do the thing I knew I was meant to do since I was seven, had passed. I thought of the world collapsing before my eyes. I thought of the people disappearing into thin air. I thought of the fact that Drayla, Caspian, Elon, Arnet, Blue, the list went on . . . could just be gone, and all because I hadn't made it back in time?! Well, I didn't know how it would go down exactly, but my imagination took over.

I couldn't believe it; I just stared at the plains, trying to process everything. I failed the attempt not to cry, and a single tear slid down and off my face.

Then I got angry. I wiped the tear away with a harsh hand and seethed.

Caspian saw my face. He realized and bowed his head to the ground.

I dismounted and stood there in my confused despair, staring out across the plain. Drayla gave a quiet whinny and nuzzled my arm. I threw my arms around her neck, rubbing my face into her familiar mane, momentarily losing my anger to panic. I was gonna lose her.

As we stood there, the sun slowly made its way to the tips of the trees. Vivid orange, red, pink, and a trace of purple washed over the sky, creating a way too beautiful sunset for the doom that awaited the world. The grass still swished peacefully, and the ocean glittered anyway. Then, Caspian lifted his head.

He looked confused. He sniffed the air and then his eyes widened. He stood up and laughed.

Drayla and I looked at him, surprised.

He laughed again and declared, "I smell something!"

My hand instinctively drew my sword slightly. "What is it?" I demanded with a frightening voice that surprised even me. I needed revenge.

"No, not that kind of smell," he said, still taking sniffs. He grinned, "This I think you'll like." And with that, he bounded down the hill.

I blinked. *What?* I swung onto Drayla's back in confusion—a nicer kind.

Caspian gently loped across the meadow, Drayla doing a light canter. I looked all around us, "Caspian . . . what—?"

"Shh," he grinned slyly, "You'll see."

His confidence caused us to follow him. But as we cantered towards the castle, strange things started happening. I brushed them away at first, but they quickly demanded my attention. I began to get dizzy and had a peculiar sensation. It felt like my energy was being drained. It didn't take long for me to feel like a sack of flour being tossed back and forth, and then I could only lay on Drayla's neck. She noticed, and I felt her tense and suddenly come down to a trot, "What's wrong?"

I blinked weird floaty things out of my eyes. "I—I'm not sure." I sounded really calm, but I bet she could feel my heart beating against her.

She stopped.

Caspian noticed and circled back. "What's wrong?" Then he saw me and came up, "Hey, what's wrong?"

"I don't know . . . I think I need Arnet." My anxiety seeped into my voice despite my efforts to hide it.

Caspian and Drayla exchanged a look.

"No," I barely managed to say, "Keep going."

Drayla seemed hesitant, but after another glance at Caspian who nodded, she took off after him as he darted ahead.

A while later I managed to look up and see the castle looming over us. Whatever Caspian had smelled seemed to be behind the white castle, out of sight. But we hadn't even gotten to the walls when I noticed my hands were like ice and I began to shiver uncontrollably. I wrapped my hands in Drayla's mane for warmth and to help steady myself.

She tensed but went all the faster.

As we traveled along the castle walls, slowly making our way to the rear of the castle, I began to hear voices and laughter, and smell glorious smells. I was weak, though—close to fainting.

As we turned the corner, a cheer went up and then died as soon as it began. I heard alarmed voices all around me; some I recognized, and others I didn't.

"Galayne! Can you hear me?"

"Your Highness!?"

My eyes rolled back in my head as someone with red hair gently lifted me from the saddle. Holding me, the person called out desperately, "Arnet, it's Galayne!"

A mix of voices and colors blurred together so that I couldn't understand anything I heard or saw. I heard what seemed to be people running through the knee-high grass. My carrier passed me to another person, and I could just make out the sound of a horse neighing in fear and the anxious barking of a dog.

Someone must have carried me into the castle because the light under my closed eyes went from bright to dim. I could feel myself being set on a soft surface, and I managed to make out an old man hurriedly mixing things in a corner. People ran around in a panic, doing things like getting sheets or water or zig-zagging aimlessly muttering to themselves about what they should do. I slowly realized that someone was clenching my hand (my left hand, to my great appreciation), saying something about how I would be okay.

I felt my mouth being gently coaxed open, and a liquid poured into it. It tasted like nothing I had ever had before. It tasted delicious and vile at the same time; I couldn't decide if I liked it or not. Before I could come to my conclusion, I felt myself fading into a deep sleep and within seconds I passed out.

FOR THE INTENDED

ROYAL PRIVILEGES

A noise came to my awareness. It sounded distant and quiet, but then became clearer. Gradually I recognized it as two people talking. My eyes were weak, and my eyelids heavy. When I forced them open, the world appeared murky, but within no time I could at least hear clearly.

"Don't worry," said a comforting voice—one I identified as Arnet's. "She should be up and about soon."

"I know, I know, you keep saying she'll be better but how do you really know? It's been two days already!" said Mildrid, my maid.

Two days! I thought to myself. I squinted so no one could see I was awake yet, but I managed to make out my surroundings. I could see that we were in my chamber.

"I just do," Arnet said, trying to keep a nice tone. "You can come back later and check on her if you like."

"I will," Mildrid stated, turning on her heel and heading out the door.

"Alright," replied Arnet, and he gently closed the door behind her.

I heard her footsteps retreating down the hallway. When the footsteps stopped and hurriedly scrambled back to the door, Arnet sighed heavily.

A gentle knock came to the door. He opened it, "Yes, Mildrid?"

"I just thought you should know that I am coming back at dinnertime, and just in case she's awake, I will be bringing a tray full of the feast leftovers. Oh, and I'll bring a nice glass of iced tea, and a change of clothes. Oh! And maybe some—"

"Is that all, Mildrid?"

She sighed dejectedly, "I suppose so."

"Good, then let's let Galayne rest," he said conclusively.

"Alright," she said, slumping away from the door.

The door closed quietly. Arnet sighed and then a few seconds later he said, "She cares a great deal for you, you know."

"I know," I said, sitting up and pulling my legs over the side of the bed.

Arnet had an amazing ability to know, like, everything—like when someone in the room wasn't really unconscious.

By that time my head had cleared up. "I was just hoping to avoid conversation just yet."

Arnet chuckled, "Well, I'm afraid you've failed. We need to talk." He bent over and fished around in a brown satchel for something as he said, "Speaking of talk, there's been a lot since your dramatic arrival the other day. The Aedine Prophecy is a particularly popular topic right now." He looked up when he finished and gave me a sly smile. He knew how much I hated speaking about the Aedine Prophecy, but he teased me with it anyway. The disappearance of the markets had undoubtedly been a prank of Arnet's doing since he knew I would think I had failed to fulfill the Aedine Prophecy. He knew the panic I would experience and couldn't resist messing with me. It probably wasn't all Arnet's idea since I knew a few officials who would've conspired with him, but I didn't doubt that he had proposed it. His amused smile dared me to express my displeasure with his sense of humor, but I knew that would let him know how successful he had been.

"Yeah, yeah," I said, trying to change the subject. I bet it *was* the talk of the castle. My incident only further proved that I was the one in the prophecy, and who doesn't like to hear gossip about the princess cantering into a party drooling over the side of her horse? But I knew it made Arnet happy because it once again confirmed he was right about me being The Summer Born.

FOR THE INTENDED

Then I remembered the oddness of my trip and said, "Arnet, this is the worst it's ever been. And I've never seen Winlit Cordial glow so bright. What is—?"

"Hold on," he said, taking a small beautifully crafted flask from the satchel. "Drink this," he ordered. He tossed it to me and immediately started rummaging through the next satchel.

I sniffed the contents, instantly taken back to the first time I met Arnet. That night so long ago. The night he changed my life forever...

Arnet had been that strange warrior—my rescuer. After breakfast that first morning in Umplidore, he told me I'd always have a home at the castle. Only a little while later, they crowned me Princess of Edgeladine and Arnet began my training.

It sounds strange and fast paced, but after all, I was The Summer Born. Arnet was pardoned from his treason, because he had been right all along. Nobody wanted to consider what would've happened if he hadn't forced his way past the guards. He wasn't fully trusted though—not for a long time—but his skill as a warrior and his knowledge of Naetera saved him. In no time, he worked his way up in the castle, and was soon in charge of several of its operations. It wasn't long before he claimed guardianship over me. Of course, he wasn't allowed to raise me by himself—I was watched over by many officials and elders—but he was the only one that felt like family.

He was like a father to me. He was a friend, teacher, and counselor, and one of the first people I'd go to for help. I would never have told him this, but I remember how he used to hold me when I cried (not that I did it often). How he used to brush the hair out of my face while I "slept," bending down to kiss my forehead. How that one time, for my ninth birthday, he traveled all the way to Turnington Tide Shore to pick the rare flowers of rinlin for me. They were extremely rare flowers that only grew there; four distinct white petals with blue pistils growing from the center. He'd sat me on his lap and told me that I was as rare as the flowers, and that one day, I'd be the greatest ruler Edgeladine had ever seen. It was just flowers, you know, but to my nine-year-old self, it meant the world.

I thought of all that in just a few seconds. I smiled in sweet remembrance and then downed the flask in a second. Disgusting sweetness poured down my throat. Nothing happened, as suspected. It would take a few minutes to work.

"Now," I said, determined to get an answer, "what about the power burst?"

"Oh . . ." I saw his face darken as he quickly turned away. "Sorry about that, it was just . . ." he paused and then lowered his voice, "a miscalculation."

I tried to not get angry, something I did a lot. But his description of what happened didn't seem extreme enough for the situation. I could have died. Like actually died.

I had experienced a "power burst," an elementary term Arnet used to summarize a complicated expansion of my abilities. My powers were constantly developing, but a power burst was a sudden, large increase in my abilities. Every time it happened, I would be vulnerable—weak and disoriented. In short, I needed to be looked after during a power burst. Arnet had predicted the first one would happen a few weeks later when I would have been surrounded by people that could help me. He was wrong.

"Yes, but you're fine now, we needn't talk about it," he said, mindlessly going through bags, pretending to look for something so he wouldn't have to meet my blazing green eyes.

"Needn't talk about it!" There was the anger. "You know what could've happened. You know what," I did air quotation marks, "a 'miscalculation' can do to me, to you, to everyone in Edgeladine!"

He said nothing, still intent upon finding something I knew didn't exist.

"Arnet! This is serious!"

"Yes," he countered back, turning abruptly and staring at me. Softening his voice, he said, "Yes, it is. I'm sorry. I'm just worried. I hadn't predicted that it would happen that soon. In my calculations, you still had a few more weeks." For the first time ever, he looked old and worn to me. His eyes were faded and hollow as if he hadn't slept in days. He came over and put his hands on my shoulders, looked me straight in the eyes and said, "I'm sorry that this happened. It . . . just means that we need to be more careful in the future."

I turned my head and nodded. I didn't want to meet his eyes. I felt bad for exploding on him. It wasn't his fault, and most likely he hadn't left my side, worried sick for me.

I watched a green leaf outside my window twist and turn slowly downwards, slipping out of sight. It reminded me to tell Arnet about the freak snow burst from nowhere, which reminded me to tell him about the varnants. But I decided to tell him later when we were both in better moods.

When I finally looked back at him, he seemed to transform into his regular self. He put his hands on his hips, and with that wide grin I'll always know said, "Now go, get changed, you have some people waiting on you."

I smiled back, disguising my somewhat sour mood. When he left, I slowly stood, shaking terribly. My legs felt like they weren't even there. As I straightened out, my back cracked several times. I sighed at the awesome feeling of being upright after days of motionlessness. I looked down to see my nightgown. Nighttime was the only time you would find me in a nonfunctional dress. I mean, besides the gowns I had to wear occasionally. I wouldn't have even worn one then, but if you could have heard how Mildrid nagged me for it.

Milly had been my caretaker ever since I moved into the castle. She was five years older than me, but no one would have ever guessed since she was so petite. She was a perfectionist, so naturally she was constantly annoyed by me. She had shoulder length brown hair and blue eyes that always followed me.

For balance, I used my furniture to slowly slink over to my wardrobe. I brushed a strand of hair from my face as I opened it to find that my regular clothes had been replaced by a beautiful light blue dress. Not fancy or anything, but *floaty* and *nice*. I instantly knew who the culprit was.

"Mildrid . . . *Mildrid*," I shouted as loud as I could but to no avail.

I sighed as I took the dress out of the wardrobe. Slipping it on, I muttered about how I would kill her the next time I saw her.

When I finished, I looked around to find my boots. Of course, all I found were some lacy blue slippers (conveniently the same color as the dress). I rolled my eyes and slipped them on.

I turned and examined myself in the mirror. My blonde hair went to the bottom of my back, but I had to keep it that long to please the elders. My eyes were deep green, and they didn't change like I've known some to do.

Most of the time I wore a green knee-length dress. I wasn't overly fond of wearing it, but it was easy to move in and I didn't really have a choice anyway. A few of my supervisors, including Arnet, said that it gave a nice feminine touch to my heroic profile that the people would see as a comfort. Yeah. *Whatever.* I would wear a dress with or without long sleeves depending on the weather. I always preferred to wear boots though. Summer, spring, winter, or fall, wearing boots suited them all. Not always, but often enough, I wore black leather armor too.

I always carried my bow with me. I usually had a sword strapped to my side, but it wasn't uncommon for me to forget it since I preferred my bow. It was a standard blade, and every once in a while, I saw people's disappointment when they caught a glimpse of it.

I should've been carrying Edral Arshine, the sword that broke that glass case so long ago. And since "Edral Arshine" literally meant "Bright star" in the Eraldine Language, their disappointment wasn't misplaced. But with my tendency to neglect to bring it with me at all times, I gave it over to the same guards that guarded all the royal artifacts. It bewildered me to think that it was entrusted to me—of all the unqualified people—*me*, so I only used it during various ceremonies where its presence was required.

Also, being the official Princess of Edgeladine, I had to wear a silver crown on special occasions. I would've normally had to wear it all the time, but I, uh . . . *insisted otherwise*. Besides that, the only accessories that I kept with me were my rarn whistle which I tied about my neck with a leather string, and of course Winlit Cordial—my curse.

I stepped out, being mindful to close the door so if Milly were to come by my room she would think I was still sleeping. I was eager to see her, but not just yet. I had a few other visits to make first before she wouldn't let me out of her sight.

I began strolling down a hallway of the castle, finding it empty. I stepped into a large room with an enormous window. I couldn't see with the light at first, but as my eyes adjusted, I looked out over a glorious sight.

There, outside that window, lay my kingdom. My view included the deep blue waters of Lake Lunadine, and the white flowers of Pludani that grew in thousands across the Plains of Andone. It was all mine, and the sickening weight of responsibility outdid the beauty every time.

FRIENDS

Lakon grinned, "Well, if it isn't Miss Galayne." His muscles rippled as he lifted a large barrel from the corner of the room and carried it to his work station. I saw a twinge of amusement cross his face as he noticed my clothes, but he thought better of saying anything. "Wasn't expecting to see you today."

"Good morning, Lakon," I said as I sat down on a stool that faced into the royal blacksmith. I studied the misshapen form of metal on his anvil and decided he must be making a horseshoe.
Lakon was enormous. He had these huge, rough-looking hands that could crush a boulder, and he was so tall he had to duck under most doorways. He had an accent that I could never place, and he didn't share anything from his past. He was probably in his forties, hence the few gray streaks in his dark brown, slightly-longer-than-shoulder-length hair. I had seen him in battle and he was a magnificent warrior, though you would have never guessed it. He was so quiet and gentle that he seemed like an ordinary blacksmith. He was almost always covered in soot and was always wearing a silver ring—a dragon coiling around his finger with a green jewel in its mouth.
I pushed hair behind my ear as I looked up above my head at the wooden "Edgeladine's Finest Armory" sign. It creaked as it swung in the light breeze. As I looked up at it, Lakon followed my gaze and laughed.

"That sign needs to be changed. Instead it should say "Edgeladine's Finest Horse Shoes" or "Edgeladine's Finest Farm Tools." He laughed again.

I smiled. I felt bad for him, though. He hadn't needed to repair a sword for months, at least that I knew of. For a long while he only had to repair horseshoes. It had been the case since the number of monster appearances had greatly decreased. In fact, the varnants I'd encountered a few days before were the first I had seen in a while. Anyway, I knew how much he appreciated a good sword, and yet he never complained. He always had a smile on no matter what work they put in front of him. But he couldn't hide the truth from me.

"I'm sorry," I said, letting him know I knew.

"Awwh, that's all right. Besides, what would the world do without my handy dandy horse shoes?" He grinned, bringing his hammer down hard onto the metal, making quite a clatter.

I gave a slight smile and slid off my stool, starting to walk away.

"Hey, Galayne."

I turned, "Yeah?"

"It's nice to see you again," a look of friendly sincerity on his face.

I grinned in response.

As I left the blacksmith, I decided I would go to the stables next. I made my way across the rundown courtyard, lost in my thoughts. Suddenly I heard a burst of laughter from my left.

"What *are* you wearing?" an obnoxious voice jeered.

Without turning I said, "Don't you have anything better to do?"

I then turned to look into a very enthusiastic face. A boy sat on a low protruding wall, sharpening a stick with his dagger. The wall was in ruins, so that when he jumped down, two corroded bricks came with him.

His name was Robert. Robert was around fourteen years old—same as me and all my friends. Robert had the reddest hair you could ever imagine, with a lightly freckled face to match. His light blue eyes always had a mischievous gleam and he had bright white teeth that were always showing. You rarely ever caught Robert without a smile on his face, him being the resident prankster of the castle. Once he put linders in Tucker's bed and didn't stop laughing about it for a whole week. But even though he messed with others constantly, no one wanted to mess with him. He was wicked with a sword. His upper body strength came from working at the blacksmith and the hours of fighting lessons that were required of all of us.

He tossed his stick and sheathed his dagger as he came up to me. He looked me up and down before snickering again.

"Is there something you want?" I glared, crossing my arms. I played impatient with him, but secretly I was so glad to see him. It had been a few months since I had seen any of my friends, the castle, or been in a place I called home.

"Oh no, Your Illustriousness," he said with a distinguished voice and an exaggerated bow.

I narrowed my eyes.

"But I think our dear friend Tucker is in need of a visitation." He looked up, "I believe he has something for you."

I put my hands on my hips. "Great! Where is he?"

"In the esteemed establishment known as the stable," he enunciated each syllable. At that, he bowed out.

As he left, I shook my head, but my grin remained. I knew he was glad to see me and to know that I was alright. He would never admit that, but I knew.

I walked into the stable and noticed something cold and mushy oozing through my toes. I looked down to see that my new lacy slippers were covered in mud, and the brown sludge was starting to seep into them. I growled a little. I really wished I had my boots then, not the frou-frou shoes. I was leaning on a stall door, shaking my feet, trying to get the mud off them, when I got tackled unexpectedly.

"Galayne! Galayne! You're here, you're okay!" said another boy my age. He hugged me so tightly I thought my lungs would collapse.

"Tucker!" I was delighted to see another familiar face.

Tucker was rather small. He had blond hair, soft brown eyes, and had the sweetest disposition of anyone I knew. I had never seen him yell or curse, and he was usually ending fights instead of starting them. He was . . . mediocre with a bow, and terrible with a sword. His true unique talent was creating things. You could've gave him some scrap metal, a stone, some long dry grass, a crooked branch, and his tools, and the next thing you knew—Ta da! He'd have made a beautiful sword, or a necklace, or invented something crazy.

Still hugging me, "Oh, Galayne, we've all missed you so much! Even Robert and Dare seemed to miss you. Are you okay? What happened?" Moving from his tight embrace to hold my shoulders and look in my eyes, he exclaimed, "Oh, Galayne! It's great to have you back!"

"Oh, I'm fine. I—wait what? Dare missed me?" I asked, somewhat surprised. She never seemed to be that kind of person.

"Yeah, she said she missed your help with the chores." He winked.

Figures, I thought, but I knew she missed me too. Just like Robert, she'd never admit it.

Suddenly Tucker burst forth, "Oh, oh, oh, I finally finished your surprise!" He darted into the tack room and came out with something wrapped in an old cloth.

"Oh, thanks, an old tattered rag," I teased.

He put his eyebrows together, clearly missing the fact that I was kidding, "No, no, inside the rag."

I pretended to suddenly understand, "Oh, I see." I carefully opened the rag, his eyes watching intently.

I found another whistle like the one I usually called Drayla with. It was made of rarn, polished to a shine. It was slightly longer and thinner than my old one, but other than that I didn't see what the big fuss was.

"It reaches a five-mile radius. That's two more than your old one!"

I blew it and found that it really did seem louder. I rolled it back and forth in between my fingers. "Thanks so much, Tucker. It's really..."

I gasped and nearly dropped it in shock when a shiny seedling rose from the smooth metal. Others formed and curled around the whistle; some began to sprout buds that bloomed. The growing didn't stop until the entire whistle was covered in flowers. I stared, speechless.

Tucker studied me and my gaping mouth. "Do you... like it?" he asked nervously.

"Tucker it's amazing!!"

A large smile returned to his face. "Sorry it took me so long, getting the flowers to grow was definitely a setback, but it was worth it."

"I'll say!" I said, studying it closely. "How do you get them to..." I started but didn't finish.

He took it, "Oh! That's my other favorite part about it. Watch." He cupped one hand around the whistle and ran it down the length of the pipe. I didn't think I could get any more blown away but was quickly proven wrong. As he ran his hand along the ornate cylinder, the flowers receded, leaving it an ordinary whistle. He smiled proudly, handing it back to me.

I threw my arms around him, "Tucker, I don't know what to say!"

He hugged me back "Don't mention it; it's your returning home present. But... could I ask a favor?"

I stopped hugging him to look him in the eyes. "Anything!"

"Could I have your old whistle? I would really like to try a few experiments on it." He asked it as if he were asking for Winlit Cordial or something.

I laughed, "Is that all? Of course." I reached for the brown string that secured the old whistle around my neck and yanked. "Here."

"Thanks." He smiled as I laid it in his cupped hands.

Both our heads turned as we heard a bell clanging in the distance. "Oh, I'm late already!" Tucker exclaimed in a panicky voice. "I'm going to get it if I don't hurry." He darted into a back room and snatched his satchel. As he ran toward the stable door, he put one hand on my shoulder and said with a grin, "It's great to have you back." Before I could reply, he darted out the door saying, "I'll see you tonight!"

"Well . . . ok . . . I guess I'll just . . ." but he already couldn't hear me.

After he left, I took a deep breath of stable smell. Some people can't stand the way horses smell, but to me, it will always be a comfort. I peered into the nearest stall and found a palomino horse chomping hay. "Hey, Pickadilly! It looks as if you've been upgraded to the premium stalls, huh? It's about time!"

The mare quickly lifted her head and smiled. She stuck her head out and whinnied, inviting me to rub her soft pink muzzle. Pickadilly, Tucker's horse, wasn't gifted with the talent of speech the way Drayla was, but she tried her hardest to convey her thoughts through motions and noises. I don't know if you've ever tried to understand Horse Speak, but it's not as easy as it looks.

I pet her nose and scratched in between her eyes, "You wouldn't happen to know where Drayla is, would you?"

Pickadilly bobbed her head and pawed the ground four times then looked at me expectantly, as if that revealed Drayla's exact location. When she saw me staring back at her blankly, she nodded her head to the right. My eyes followed her motions to the other end of the stable where the doors were hanging open.

"Is she in the pastures?"

A nod.

"Thanks, Pickadilly!" I called as I ran out the stable doors. She whinnied in farewell.

I thought it was strange that Drayla had stayed in the pastures. She preferred free roaming despite my protests. I liked to know she would be safe at night, and if anything happened I'd be right there. But she said that she could take care of herself.

The back of the stable looked out over acres and acres of fenced-in lush green grass. There were many horses boarded in Umplidore's stables, sometimes hundreds, so finding Drayla would be a pain if not for a certain gift I'd just received.

I rolled the new whistle back and forth between my fingers and couldn't help but smile. As it transformed, I blew it, fully appreciating its range. There were lots of horses, so lots of noise—chomping, neighing, and hooves thundering. I began to worry that she might not hear it, or because it was a different whistle that she might not come.

I strained to hear or see her for some time but failed to do so. I put it in my mouth to try again when a loud neigh burst through the chaos. I turned my head to see a flurry of black and white emerge from a cluster of horses and fly towards the front of the pasture.

I ran towards her, scurrying over the fence.

When we reached each other, she neighed happily in greeting.

I put my arms around her, clutching her mane.

She gave a gigantic horse hug, nearly crushing me. Shakily she asked, "How are you? Are you better?"

I took a step back and hugged her head, stroking it comfortingly. "I'm better. Apparently, it was just an accident—a 'miscalculation' I guess. Arnet didn't realize it would be so soon..."

She pulled away and forced me to look into her eyes. That's when I realized how poorly she looked. Her coat had lost its sheen. Her mane had become stringy and her eyes seemed cloudy. She had obviously strayed from her normal grooming routine and seemed to have been sick with worry for me. "No more accidents?"

I didn't think I could help that, but I hugged her, "No more."

Haven Berg

OCCUPATIONAL HAZARD

The rest of the day I tried to find the rest of my friends. I looked for Lily, but I knew she was busy with her daily tasks just like Tucker. Dare was occasionally assigned as a scout, so she was probably inaccessible at the moment, too. I decided to look for Blue. Blue would be busy too, but we usually shared the same schedule. I knew where he should be at what time.

I couldn't find him anywhere. I had the thought to go and ask his adopted father before quickly tossing the idea aside. I would probably find his father drunk, as usual, and it wouldn't be worth my time. I could've stopped by the house just to check, but Blue was never home. Not that home, at least.

All my friends had adopted caretakers. Most of them got lucky, but not Blue. Blue had been adopted by a drunken, sour man with a rundown house full of broken bottles and grime. His adoption happened when we were seven, and nobody argued because his father used to be stately and still held some influence. He named Blue "Vir," a cruel name meaning "Worthless" in the Eraldine Language. Only a few people knew what his name meant, though, so people called him worthless all throughout the day without knowing it. Blue and I knew, though, and I had made it a point to never call him that.

The past few months he had been growing more and more distant. We used to do just about everything together, but lately . . . it seemed like he tried to avoid me. I had originally been angry with him, but then I was just concerned. It wasn't like him to not be there when I got back. And surely, he must have heard about my fainting episode. I should've seen him by then.

After searching at length, I finally decided to ask a maid carrying a basket of freshly washed clothes where Blue was. The gossip that happened in the castle was insane, so I could count on her to know the answer.

At first the maid seemed surprised that I was asking her a question, but then she suppressed a smile. She acted as if I were asking about my crush or something, "I believe Arnet sent him on a long quest, I'm not sure when he'll be back."

"Long? How long?"

She gave a large smile, probably proud to have something important to say. She shifted the basket to her other hip. "Well, he's been gone a long time, dearie. He left right after you did."

My confusion must've been evident.

Her smile faltered, "Is everything alright?"

I smiled, "Yes, everything's just fine. Thank you." As I turned, I saw her grin and run to tell her friends who she'd just talked to.

It was strange though. The longest quest Blue had ever gone on only lasted a few weeks. And not only had Blue been gone for months, but Arnet didn't even think to mention it?

I thought about it and other things until I suddenly realized I'd walked all the way to the shores of Lake Lunadine. It was located pretty far to the southeast from the castle, so I couldn't hear the fresh markets. Normally, I would've been able to hear the slight buzz of talking, arguing, and trading, but the merchant tents were still being set up from when they'd been taken down for my return. I smiled to myself when I looked to my right to find a large oak tree; I had subconsciously walked to my favorite thinking spot.

I slumped against the tree, slowly sinking down the trunk. The sun fell on the other side of the tree by then, giving me some awesome shade. I sat only a few feet away from the water and I watched the breeze create ripples on the surface. For a moment, I forgot everything, retreating into the peacefulness of my surroundings. I closed my eyes and spread my hands in the cool, green grass. I loved the way it felt, but then my right hand bumped into something. I looked down at the smooth stone that blocked my hand's path and everything flooded back to me. I had a flashback to when I was eight years old.

I had pouted at the base of that very same tree. A bow and arrow lay strewn apart a few feet away, just tossed. With my head resting on my knees, buried under my arms, I yelled, "I can't do it!"

Arnet came over and set his bow against the trunk calmly. He sat next to me and put one arm around me, "Can I show you something?"

I didn't expect him to say that so I raised my tearstained face. He smiled as he picked up a stone; he bounced it up and down in his hand and then handed it to me. He found his own and pulled me up. "This will help you. You'll get a bull's-eye in no time." We faced the lake as he instructed, "Throw all your anger and frustration away as you throw your stone."

I frowned, confused.

He laughed at my expression and challenged, "Just try it. One... Two... Three!"

We both threw our rocks as hard as we could. He picked up another one for both of us and we did it again. We did it until I slowly began to smile, and then laugh. I had way more fun than I expected. At one point, Arnet pretended to throw his rock so hard that he lost his footing and toppled into the water. I burst into laughter when he came up. He splashed me and I splashed him back. Before I knew it, we were having a blast.

When we were done, we rested our soaking wet bodies against the oak tree, the sun setting behind us. We were laughing for no particular reason when he said, "Would you like to try again? Just one more try?"

My smile broke, and with a determined face, I nodded. He nodded back and we got up. I retrieved my bow and arrow, and with my hair dripping, I notched the arrow in place.

FOR THE INTENDED

He watched me carefully, looking for any errors as I drew the bowstring. I took a deep breath, trying to relax. I don't know what I did differently, but that arrow flew straight towards the middle of the target fast enough to break the arrow on impact.

Within a second, I was being twirled around in Arnet's arms, "You did it! You did it! I knew you could!"

I laughed and giggled, so proud of myself. When Arnet finally stopped circling, I gave him a hug. "I love you, Arnet," I whispered into his ear.

He hugged me back, "I love you too, Galayne."

It was usually one of my favorite memories, but right then, it just reminded me of how hard my life had been. The memory should have started with us throwing stones, not an archery lesson. I only needed an archery lesson because my safety required it—I had no choice. My whole life had been that way, and negative memories poured in after the positive one. Abruptly standing up, I snatched the rock. My right hand glowed with light. It got hotter and hotter until the stone looked like a blazing ball of white fire. Before I could even consider wisdom, I chucked it as far as I could. I staggered backwards from all of the energy that took but smiled triumphantly anyway as I saw it sink under the dark water. *Hah! Take that rock!*

I turned to walk away, and my smile disappeared as I heard a small explosion behind me. I slowly turned around . . . there was nothing except some large ripples from where my rock had landed. I thought I'd imagined it until I watched in horror as my small rock exploded making a sound like a sonic boom. Pure white energy shot out from it, forming large waves. As the light passed me, I gasped as I got knocked over by its power, the heat intense. The grass in the explosion's radius bent over, and some of the leaves on the tree blew away, crinkling in the heat. Honestly, if I didn't have the powers of summer, I could've been seriously injured just from the temperature.

When the energy died out, the light slowly diminished and the heat began to subside. I quickly looked around, making sure no one had been affected. I breathed a sigh of relief. No people. Not only could I have hurt someone, I could've set the grass on fire. *Yeah, way to go, hero!* I thought. If Arnet found out he'd kill me.

I stood up, checking one last time for damage. I didn't see anything except for a pair of seriously freaked out birds. I brushed myself off and headed back to the castle, making sure not to cause any more explosions on the way.

FOR THE INTENDED

SISTERS

I drifted around the castle until evening. I exchanged several of the customary pleasantries with various servants. "How was your journey?" asked one. "How was the weather?" inquired the next. "You didn't see any monsters, did you?" asked another.

Of course, I wasn't going to give out anything juicy; the whole castle might go into panic. So, I pretty much just said, "Great. Perfect. No, not really." Most of them looked too busy to press me much.

Once or twice I asked if I could help with the chores, but the answer was always the same. "Don't you dare lift a finger, miss! I can manage. Why don't you go rest yourself?"

Usually, in spite of being the princess, I had my own chores and duties. I only occasionally had to actually be a princess. The rest of the time Arnet called "character building." But it seemed like there wasn't going to be any of that for a while. It all had to do with my little showcase at the feast. To tell you the truth, it made me mad. Usually everyone respected me as a tough warrior who could handle almost anything. But after my incident, they treated me as sweet, little, delicate thing that couldn't be bothered to do zilch. I was sure it was the dress.

The sun started to set when I realized I hadn't found Caspian or Elon yet. I figured Caspian had started up his usual hunting schedule. He was really good at catching his prey without totally dismembering it, and actually brought in a considerable amount of food to Umplidore. Elon was probably in his normal messenger position. He was my personal messenger when needed, but mostly he took minor information throughout the castle. I searched a little longer for either one of them, but noticed the light failing, and made my way back to my chamber.

I headed down the empty corridor to my room in a groggy haze. I jumped at the sound of a voice.

"Galayne?"

I turned around. I saw a girl my age standing in the entrance of the hallway, her sword in her right hand and a satchel in her left. Her sparkling light blue eyes shimmered in the fading sunlight. Her usually soft, flowing, light blonde hair was sweaty and confined into a tangled ponytail. Smudges covered her face. Even though she looked really unkempt, it couldn't hide her natural beauty. With those shining eyes and rosy cheeks, she was definitely considered by the rest of the castle to be the prettiest one in my group of friends. Her mouth hung wide open, and her things slipped from her hands and clattered to the floor. Her mouth slowly curled into a smile. "Galayne!"

"Lily!"

She ran towards me without bothering to pick up her things, "Galayne! It's really you!" She threw herself at me and we spun around and around—she laughing like a little girl, and me with a silly grin on my face.

"Oh, it's been so long!" she laughed.

"I know! I can't believe how long it seems!" I smiled.

"Well, two months *is* a long time!"

She gave me one last squeeze before going to get her things. "Soooo how did it go? Oh, and I love your dress by the way," she smiled slyly.

"Oh..." the question caught me off-guard and I fumbled for words. Normally I could tell Lily almost anything, but I couldn't then. I didn't even notice the bit about the dress.

FOR THE INTENDED

"Um . . . you know . . . the usual. Nothing new." I was disappointed at how bad that sounded.

She made a puzzled face as she bent down for her things, noticing my bluntness. But being Lily, she didn't press me. She always knew when I was in trouble or just not in the mood, and never bothered me during those times. She collected her things and smiled a perfect smile, "Let's go, we have some catching up to do."

We went to a parlor down the hall and sat on a comfy couch. We talked and laughed for at least an hour until we heard the great silver bells that rang throughout the castle letting people know the time. Lily never once mentioned the accident. She was one of those optimists who don't like to linger on past events. She was always "look ahead" and "even thunderstorms must pass." Her smile never left her face and she refused to say anything that might upset me.

After the bells rang for dinner, Lily stood and gathered her belongings. She turned and asked, "Aren't you coming?"

"Um . . . I think I'll just go to bed." I didn't realize it until then, but I was exhausted.

She smiled gently, "Okay, see you tomorrow."

We gave each other one last hug and parted.

Servants were lighting the torches as I went down the hall to my room. The halls were empty besides them. I took a long time to reach my room, not in the mood to go fast.

I practically crawled into bed. I pulled back the covers, kicked off the dirt-caked slippers and got in. *Ha ha, no nightgown.* It would get Milly back for the frou frou dress. I looked around my room one last time, and peace washed over me. I closed my eyes. I was home. Finally home.

RESPONSIBILITIES

The bells sounded abnormally loud the next morning. I groaned and pulled the blankets over my head. Arnet walked in precisely as the last clang reverberated.

"Gooooood morning!" he quipped cheerfully. Then, with a failing grin, continued, "I see you're *not* following the schedule I gave you."

"Ghhh... what schedule?" I removed the covers from my face and squinted in the light of the room.

He walked over to my nightstand, "This one." He lifted a piece of paper from the stand. "I put it here for you last night." He began to read from it. "At 6:00, feed the horses in section four of the stables. At 7:00 go to the armory and help Lakon. At 8:00 go to the docks and..."

I zoned out then. Reading his list was a way to lecture me on how careless I was. Like I should have noticed his small, hard to see, nearly invisible note on the nightstand!

I didn't pay attention until I heard in the back of my mind, "... help with the ball decorations."

"What?"

He looked up.

"Ball?" I asked fearfully, the dread already passing over me.

"Yes, I mean the grand ball for your return."

I threw the pillow over my head, groaning.

He smiled, "Since you... uh... 'fell ill' during the last one, the people want to throw you another."

I didn't respond.

He put the note on the stand, "Come on, Galayne, it won't be that bad. It's just a few hours."

I took a deep breath, realizing I didn't really have a choice. I removed the pillow and slung my legs over the right side of the bed, my back facing Arnet. "I'll be down in a minute," I mumbled.

"That's the spirit!" He strode out of the room, closing the door behind him.

At least I felt like myself that morning; cranky, grouchy, and tired. I stood, stretching my arms back and yawning. I rubbed my eyes, trying to get them to focus. I dragged my feet over to my wardrobe. I opened the thick wood doors and my mood lifted a bit. My regular outfit was waiting for me, boots and all.

After that I moved a little quicker. I threw my dress on, tightened my belt, attached my sword, and shoved my feet into my boots. I felt ready to take on my crazy world.

I bounded down the kitchen steps and whizzed past Arnet so I wouldn't have to talk to him. The kitchen we were in wasn't the main one in the castle. In fact, it wasn't really even a kitchen but more of a sitting alcove. It was about the size of my room, with a cheap wooden table and benches. The maids had brought two bowls of various fruits, a plate of toast, and a platter stacked with a mountain of bacon and sausages. That bacon also had a little magical effect on me.

"Hmmm . . . someone's had a change of attitude," Arnet smiled.

I snatched a muffin and about fifteen pounds of bacon and slid next to Lily who delicately buttered a piece of toast, "Hmm . . . what? Oh, I guess." I shrugged it off. I didn't want my friends to know I had been crabby that morning, though they'd seen me far worse.

Tucker walked in then. "Good morning," he smiled cheerfully. Lily nodded in acknowledgement since her mouth was full. I didn't really care for manners so I said a muffled good morning through a mouth full of bacon. He headed straight for the fruit bowl, grabbed a banana, and leaned against the counter. As he peeled it he asked, "Where's Robert?"

"He had to go straight to Lakon's this morning; he should be here any minute," Arnet said.

Dare walked into the room, blocking the sunlight. I loved her just as much as my other friends, but some people would have found that hard to do. She never gave so much as a smile and never spoke unless she could give input on a battle plan. She always stood straight with a look of power. She was the best dagger fighter I had ever seen, and her sword fighting came close second. She knew how to use a bow and arrow, and I had seen her shoot one pretty accurately, but she never chose to use one. Her straight, waist-length black hair, her dark apparel, and her purple eyes gave her a chilling aura.

She walked silently to the fruit counter and picked up a blood red apple. She turned it around in her hand, inspecting it. She then turned to me, nodded, and then without a word strode outside. Her eyes said she was glad I was back, and her silence reaffirmed it. Right as she walked out the door, Robert just about ran her over.

"Whoops, sorry, Dare!" he apologized and dashed to the side, continuing his fast pace to the meat plate. I could swear I saw Dare's murderous expression through the back of her head before she continued out the door.

"Hey, thanks for saving these last six sausages for me," he beamed as he grabbed all of them plus a handful of bacon. He slid onto the bench across from me and Lily.

Arnet, leaning against the wall silently, didn't even look up from his list. "Don't you think you should try to get something other than protein in your body, Robert?"

Robert looked up with a mouth bursting with various meats, and took a second before making a triumphant sound. He reached over and grabbed the entire jug full of orange juice and took a long guzzle before putting it back.

"Good job, Robert," Arnet said sarcastically.

FOR THE INTENDED

Robert looked over and grinned at him.

"You too, Galayne," Arnet said, turning the page in his leather-bound notebook.

I looked down at my pile of bacon, then over at the counter. I sighed as I got up and went to get a nectarine.

As I sat down, about to take a big, juicy bite, the bells clanged. Tucker nearly choked as he lunged for his satchel and shot out the door. Lily quickly stacked her silverware on her plate and put it on the counter. She wiped her mouth with a napkin then strode outside. Robert shoved an amazing amount of food into his mouth and snatched the juice jug before lunging over the table and leaping out the door.

I just put the fruit back on my plate and sighed. "Okay, what's first?"

Arnet, without looking up from his reading, said distractedly, "What? Oh, um, over there on the counter. I made you a revised list."

I went and picked it up. I pretended to glance it over, but I was really just thinking about Blue. I considered asking Arnet what kind of quest he was on, but I just wanted to get out of there. Arnet was particularly irritating that morning and the sooner I got away from him the less chance there was that he would add more chores to my schedule. And besides, all my friends went on random quests from time to time—it was part of our training. So it wasn't really that concerning that Blue was on one. Yeah, it was longer than usual, but we were getting older so more was expected of us. Blue could tell me all about his journey when he got back. I brushed him from my mind and attempted to evade Arnet.

I shoved the list in my hidden side pocket. "Okay. See ya later!" I rushed towards the door.

"Oh, Galayne," he said, looking up.

I stopped abruptly. I sighed, "Yeah?"

His face looked concerned, worried or something. "Um, I . . ." He blinked, and his face returned to normal, "No slacking off today." I was sure he had been about to say something else.

That was weird. That was all I could think as I slow-jogged to the stables. He just seemed so . . . not himself. We always talked about everything and discussed every idea together. Never did we ever hold back information. Normally, I would've been angry, but I mean, I wasn't telling him everything either.

I was just beginning to feel bad about that when something slammed into me. I flew sideways and slid in the dirt. Rage fueled my instincts. I lashed out for my sword but didn't get the chance before getting smothered with doggy kisses.

Caspian made whimpering sounds and could barely hold still as he coated my face in slobber. That was one of my favorite things about Caspian. In public, Caspian was a general with an army of wolves at his command: hostile, fierce, unyielding. But when it was just me and him, he was my puppy dog.

"Caspian!" I laughed.

Contented whimpering. Finally, he breathed, "Oh, you're alright! I was so worried." His golden eyes glistened.

"Yeah, I'm alright," I smiled and hugged him.

He rubbed his soft face against mine and my arms drew tighter.

He started to sit on my lap when we heard an excited, "Galayne?"

Caspian bounded out of my arms and resumed his professional stance just as a brown blur rushed towards us. It fluttered around my head excitedly, giving happy little chirps. "Oh, Galayne!" Elon exclaimed. "It certainly is good to see you again!"

I held out my hand and he quickly landed in it. I brought him up to my face and he snuggled up against it. After one last cuddle he flew up a little and then back down into my hand, tucking his wings in gently and rearranging the feathers. He always did that before he said something important.

"Yes. Well, I have a message," he dutifully proclaimed.

FOR THE INTENDED

I laughed at his self-important pose. I leaned back on one hand, "Hit me."

He cleared his throat and then announced, "You are late for history class, and Witherbore is having quite a fit."

Me and Caspian just looked at each other with our mouths slightly ajar.

"Elon!" I yelled angrily. I jumped up and took off.

Witherbore was a stingy, stuck-up, middle-aged man. He was tall and thin, and his nose came to a point. Every word that came out of his mouth was greatly exaggerated. He couldn't stand tardiness and I personally think he just couldn't stand me. He always found something to lecture me on. And if I did anything wrong—*anything*—he went straight to Arnet. That meant two lectures in one day.

Lily was his class pet, always on time and focused, but not on purpose. It just came naturally to her. Any time I mentioned something bad about Witherbore, or cracked a joke about him, she would shrug it off and say, "He's just misunderstood." Yeah. Whatever.

So yeah, class stunk. It mainly consisted of Witherbore giving me a twenty-minute lecture while Robert snickered in the back of the room. Tucker and Lily pretended not to notice, both of them being too sweet. Dare I think really didn't notice, her face buried in a battle tactics book the entire time.

The bell rang, and everyone ran out of the room, except Dare who always took her time. I snatched my homework off my desk and flew to the door, but Witherbore beat me there.

"Ahem," he coughed loudly and held out his hand, a letter to Arnet in it. I rolled my eyes and grabbed it. He silently pointed out the door for me to go.

I hate him so much, I thought as I looked over the letter. It read:

Sir,
Pardon me, but your Galayne was tardy for the fifth time this semester.

Arnet was a great warrior held with high esteem in Umplidore, and his fame spread out through many of the surrounding provinces. So naturally, everyone who approached him was always a little nervous.

I know you say she is trying but I just cannot tolerate it anymore. The next time she is late, I will have no choice but to expel her . . .

I sighed and proceeded to tear it up. It went on to say something about how sorry he was and he hoped it would not create tension between them or whatever. I tossed the pieces at the base of a tree and took out my to-do list: A few chores, then lunch, and a few more chores. After that, my worst nightmare: Dress Fitting.

FOR THE INTENDED

DRESS FITTING

I headed back to the castle in the evening. I looked down and saw myself caked in dirt; my shoes probably had horse manure on them, and I had various leaves sticking out of my hair. Normally I didn't mind being so dirty. In fact, sometimes I liked it. But I had to go and get ready for the ball, and you don't know Mildrid's standards. She always scrubbed so hard and put a gallon of soap in my hair. She cleaned under each fingernail and put gnolie oil in my hair to soften it. She put a fountain of perfume all over me until I couldn't breathe. After all that, we could finally start the dress fitting.

Milly actually gasped in horror when she saw me. "What did you do!?"
"Um . . ." I tried to smile it off.
She moaned, "Well. Let's get started." She grabbed my arm and led me to the bath.
I thought she'd be so excited to see me up and going, but she had gotten used to me being in trouble by then. Since I was well, there wasn't need for any more concern. She was a good enough caretaker herself to know I would be fine, so she wasn't surprised when I recovered. Also, she was in charge of making sure I was presentable, and I think that responsibility took over her ability to be excited.

The cleaning process commenced with a little more rigor than I had originally thought. After my skin burned from scrubbing and my nose burned with the smell of roses, Milly led me to the podium set in front of a folding mirror.

Then the seamstresses came in and got to work. They picked out a silky, blue fabric with tiny, silver beads that twisted into an elaborate design. Milly watched in pure joy as they quickly put a beautiful dress together, finishing in about an hour and a half. A few maids brought in several cases full of various pieces of jewelry and set them on the tables on the left-hand wall of the room. Then they departed, leaving me and Milly alone.

Milly couldn't stop smiling as she selected a silver necklace lined with diamonds and placed it over my head. She picked up a matching bracelet and to my surprise whispered decidedly, "No. I think that would be a bit too much."

My hair had dried by then, so she grabbed a brush and styled it to perfection. She ambled over to the dressing table. With an air of importance, she unfastened a marble box lined with light blue velvet. She held her breath as she lifted my crown from the case and carefully made her way over to me. She gingerly set the crown on top of my head, sighing in relief. She then set to making sure each strand of hair fit perfectly under it.

"Now remember your manners. Curtsy to all, keep your back straight and shoulders reigned in, say please and thank you, try not to belch, and—" She noticed me not responding, just staring blankly at myself in the mirror, and let her voice trail off. "Never mind, I'm sure you'll do just fine," she gently reassured.

Finally, she wrapped a transparent, silver shawl around my shoulders and stepped back in admiration. "You're perfect!" she grinned.

I offered a slight smile. I did feel kind of happy for her. That was how she always wanted me to look and she finally got to see it happen.

FOR THE INTENDED

Another maid came and whispered something in Milly's ear. Milly smiled even larger, "The ball begins in five minutes! We finished just in time!"

She strode out of the room and I watched as the large doors closed behind her, echoing loudly, making the room seem a whole lot larger than before.

I looked at myself in the mirror and sighed sadly. I stepped down from the podium and stood on the ground in front of the mirror. For just a moment I let my guard down. I grabbed each side of my dress and swished it back and forth gently. I thought for a second that I actually looked beautiful and graceful, and for once, I didn't really mind. In fact, I kind of liked it. My expression had just begun to show it when a face suddenly appeared above my shoulder.

"Well, that's an improvement."

I whirled around, "What are you doing here!?"

Robert grinned, not noticing my anger since I was almost always annoyed with him, and held out his arm and bowed, "I am to be your escort for the evening."

"Oh," I calmed my voice down. For a second, I thought he had seen me admiring my dress. There was a certain reputation that I had personally sworn to maintain since an early age, and that was the rep of a fierce, ferocious, warrior. When I was nine, I took a private oath to always protect Edgeladine, with my life if needed, and to always be there in the time of its greatest need. It sounded a little more childish the older I got, especially since I knew it had been the plan for me all along... Anyway, I thought the people wouldn't look to a weak princess for guidance; they needed to feel secure and protected. Arnet felt differently though. He said, "There is a sense of protection and order for the people if they see a kind, gentle ruler"—hence I was required to attend all the balls, wearing various ornate costumes.

I hooked my arm through Robert's and we moved to the majestic doors that led into the ballroom. As we walked over I noticed his ball attire, and had the faintest twinge of amusement. He was decked out in dark blue velvet with silver etchings, and I know he preferred red. The top was decorative but not unbearable. At least he didn't have to wear the puffy sleeves. He did have those ballooning pant things on his thighs, though, and he sported thick tights. A short cape draped over his shoulders and it seemed to get in the way in spite of its length. A shiny black belt circled his waist, and matching fancy shoes completed his look. His sword was safely attached in a brand new black scabbard at his left. Overall, he looked pretty uncomfortable. We made quite the pair.

I suddenly realized it would be the first time Blue wouldn't be my escort. He had always been with me for every ball and festival, somehow bringing out the fun in them. Robert would be fun too—he always made sure the people around him had a good time—but it was still breaking tradition. I wasn't a huge fan of most of the traditions I had to keep up with, but that was one I didn't want to break.

We arrived at the doors where the festive music and the voices of thousands made their way to us.

Robert grinned from ear to ear until he noticed my face. "Hey. Are you alright?" There were rare moments when Robert didn't joke around and actually took things seriously. It was one of those times and he looked at my face with genuine concern.

I looked at him. "Yeah, I'm good." I gave a small smile.

He nodded and looked back at the door. He sighed almost apprehensively, pulling at his tight-fitted collar. I realized he probably hated balls almost as much as I did. But then he heard the announcer's voice through the door and he rolled his shoulders and put on a grin.

The announcer's voice boomed, "Introducing... Princess Galayne of Edgeladine, and her escort, Robert Devin." Thunderous applause sounded.

"You ready?" he asked through his teeth.

I put on the biggest fake smile ever, and without turning, lied through my teeth, "You betcha."

FOR THE INTENDED

Just then the doors opened, and the light of the grand chandeliers and hundreds of candles flooded over us. The applause grew louder and the faces of the smiling people became merged into one great mass. I forced my mind to go blank and waved gracefully as we waded out into the crowd, becoming nothing more than a beautiful princess.

SOCIAL CUSTOMS

When we first strode out I heard several people mumble something like, "Is she okay?" and, "I wonder what happened, she looks fine to me." I pretended not to hear, though, and smiled blindly.

After that our job mainly consisted of strolling around and making conversation with various dukes and duchesses, the general nobility, and a few famous wealthy merchantmen. Robert did most of the talking. He made all the different people laugh at least once during the conversation, but usually the conversation ended because the people couldn't stop laughing and were gasping for air. I just stood there and performed my duty of the night—look pretty. I smiled and bowed, and smiled and bowed. Then just to shake things up, I bowed and then smiled. Arnet passed me every once in a while and smiled approvingly before moving on. I couldn't decide if that made me happy that he was proud of my efforts, or angry that I was there in the first place.

I saw Dare appear and disappear from my sight a few times. She wore a black feather dress with a purple sash that accentuated the intensity of her eyes. She was always retreated against a wall, glaring at everyone who passed. Once I saw a young gentlemen go up to her to start a conversation, but left within seconds as she stared him down.

FOR THE INTENDED

I saw Lily and Tucker a few times laughing and smiling together. They were perfect for each other, and I don't usually dabble in matchmaking. They'd blush and deny they were a couple if you hinted anything, but everybody knew they were.

Once I glimpsed Witherbore standing importantly, his nose towards the ceiling, discussing teaching techniques with tutors from other provinces. One tutor said he continued to have an impossible time with one of his students. "Really?" Witherbore asked, astonished, his chest puffed out, "I have never had that problem. My students are all so well-behaved and are quite the geniuses as well." *Classic Mister Witherbore.* He had apparently already forgotten the note to Arnet regarding a certain rebel princess.

I'd forgotten how tired one could get from standing around for hours. I was exhausted and I was only two hours in! My toes were almost totally asleep, and the few parts that were still awake throbbed terribly. Both my heels were sure to have blisters, and my lungs felt completely deflated. My mouth ached from the constant smiling, and the many layers of skirts began to feel heavy and hot.

Sometimes, to try to distract myself, I would glance around the room, taking in the splendor. The entire ballroom was made with marble and the floor had designs inlaid with silver. The ceiling was also ornate, with difficult swirls and curves coming to the center. The walls were almost entirely made of glass. Two large balconies with glass doors and white curtains were to the north and south. Grand, silver chandeliers lit every corner of the room brilliantly. Silver candlesticks and large vases of white and light blue flowers adorned the white tables. If I wasn't totally suffering right then, I would have thought it was breathtaking.

Later, the announcer asked everyone to gather around the table. I was so thankful for the tiny break from standing, but I was dreading the part that came afterwards.

Robert pulled my chair out for me. Both of our chairs were at the head of the table and it took every bit of willpower in me to not just fall back into it. Instead I managed to sit gracefully as Robert scooted it in.

When everyone was seated, the servants began to lay the table with mouthwatering foods: Succulent seasoned meats, shiny fruits, vibrant vegetables, and warm decorated pastries of all kinds. Everyone toasted to the queen, who for whatever reason couldn't attend, and then dug in. Well, "dug in" is a bit too much. They ate as quickly as their manners would let them. Whatever they took from the platter, a servant instantly replaced.

Now normally, that would be my kind of thing. You know, stuffing my face with a never-ending source of food. But as I looked around, nothing looked appetizing. All I could think about was how exhausted I was, and filling my stomach with food didn't sound like it would help. Also, I could barely chew with my mouth so sore from smiling, and with my dress so tight it was hard to swallow anyway.

Although I didn't have much of an appetite, the water became one of the best things I had ever tasted. There were various wines, juices, coffees, and foreign teas, but my eyes were on the water.

One time, Milly refilled my cup, and she feigned a cough.

"What?" I whispered.

She stood and pulled her shoulders back, staring at me expectantly. I didn't know that I could possibly sit any straighter, but I must've, because she smiled, satisfied, and went off.

I downed my fifth cup of water when all of a sudden the trumpets sounded, and the announcer's voice echoed, "Let the dancing commence!"

Music immediately filled the room. People leaped up from the table, almost abandoning their manners, and whooped. Everyone snatched a partner and darted to the dance floor.

Robert flew out of his chair and made a run for it.

FOR THE INTENDED

"Robert! Wait! We need to . . ." I tried to shout over the noise, but he disappeared in the mass of swishing skirts and large extravagant hats.

I went to go after him but someone stepped in my way. "Care to dance, Your Highness?" a boy about my age asked. I vaguely remembered him being introduced as the son of Lord What's-His-Face with the snobby voice, massive ego, and large feather hat. His son had a mischievous gleam in his eyes and seemed to have more bad than good about him. The way he asked almost felt like a dare.

I wanted to flick his nose and storm the other way, but remembered Milly's instruction to *never* turn down a dance invitation, so I held out my hand and nodded.

So, after a painful "dance" with the Lord What's-His-Face's son that mainly consisted of him tripping me and "apologizing," I went to go find Robert. Of course as soon as I turned around, another hand reached out for me. So of course, I danced. Then when that dance ended, I got asked again. So, I danced again. And thus proceeded the night.

After about the seventh dance I wanted to scream, the evening nowhere near over. My feet were shrieking in agony for me to stop, and my lungs refused to provide enough oxygen. I felt dizzy and lightheaded and could no longer focus on the people we were swirling around.

After the twelfth dance I bowed as quickly as I could and refused to turn around. I barreled forward towards the crowd around the edges as gracefully as I could and vanished into it. I immediately made my way to the wall and tried to hide my face without looking too conspicuous, but I was spotted nonetheless.

"Your Majesty?"

I rolled my eyes, but was relieved when I turned around, "Good evening, Jack. How are you?" It was way too formal compared to how I talked to him every other day, but the atmosphere required manners.

He bowed slightly, "I'm doing well, Your Majesty. I was about to ask the same of you."

Jack Larren was the same age as me, but he had a professional demeanor that aged him at least a decade. I only saw his teen side on occasions where he let himself forget about duties, and that was a rare occurrence. He was one of Arnet's favorites and a top contender for the next generation of Royal Guards, and no one else in Edgeladine was more suited to fill both roles. He had dark brown hair and eyes—eyes that constantly watched for danger.

He continued, "If I may say so, I know you have not been feeling too well of late." I could feel extra eyes look over when he said that, as discreet as ever, as their owners pretended to continue their own conversations. They tensed, knowing it was an inappropriate remark for him to make, at least to my face.

I laughed a little, "Of course you may, it's a fact, isn't it?" But I could feel my face get hot. "I'm alright. Really."

He nodded, but he could see my embarrassment. He looked down, bowing again, "Forgive me, Your Highness, I know a guard isn't supposed to notice such things. It's my duty to protect the royals from assassins, not comment on their well-being." He met my eyes apologetically, "It was not my place."

I could feel the crowd around us relax as he stated the obvious, and the air got even haughtier. My indignation flared, and I suddenly didn't care who was listening in, "Don't worry about it, Jack." I put my hand on his shoulder, savoring the crowd's repugnance, "Thanks for thinking of me. I'll see you at sword practice."

He bowed out.

I watched him go until I remembered my quest. I surveyed the room, finally successful as I barely managed to glimpse Robert's red curls by the balcony.

I made my way over, occasionally shielding my face from potential dance partners. When I had almost reached him, I realized he was talking to someone and I stopped. He did his normal joke routine, but his audience wouldn't even break a smile. He tried his very best, but with her arms crossed, Dare just glared, her purple eyes radiating.

Robert had just finished a joke and was bent over cracking up, but looked up and saw Dare's unresponsive form and his laughter died. Dare sighed, "Look Robert . . . I have to go." At least she didn't say it harshly.

"Oh . . . yeah," he said, trying to sound upbeat. "That's fine. I'll be over here if you want to . . ." but she had already disappeared into the crowd.

He sighed and lowered his head, rubbing his face, looking so disappointed. But I could only think, *He likes Dare? Well, that's obvious. Have I just never noticed before? Is this a new thing?*

I walked up to him, "Hey."

He brought his head up quickly and grinned, "Hey, where you been?"

"Where have *I* been? You ditched me! Where have *you* been?"

He laughed, "Oh yeah. Sorry about that. I've been around, just doing the normal ball routine: spew spitballs at the snobs, flirt with the clueless, and cause overall ruckus."

"Good ol' Robert."

He grinned.

"Have you seen Dare? I haven't seen her tonight," I asked innocently.

"What, who Dare?" he acted surprised. "No, not really. I mean I think I passed her once or something, but not really." He played it real cool.

"Hmm . . . okay. I'll keep looking."

He just nodded, looking around.

"Hey, do you know what time it is?" I asked hopefully.

"It's about one or two in the morning."

I smiled. People usually started leaving then.

"Lily and Tucker have already gone to bed."

It was a great injustice, but they were allowed to leave early. Robert and I had to say goodbye to everyone though, me being the princess and him being my escort. It was so boring and long considering the thousands that attended the party.

"Looks like I'm stuck with you now," he said as he held out his arm, and we strode to the doors everyone would exit out of.

We stood there for about an hour and a half as small sections of the crowd slowly made their way to the door. I bowed so many times that bowing felt almost awkward. It felt more like bouncing up and down since I would have to bow to like ten people a second. But after most of the crowd had gone, only a few people would leave at a time, giving me adequate time to bow gracefully.

Finally, the last couple headed through the doors, engaged in a conversation with Arnet. He offered to walk them to their carriage.

Robert and I bowed as they passed. Arnet turned to close the doors behind them and winked at us. I playfully stuck my tongue out at him, and I saw him smile as the doors shut.

We were alone, just me and Robert in the massive room. We both just looked at each other, smiling maniacally as the same thought popped in both our heads. We both whooped as Robert immediately attacked the cape around his neck, and I fell to the floor clawing at my tight pointy shoes. I tossed the hot shawl and he kicked off his shoes. We both sat in front of the door for a moment, enjoying the freedom.

"Oh, I am *so-ho-ho* ready for bed," he said as he helped me up. "See you in the morning." He gathered his strewn clothes and walked towards the hall that led to his chamber.

I collected the shawl and shoes, "See ya."

The sound of the hallway door closing echoed throughout the gigantic ballroom. Once empty, the space seemed twice as large. I stood in the middle of the dance floor and put my stuff down. I glanced around, making sure no one could see me. My only company was the occasional voice of the chilly night wind coming through the open balconies, which made the silky white curtains float gracefully. Knowing no one was watching, I twirled around freely. Being able to spread out my toes and arch my back felt delicious. I may have even given a small laugh. Then I had an even greater idea.

I ran to a balcony and bounded through the door frame to the outdoors. And I just inhaled. The chilly night air felt the best after the hot confinement of the ball. The sky displayed itself clearly, the moon shining exquisitely with millions of little stars to accompany it. The balcony faced the sea, which shined in the brilliance of it all. If I closed my eyes, I could just hear the crashing waves.

I stood there for a few minutes, escaping everything, when I heard a door open and close in the ballroom. "Galayne?" Mildrid's voice quietly echoed.

I sighed, realizing my moment of freedom had ended. "I'm here, Milly," I responded reluctantly.

I heard the patter of her steps coming across the ballroom to the balcony. "What are you doing out here?" She asked as if I was stupid. "Don't you know you'll catch a cold?"

I sighed again, but just said, "Sorry, Milly, I'll come in now." She nodded and held her arm out for me. I went to her and she put her arm around my waist, leading me to a hallway. Her excited smile from earlier returned as she said, "As we get you ready for bed, I want to hear *every* detail." She rubbed my arm giddily as we headed through the door. I thought the day had finally come to a close. And, as usual, I couldn't have been more wrong.

IN HOT WATER

Mildred asked various questions on the way to my private bathroom: what did this person wear, was this duke or duchess there, what was my favorite dish, and so on. I answered everything, trying to make it as interesting as I could for her.

I started telling her about Lady Darmian's gown when someone suddenly stepped right in front of us. Lord-What's-His-Face scoffed, as if we were the ones who got in his way.

Milly gasped as she bumped into him and immediately bowed, "We beg your pardon, Lord Rothaldo." It took me a second to realize I should bow too.

He took a moment to look us up and down, then turned abruptly with a look of disgust and strode down the hall in the direction we'd just come from.

I had the thought and asked Milly, "What is he still doing here?"

"Some of the guests are staying the night. Which reminds me, I need to hurry so that I can help service the rooms." With that she quickened her stride and dragged me along.

The warm, soapy water felt amazing as I slowly sank into my bath. I closed my eyes and slipped into such extreme relief that part of me was worried that I'd fall asleep and drown.

Milly laid out my nightgown and slippers and her own night attire. It had to be a secret, but I'd always let her use my bath.

FOR THE INTENDED

When she'd just laid out my towel, I held up a finger and said, "Just one more bucket, Milly, then I'll be done." She smiled and brought one of the buckets by the door over and began to pour it in by my feet. My eyes flashed open and I quickly pulled my feet towards my chest. "Milly!"

She immediately stopped pouring, splashing some on the floor, "What?" she asked a bit frightened.

"Um," I said, calming my voice down, "the water, it's freezing."

She stuck her finger in and immediately pulled it back out. "Oh, you're right. Sorry about that." She walked back over to the door and picked up a different bucket and poured it in. I sighed in complete bliss.

After a while of lying in pure pleasure I opened my eyes, "Alright, Milly. I'm done."

She smiled as she came over from where she sat, ready for her bath. I stepped out of the tub and grabbed the towel. When I finished drying off, Milly held out my nightgown.

"Uh, actually, Milly, I was going to wear my outfit for tomorrow. That way I can get straight to work," I finished quickly.

She sighed but didn't argue. Since the next day would primarily be scouting, she brought over my tan riding pants, a white blouse and a black vest. As I put them on, she placed my boots by my bed.

As I buttoned the last button on my vest, I had a thought. "Milly?"

She continued preparing her own bath, "Yes?"

"What was that bucket of cold water doing here?"

No answer.

The only reason buckets were brought to my chamber were for baths, and they were steaming hot from the furnaces.

"Whose bucket was that, Milly?" I said gently but firmly.

"Um . . . it was mine," she said hesitantly.

"What? Why was it so cold?"

"Um . . ." she said nervously, shifting her feet.

"It's okay, Mill, just tell me why."

"Well, with all the guests . . . there isn't enough time to heat water for everybody. Therefore, all the servants," she swallowed, then finished quickly, "get one bucket of unheated water."

Wait . . . what? The servants were the only ones that did anything, and they can't even get a decent bath? But I tried to act reasonably. "Are the guests aware of the issue?"

"We let everyone know, and thankfully some were understanding and stopped asking for more. But some . . . some asked for even more."

She saw the look of growing fury on my face and smiled quickly, trying to make the whole thing seem fine. She thought she'd try for humor so she said, "Oh, you should have seen the orders piling up down there. Why, Lord Rothaldo down the hall has ordered fifteen buckets of water in the last twenty minutes. When we told him about the backup of bathwater and how the servants wouldn't get any, he got angry and said, 'Why should he care about a bunch of useless peasants?' Oh, Galayne, it was terribly funny." She smiled, using her hand to hold back giggles.

Terribly funny? **Terribly funny?** I didn't know how she could remain so positive all of the time. He had just called her a useless peasant after she had served him all night, and then he was going to deprive her of a warm bath? Between my aching toes, sore muscles, and drooping eyes, and being pretty sure he was the guy I couldn't stand, I still had enough energy to defend an abused Milly.

I thrust my boots on in anger.

"Galayne! No! Galayne, listen to me," she said, running over to me. She tried to grab my boot, but physically trying to stop me wouldn't work. Practically twice her size, I turned the opposite way and shoved it on.

"It's fine," she said quickly, "I didn't even want a bath! And anything he says doesn't bother me!"

But as usual, I didn't listen.

FOR THE INTENDED

I flung open the door and pounded down the hall, growing angrier by the second. For a minute, Milly tried to stop me, pulling on me and pleading. After a bit, she gave up. When I turned around to see where she went, I saw her scurrying back down the hall.

When I finally located the right room, I didn't hesitate for a second. I burst through the door of his room with a vengeance.

I regretted it instantly.

We made eye contact immediately. He lay in his bathrobe on top of his bed, holding a book. His hair dripped from his extra hot and long bath. His chin brushed his chest as he gaped at me.

I suddenly felt really hot. I hadn't even considered the fact that he could have still been in the bath. I didn't want to think about what could've happened had I been a few minutes earlier...

I swallowed, my throat uncomfortably dry. Arnet would kill me if he found out. We just kept staring at each other in stunned silence.

I considered apologizing and retreating quietly out the door, hoping he wouldn't spread my second embarrassing incident throughout the castle. Just as I made up my mind to leave, I was reminded of why I went there in the first place.

The nobleman snapped the book shut, "How dare you intrude upon our peaceful evening? And after we came all this way to be present for you and for your return! You... you little ingrate! When the queen hears about this she—"

"Hold it, Mister Ritho-Ratho—whoever you are! First off, I'll have you know that I'm allowed to do as I please in this kingdom, hence being the *princess*!" I spouted savagely, gesturing to the place where my crown usually sat.

His eyes opened wide in disbelief.

"Second off, how dare you request more water for you and your family when you know full well that means the servants will go without? You pretend to be well-bred, but a true gentleman shows decorum toward royalty and servant alike!" It sounded professional and princesscy. I continued.

"And third off, do you think I care if you and your pompous, ungrateful, snobby little family show up to my ball? And the queen? You're trying to scare me by using the queen against me? My authority is just as good as hers and she can't touch me. In faaacccct," I stretched the word, "I can make some pretty big commands as well . . . including the arrest of some certain arrogant guests!" I announced pointedly, nodding in his direction.

He seemed to choke on all the insults. His face was a few shades paler than when I first made my entrance.

I smiled smugly at my victory. Was I allowed to do whatever I wanted because I was the princess? No. Did I really believe the queen couldn't send me to the dungeon for harassing her guests? No. But was telling him off and scaring him out of his wits worth it? Totally.

I glanced around the room. His wife and son looked just as stunned and fearful as he did. I made sure everyone saw my pleasure before saying, "Good evening," turning on my heel. As I swirled around, I bumped into a tall figure in the doorway.

I slowly, painfully, raised my eyes to meet Arnet's. He looked more than furious. Milly stood behind him, hands over her mouth, looking completely horrified.

"Oh, hi, Arnet. I was just . . ." I looked into his eyes and saw that no excuse could excuse my actions. He had heard enough.

Without a word, he firmly grabbed my upper arm and stormed us down the hall, leaving the nobleman and his family in stunned disbelief. Milly stood frozen, not knowing what to do. Arnet continued down the stone hall and led us out a wooden door into the chilly, moonlit night.

We rushed through the door before he finally released me. I crossed my arms and walked forward a bit through the grass, readying myself for the worst. I knew how it would come. He would shout angrily at me for a while, saying things like "I can't believe you would do this," and, "I have never been so disappointed in my life," and, "You are better than this." His voice would lower for a moment, but then he'd be shouting again the next. The next part, after he had finally calmed down enough, would consist of him listing all the consequences of my actions. And finally, after a good long while, he would just sit down and rub his eyes. "Galayne . . . I just . . . I can't do this myself. You have to try harder, Galayne." Then he'd look up and say plainly. "Try harder." Then he would leave. Without a goodbye, without an, "I love you no matter what" like he used to. He would just leave.

I used to look up to him, and I supposed I still did, but not as much as I used to. He was always agitated. Between making sure I stayed in line, or being away on trips serving Umplidore, we didn't have time to have a real relationship. The worst part was, I cared what he had to say . . . but I'd never let him know it. And I wouldn't have admitted it to myself then, because I felt too hurt to care.

I took a deep breath and turned, facing him, as he would expect from me. You see, he was not only my guardian by law, but my commanding officer. He would require me to stand erect, make eye contact, and remain silent until he finished. And also, he was raising the princess, so multiply the expectations of good behavior by ten.

He glared at me with his arms crossed. He looked like he wanted to say something, but instead just breathed out angrily and started to pace back and forth. He continued for some time, and then stopped and asked, "Do you have any idea what you just did?"

Silence.

"That was *Lord Rothaldo.* He influences many of the leaders in the Royal Assembly. If he tells anyone of what just happened . . ." he rubbed his face stressfully.

I swallowed. *Oh. He didn't look that important.*

He continued rubbing his face as he sat down on a boulder under an old apple tree. He breathed slowly in and out, giving me time to realize how quiet the night had become. There were no crickets, and usually one or two nightingales would sing. But that night, only the noise of the cold wind that blew through the aging orchard could be heard. The night felt chillier than normal, seeming to drop a few degrees by the minute, but if Arnet noticed he didn't show it.

Arnet continued to sit there with his head down, his face covered with his hands. I felt tired and defeated, wanting to just leave. To just walk away. My eyes drifted to the moon above—so round, so full, and providing a silver lining to everything it touched. I then watched the leaves rustle in the wind, some falling off and floating away.

I glanced back at the moon. I thought about how unusually cold it had become until Arnet finally stood. We made eye contact again. He managed to be calm. "Go to your room. Tomorrow you will apologize to Lord Rothaldo and his family. You will also inform the queen of your rash behavior and do anything she requires you to do to fix the situation." He finished firmly, disappointedly, emptily.

I looked away. My eyes were fixed on the moon when I whispered, "No."

He had already started to walk to the door but stopped abruptly and turned on his heel, "What?"

I looked back at him in composed defiance. "No," I said once more. I don't know where it came from. I felt unnaturally serene and strong. "No, I will not."

His anger fueled up, "*What?*"

"I said no, Arnet." I wouldn't back down. I would normally never have had the guts to speak up at all, much less to completely contradict his order. I said smoothly and calmly as if we were just having a chat, "I will not apologize, and you cannot make me. He deserved everything I said about him. I do not care how important a person thinks they are. If they are not respectful to me and my . . ."

"That's enough, Galayne," he said firmly.

I carried right on through, "friends, then they do not deserve respect . . ."

"Silence," he demanded, his anger increasing.

I continued, my voice rising with each word, my heart beating faster. "You of all people should understand why I said what I did. You taught me to treat everyone as if they are important . . . not just the royals! The past few years you've let things like this slide! You always said being the princess is about power and what to do with it, but you never let me use it! You say it's to protect people!" I finished calmly, "You may be my commanding officer and think you own me, but you do not, and I will *not* do as you say. Not this time."

"Silence!"

My heart leaped into my throat.

"I have never seen such unruly, disrespectful conduct in my life!" he snarled. "And in spite of what you think, in the eyes of the law, *I do own you!*"

I blinked. Wrong thing to say. In the back of my mind, I had wanted to make him proud. I hadn't planned to confront him, but I already had and he had counterattacked.

"*Oh.* Is that what you think? . . . You *don't own me!* I'm the *princess*! You've made that clear all my life. I can leave *anytime I want*. No one would *dare* stop me." I gritted my teeth and glared. I hated to use authority to get what I wanted. It made me uncomfortable, but right then I was all too glad to rub it in his face.

As my insubordination spiraled out of control, the air dropped at least another ten degrees and the wind picked up a bit.

Arnet's face had turned into a boiling pot of anger, but when the frigid wind tousled his hair, he finally noticed the temperature. A baffled expression of alarm formed on his face. "Galayne?" He spoke with urgency, his voice no longer angry. "I think we should continue this discussion inside." He glanced around anxiously.

His complete change in behavior should have been more of a warning to me, but I stood firm, stubborn and enraged. He stepped toward me but I dodged him by backing toward the shadowy trees. "I'm not going anywhere with you!"

The wind picked up even more, twice as cold as a moment before.

"Galayne! We need to go *now*!" His insistent demands turned into pleading. He knew if he lashed out for me, I'd turn and bolt. So, he reached out in a panicked state I had only seen one other time . . .

My hair took to the wind as I shouted, "No! You've told me to fight for what I think is right, but you don't actually believe all the stuff about morality and justice that you've taught me. You're only worried about your and the castle's reputation, and I'm sick of following a blind tyrant!" I wanted to say something really smart, and it bugged me how much like a child I sounded.

The trees rustled behind me. *It's just the wind*, I told myself. But part of me knew better.

"Galayne! *Now*!"

I wouldn't allow him to scare me. He just wanted me to come inside so he could confine me in a place where I couldn't run away.

"No!" I had just thought of something really awesomely clever to say, when a snowflake floated past my face.

All of my courage and composure dissolved as I became aware of my surroundings. The night had dropped below freezing, in the middle of summer, *again*. And not only that, but snow began to fall in quick, thick clumps.

"Arnet?" My tone sounded like that of a frightened child as I peered into his troubled eyes. I felt weak as if all the strength had been sucked out of me. I thought my knees would buckle like before. Every snowflake that fell on my skin drained a little bit more of me. My startled thoughts were pushed aside when I gasped quietly as something heavy landed behind me. My heart doing a million beats a second, I turned to see the newcomer.

The form was crouched in the shadows but then it slowly stood up. The wind immediately tapered down and the snow fell gracefully to the frozen ground. I could make out short hair which blew softly in the breeze, but everything else was hidden in darkness.

"Galayne!" Arnet ordered even more urgently, "*Get inside!*"

My ability to think went with the wind. Paralysis overtook me. My inability to do anything made me start to panic. I couldn't move at all as I stared into the shadows at the figure. My thoughts were so jumbled together, that when I finally came to the realization that I really should get inside, I just turned slowly and faced Arnet.

Arnet stepped closer, "That's it, Galayne! Come on!" He eyed the shadow behind me, which hadn't stirred yet.

All of a sudden, Arnet gasped and dashed towards me.

Too late. My breath immediately got knocked out of me as an arm lashed itself across my waist from behind and launched me into the air at an alarming rate. The wind was biting, as if tiny ice arrows were being shot at my face.

Already thirty feet in the air and gaining fast, Arnet's shouts quickly disappeared into the background.

RAPTOR CAPTOR

My mind continued to be tangled and shaken as I darted upwards through the dark icy sky. My brain desperately tried to form a distinguishable thought and all it could come up with was an agitated *Um . . .*

I tried to get a glimpse of my unwanted flight partner but could only make out a pair of gigantic wings attached to a dark form above me, its arm wrapped securely around my waist. We had started to level out but were gliding just as quickly over the trees.

I yelled, kicked, and clawed viciously at whatever I could manage to grab of the mysterious figure above. A few times it seemed like I slowed us down, or at least made it more difficult to fly.

Finally, as we were descending, I saw my opportunity. When we were about fifteen feet away from the ground, a large gust of wind made the form above me do a sudden flap to avoid tumbling out of control. He lost his tight grip on my waist, and his arm slid up just far enough for me to sink my teeth into it.

With a strangled yelp, his arm fully released, and I toppled downwards. Ooops. Even though we were only ten feet from the ground, it didn't make me skidding five feet in the dirt any more fun.

The figure landed softly about ten feet behind me and exclaimed, "*Come on, Galayne!*" He began to rub his arm.

FOR THE INTENDED

"What in the world?" The voice was very familiar, but I was too adrenalized to recognize its owner. My captor had landed under a large oak tree, but again clothed in darkness, I could barely see him.

Furious for the unwanted ride, I scrambled to a defensive stance. I clawed my side for my sword, but I painfully came to the realization I had left it in my room. My eyes darted around for something to throw, perhaps a large stick or something. Finally, I found a pointy rock and raised it, ready to hurl it any second.

Rubbing his arm still, he glanced up and saw the rock about to smash his head. His hands shot up in surrender as he said "Whoa, come on, Galayne. It's me."

The figure carefully stepped out from the shadows and into the moonlight. I took a step back in disbelief. Blue's face immediately illuminated in the full moon, and he gave a slight smile when he saw my surprise. His black hair whipped gently in the wind and his eyes gleamed. To my astonishment, he shuffled his wings before gently tucking them in against his back. I lowered my weapon in shock.

Blue. Had. Wings.

Was that possible? Well obviously it was, but Naetera were incredibly rare, and Naetera with wings were even more so.

"Sorry about the sudden flight thing. It seemed like my only chance," he apologized, sliding his hands into his pockets.

I stared. What was that supposed to mean?

There were a few moments of silence before he broke it.

"So, how have things been? You know . . ." he shuffled his feet and lowered his voice, "since the last time I saw you."

No response.

"Are you okay?" He stepped closer. "I didn't bust your brain, did I?" he asked jokingly.

Where should I begin? I was furious that he had scared me like that. He also had *wings*. How long had that been a thing? Also, he hadn't told me that he was leaving for a quest, and since his first sentence wasn't explaining where he'd been, I was spitting mad.

:The rock might've come in handy . . . but I finally tossed it aside and studied him.

He looked the same; pale face, black attire, and those amazing blue eyes. Nothing that hinted where he'd been.

My glare hardened. I had missed him, don't get me wrong. I was also relieved that he came back from his quest unharmed, but I was still mad at him for not sharing everything with me like he used to.

I glanced at the feathery appendages on my closest friend, and he suddenly felt the need to explain himself.

He let out a little snicker and exclaimed, "Oh yeah." He stretched them out completely and I backed up in awe. They were long and sleek and pitch black like his hair. "I guess this is probably a little weird for you. Here, just one sec." He closed his eyes and concentrated, his wings slowly retracting and disappearing.

I gaped in amazement as he became just Blue instead of Blue Bird.

He watched me appreciate his new power until he asked again, a little more concerned, "Are you okay?" I suddenly realized why.

I must have looked pretty messed up. It had to be about five in the morning, close to sunrise, and I was exhausted. I was also hungry from not eating dinner, and I was freezing. I glanced around for the first time and saw that the snow had resumed. The wind stayed fairly calm, blowing smoothly through occasionally. I crossed my arms and shivered, feeling pretty miserable. I glanced back at Blue to see how he responded to the freak change in weather, but he didn't seem to notice. I realized he was still waiting for me to respond so I did. "Yeah, I'm great. *What about you?*"

"Oh good, you can still talk. I was getting worried," he smiled playfully.

I wasn't in the mood to play.

We just looked at each other for a moment, his blue eyes glinting in the moonlight. Then he shoved his hands in his pockets again and gave me an answer even though it was rhetorical. "I'm pretty good," he looked around at the trees. "Things are great. You know, away from the castle . . ." again he seemed to lose his normal self as he looked down and kicked at the grass.

"Why'd you leave?" I asked, crossing my arms and setting my jaw.

"Because—" he began, but then looked up and asked, "Wait. You don't know?" He sounded really surprised.

"No. I don't," I said, pretty mad. "Do tell."

He blinked, clearly shocked I didn't know. "Look, Galayne," he began, his voice lower. He swallowed, "Things have changed." He made eye contact, his eyes intense, "I've changed."

I blinked and I lost my anger for a second, "What do you mean?"

He seemed to be deciding whether to tell me or not.

"Blue," I said firmly, "What's changed?"

He looked at me skeptically, and then after a moment said, "Give me your hand."

He reached out for my hand and I stepped back in surprised defiance. "Why?" I asked hesitantly.

He laughed, "You'll see."

He reached out again, and I stepped farther away

He laughed again, "Come on, Galayne, it's me."

I thought about saying no when he lashed out without time for me to react and got a firm grip on my wrist.

I exhaled sharply in terror as he did. I felt as if a human icicle had latched itself to my wrist. Not like his hands were "cold," they were *ice cold*. I watched in horror as frost began to travel up my arm slowly.

"Isn't that awesome?" Blue asked, grinning, but then he saw my face. "Galayne?" He filled with concern.

I began to gasp for air, and then my legs gave in.

He let go instantly, "Galayne!" he cried, falling to my side.
I bent over, choking due to the sudden ability to breathe.

"Galayne! I had no idea . . . I didn't mean to . . ." He laid his hand on my shoulder but exclaimed and snatched it back when he saw the frost spreading from his fingertips. After that he scooted back from me, looking pained with his uselessness to help me.

After a minute of trying to get my breathing under control, I finally rolled back onto my hands in a sitting position. I thrust my chin upwards and breathed in the extremely welcomed brisk air.

When he saw that I had finally recovered he said, "Galayne, I'm serious, I had no idea. Are you alright?"

I tried to say yes but had to cough out the raspy-ness before it sounded like it.

"Galayne, really you have to know, I didn't—"

"It's alright. Really." I said it calmly, but I was freaking out.

He looked really shaken. He clutched his knees to his chest, observing me.

After a few minutes of silence, I tried to distract both of us from our shakiness and thus gave up my anger. "So, this," I said, looking around at the snow, the ice spreading slowly over the pond to the right, and the frost spreading in a circle from where Blue sat, "is all you."

He looked around. "Yeah, it's me." His voice lowered, "all me."

We both sat in silence, contemplating everything that had passed, when I had a thought.

"Hey, the other day in the woods, on my way to Umplidore . . . the freak snow blast . . . that was you too, wasn't it?!"

His face washed over with pink as he looked down, a nervous smile on his face. "Yeah, that was me."

"What were you doing? Why didn't you show yourself?" I paused for a second before adding, "And why would you do that?"

"I didn't do it on purpose," he said hurriedly, "I was just keeping an eye on you. When I realized the ruckus I was causing, I left."

"Yeah, but why didn't you let me know you were there?"

He looked down again, "Because the time wasn't right."

"What?" I asked, totally frustrated with his bluntness.

"You know, it doesn't matter . . ." He looked up, "What matters is now you see me. And we have to talk." He looked dead serious. He sighed as he gazed at the sky, preparing himself. "Galayne, as I said before, things are changing."

I looked at him intently, dying to know.

He continued, "And, as you may have noticed, I haven't been at the castle for a while now . . ." he looked down, "and it has to stay that way."

"What!? Why?"

He looked up, and he seemed like he was about to give me all the answers I wanted, when someone else did it for him.

"Vir Mithe!" Arnet's voice boomed through the air. Arnet, Robert, Lily, Tucker, Dare, and a handful of guards, including Jack, poured into the small opening, weapons drawn.

Blue and I jumped to our feet.

All of them seemed edgy, ready to pounce on us. Robert was furious and irritable, his eyes fixed on me. Lily appeared so shaken I thought she'd burst into tears any moment. Tucker looked shocked and pale; his sword seemed awkward in his hands. Dare stood ready for action. Jack was resolute, but I could see a trace of panic hidden deep within his solid stature. His eyes met mine determinedly, promising me he'd get me out of there safely. Arnet appeared undaunted, but no matter how hard he tried, he couldn't hide his unusual fear from me.

A guard carefully said, "Your Highness, please step away from the traitor."

I blinked. *What? Traitor?* It took me a moment to put the pieces together. I turned slowly to face Blue.

Blue just looked back at me apologetically.

I was shocked. Stunned. I couldn't speak. I lost myself in his pained eyes, the eyes that tried so hard to apologize for everything but failed. *Traitor.* That wasn't thief, or hooligan, that was traitor. Traitor meant much, much more crime had been done, and much more punishment . . .

"Galayne." Arnet's firm voice woke me from my trance.

I looked back at him, my eyes displaying my broken self. Still in a daze, I woke to hear a voice beside me.

"If I may, sir—" Blue began gently, but got cut off immediately.

"Silence!" Arnet's voice boomed with fury. "Vir Mithe, you were banished from Umplidore due to your traitorous deeds, and the penalty for your return is lifelong imprisonment in the dungeons of Kor."

I watched Blue flinch at his real name. Blue raised his chin slightly in his last attempt to keep it together. He swallowed, "Very well, sir." Despite his relatively calm outside appearance, I could see Blue breaking on the inside. No one else would know it, but it was evident to me.

I saw the guards begin to shuffle their feet a bit, taking a step forward every few seconds. Blue looked up at the sky and smiled gently at it, his wings opening slightly and shifting a bit, then he said, turning to each of us in our turn, "Sir," he nodded to Arnet, "friends," he nodded to Robert, Dare, Lily and Tucker. Lily and Tucker just stared in shock, Dare looked indifferent, but Robert narrowed his eyes and looked even angrier than before. "Galayne," his eyes drifted to mine, and I saw his hurt. He nodded with a slight smile. "Farewell," he said mostly to me, giving me one last smile that I would always know.

In an instant the guards rushed him, swords high. Dare, Arnet, and Robert were close on their tail, leaving Lily and Tucker frozen stiff. Before anyone had taken two steps, Blue thrust himself into the air and shot off into the sky.

"No!" I yelled and tried to lunge after him as he took off. I just missed him.

FOR THE INTENDED

I saw the dark spot in the sky veer to the southwest.

"Follow him!" Arnet ordered the guards, and they dashed after Blue, Jack at the head. Arnet looked up for a second at the shrinking dot in the sky, and then started after them.

I was about to do the same, but my friends suddenly surrounded me. Lily threw herself at me and exclaimed, "Oh, Galayne, I thought you were gone for good." I really thought she might cry. Tucker just stood there, watching us hug, looking so relieved. Dare sheathed her daggers after looking around once more for danger, and then she nodded at me before walking back to the castle. Robert still looked just as edgy as he watched me. I'd never seen him like that before. Finally, he sheathed his sword, but he still looked so tense.

"Come on, guys, it's Blue." I looked at all of them, shocked at their behaviors.

Lily looked down, almost shamefully.

"But, Galayne," Tucker began quietly, "he was banished."

"For what?" I burst forward with anger and frustration. "What could he possibly have done?" I pushed Lily away, somewhat gently, but enough for her to know I was mad. I felt a little bad about it, but not bad enough.

Robert walked up, his hand resting on the hilt of his sword, and said, almost sternly, "For his traitorous deeds." Then, emotionless, he added, "Weren't you listening?"

"But what did he do?" I asked indignantly.

Robert squared his jaw. Tense and serious, looking almost dark, the normal gleam in his eyes vanished.

I almost lost it on all of them when Lily burst forth, flinging her arms around me. "Oh, Galayne! I'm so sorry! I wanted to tell you, but—"

"But what?? What did he do??"

She paused, but out of confusion, not hesitancy.

I persisted, "You must know what he did; It's always announced in The Records."

"Attention!" Arnet stormed into the glade. Lily's arms fell from my neck in surprise. She straightened along with everyone else. I decidedly remained slumped and angry.

I glared at Arnet, but he wouldn't look back. I had forgotten I was mad at him and it all rushed in twice as strong as I realized he was hunting down Blue. But his next words surprised me.

"All of you are not to be seen with Galayne. You are not to communicate in any way or have any interaction with her. Punishments will vary, but I assure you they will be severe."

Everyone was silenced; no one dared to speak.

"You are to go immediately to your chambers and speak to no one of what has passed this morning. You are to report to your normal duties, leading no one to believe anything unusual has happened."

I bit my tongue, my hate growing for him in that moment. He existed as a second father to them, and instead he treated them like strangers.

They all looked at me. Lily and Tucker looked apologetic and upset, but Robert just looked surprised.

"*Is this understood?*" Arnet's voice menaced.

They all bowed in quick unison, "Yes, Arnet." With that, they all left quickly in the direction of home, leaving us alone.

I looked at him. I felt confused, angry, and worried—the first two for myself, the last for Blue. With all the emotions I could only glare.

He looked at me, his eyes squinted a bit, but he said nothing. Without a word he signaled for some guards to be my escorts. I could've fought them, I could've run, but then the guards who went after Blue returned.

The guardsen bowed respectfully, "I am sorry, sir, but we lost him. He vanished from our sight."

Jack's entire body revealed his disappointment—not in their collective failure, but his own.

Arnet seethed but said, "No matter. He is by now far from our borders, and will most likely stay that way for some time.

But to be absolutely clear, if you see him step one foot into Umplidore, if one *feather* falls on our ground, you have orders to make sure he never leaves again. Whatever that may mean."

I gaped into the emotionless face that had just made the order to kill my best friend, once again shocked. Blue was close to him as well. My only guess was that he was trying to get back at me, and unfortunately, it was working.

Jack noticed, and I witnessed conflicting thoughts enter his mind.

I saw some of the guards were younger and I thought I recognized a few faces. Then I realized they used to hang around Blue and knew him pretty well. I saw a few swallow anxiously. They shifted and murmured a bit amongst themselves.

"Is there a problem?" Arnet asked loudly.

The guardsen immediately spoke up, "No, sir." With that they all bowed nervously, and Jack's concern for my feelings faded as he adopted his commanding officer's latest order.

"Good. For now though, you will escort myself and Her Highness to her chambers. There, you will post your best guards outside her room. She should never go unguarded or be allowed to leave her room."

Shocked, I looked up into his face, but he didn't look back.

Jack actually had an easier time accepting the second order—it would be easier to keep his royal safe.

With that Arnet pushed me forward and the guards formed a circle around me and led me back home. As I walked on, I glanced back at Arnet who finally made eye contact with me. But he turned away completely indifferent and continued behind the pack of highly trained guards who I knew I couldn't escape from.

We all made our way back to the castle in silence. We halted for a moment outside where Arnet and I had fought earlier, waiting for a guard to open the door for us. It gave me a chance to notice the sun rising. It had just broken the surface, shedding the brightest orange color over everything.

Everything in the distance became a black silhouette. The sun on my face gave me some sort of comfort, though I didn't know why. I breathed in the peace it brought until someone gave me a slight push from behind and told me to move on. I regretfully stepped into the dark castle, away from the freedom of the outside, knowing it might be a long time before I would get to enjoy it again.

I didn't know if I would be able to manipulate my way out. I *was* the princess, but I was also The Summer Born. People were afraid of me running away or establishing negative associations with them. They were afraid of losing me or my loyalty . . . so I knew why they were locking me up. Blue had taken me, so they were freaked out. It was time to get their princess under control even if it meant destroying my trust.

We were marching down the hall when I saw Milly. She looked frightened and confused as she watched the group of guards escorting me. She began to walk up to us, about to say something, but Arnet held his hand up, and she retreated quietly against the wall. I glanced back at her, and her eyes showed the sorrow and anxiety she had for me. Even she knew there were limits to my power.

We reached my room and I stepped in silently, my rage boiling. Arnet stood a few feet away from the doorway, and we just looked at each other. Well, I glared, he looked. Somewhere in the back of my mind, in the region that hadn't been completely taken over with hate for him, I noticed his disguised relief. That little, small part of me felt thankful that he cared, but the rest of me loathed his guts.

The guardsen appointed two guards to the door, and they immediately took their place. The guardsen bowed low to Arnet, then he and the rest of his guards continued down the hall, Jack looking slightly apologetic as they did.

Arnet took a step after them, but then turned and said, "I wouldn't try anything, Galayne. You have no chance of escape."

FOR THE INTENDED

I glared harder if possible, my breathing becoming deeper. I knew he was right. He had trained me all my life in combat, so we both knew it.

"I will be back in a few hours," he said to the guards, "Any unusual activity should be reported immediately."

"Yes, sir," they bowed in steady unison.

"Sleep well." With that he turned and strode down the hall.

I watched Arnet leave, every step increasing my anger. When he got out of sight, I yelled and slammed the door as hard as I could. I heard the lock turn and click into place.

I sunk against the wall and seethed in my anger. Then, slowly, my thoughts bunched together in a stressful mound, and panic filled me. Blue had been banished, I imprisoned, and it all meant I couldn't get to him. I didn't know if I would ever be let out of my room, and if I would ever know what he did . . .

SOLITARY CONFINEMENT

I woke to the sound of water being poured into a basin. My back and left arm were so sore from the nap I had taken on the cold stone floor. I brushed the messy hair out of my face and blinked in the startling light pouring from my window.

I saw Milly setting a towel down on my nightstand.
"Hey, Milly," I croaked, trying to sit up.
Startled, she whirled around. "Oh, Galayne," she exclaimed, tears rising in her eyes. She ran to me and hugged me tight. "I thought you were doomed! When I saw the guards, I thought..." she tried to say, her voice breaking.
"It's okay," I whispered reassuringly, hugging her tight and patting her back. "I'm alright." She didn't need to be *that* concerned. I hadn't gotten a death sentence—maybe just lifelong imprisonment.
We sat for a moment while I let Milly get a hold of herself. Finally, she seemed ready to talk, so I whispered, "What time is it?"
She let go of me, and glancing out the window said, "Near noon."
I signaled for her to whisper and pointed at the door. It took her a second to realize that the guards right outside the door might be listening, but she bit her lower lip when she did.

"Has Arnet come back yet?" I continued.

"No, but it should be soon," she whispered.

I nodded, glancing around the room that had become my prison. I thought about how long it could be before I could leave it. Maybe never. I felt indifferent. It meant no chores, no ball invitations, and no pompous royals. My only concerns were for Blue. I had to see him or at least get some answers.

When I looked back at Milly, I saw her face distorting.

"Milly, what is it?"

She sniffled, "We're not even supposed to be talking to each other. I had to beg to bring you some water this morning. Oh, Galayne, what's going to happen to you?"

I wrapped my arms around her. "Nothing, Milly. Absolutely nothing and you know it. I'm just stuck here for a while. I'm sure I'll be out of here soon."

She hugged me back. We sat there for a moment in peace until she gasped. We both heard heavy footsteps coming down the hall. "Milly, everything's going to be fine. No one's going to hurt me," I whispered hurriedly, hugging her all the tighter. I let go and smiled reassuringly.

She scurried to the nightstand. She began to pretend to fill the water basin. She had just got herself under control when the door opened.

She turned, acting surprised, "Hello, Arnet, nice to see you! I was just finishing up here." She said it with such strength and composure that it made me proud.

He eyed her suspiciously, but then glanced down at me still slumped on the floor. "Nothing has changed. You are to remain in your room."

My face was unimpressed.

I saw Milly glance sorrowfully at me, but she quickly turned back around and pretended to be busy.

Eventually I got left all alone. It was surprising how painful just one day of that room could be. I sat and thought of everything I'd done wrong, every stupid decision. I should have at least tried to escape in the woods. Or maybe I should've just listened to Arnet in the first place... but then I wouldn't have seen Blue. No, I was glad I did it. It was worth it. Then I thought about Arnet, growing increasingly angry each time he crossed my mind.

And so the days passed. Milly became my only company, and she only came to bring me meals, clothes, or bathwater. Even then, it didn't feel like company. She could only whisper, and only for a few minutes.

Sometimes, Arnet would come by to check on me. The first few days, I would glare. Then, after about a week and a half, I grew tired. Not exactly physically tired—though I did feel groggy and not myself—but mentally tired and weak. I dipped into the depression that my actions had created. I hadn't seen my friends, or really talked to anyone in so long, and I got tired of everything. I began to eat less and less and sleep more and more. The days passed slowly and steadily, merging into each other.

One day my heart leaped at the sound of a familiar chirp outside my window. "Elon?" I called with hope.

"Galayne?" A voice called back. A brown bird flew through my window.

"Elon!" I exclaimed, ever so happy.

He darted to me. "Galayne!" He cried happily as he landed in my hands. "I've been searching for you for days!"

"I've been in here this whole time."

"Yes, but every window looks the same I'm afraid."

I thought for a second, *he's got a point.*

"Galayne, what's happened? No one knows where you've been, or what's happened. Are you alright?"

Nobody knew? Someone was playing a dangerous game. I opened my mouth to respond when once again I heard the sound of heavy footsteps in the hall. Elon began to dance anxiously in my hands.

"Yes, I'm alright," I said quickly. "Let everyone know I'm okay." The footsteps were right outside the door when Elon took off. "Don't forget Drayla," I shouted after him, my heart dropping. Arnet walked in just in time to see Elon flap frantically out the window.

He glanced around the room, his eyes resting on my fury-filled face for a second before he walked out and closed the door.

Elon never visited again.

After that, I lost count of the days, but it must've been a little over two weeks since the start of my imprisonment when I heard a rap at the door.

Late in the afternoon, close to sunset, I lay on top of my bed, covers untouched. I woke from a deep, depressed sleep to the sight of Arnet coming into the room.

Unlike before, I didn't feel angry. I just sat up and looked at him, feeling half alive.

"Galayne, the queen has summoned you." He motioned for me to come. "I would be on your best behavior if I were you."

The queen. If there was one person I didn't want to see right then, it was her. I felt my heart sink lower as I slid from my bed and made my way over to Arnet's side.

I didn't make eye contact with him as I stepped out into the hall. Arnet had ordered two pairs of guards to escort me to the throne room, and they immediately secured me in between the four of them.

I didn't even consider fighting back or causing trouble. I silently began to walk down the hall, flanked by the guards. I felt Arnet's eyes on my back as we departed from where he stood, leaving him wondering how I would behave.

I didn't notice the trip there. Most of time I thought about how messed up everything had become. What would the queen even say? I was only slightly aware of the fact that it was the middle of the day and the halls were completely empty on the way there. I was able to appreciate that fact a little, though. It meant no unwanted attention. No one could see that I was a prisoner in my own castle.

Still lost in my thoughts, we finally stopped. We were standing in front of the doors that led into the throne room. I looked up at them in silence, not enjoying the splendid glory of them as I used to.

One of the guards who seemed slightly higher in rank went in first, and I could just hear him say, "The princess has been summoned at your request, milady. Shall we bring her in?"

A beautiful voice could just barely be heard approving. With that the doors opened, and I walked inside the magnificent room that brought back unwanted memories.

They escorted me all the way to the foot of the large podium which held the grand throne. The queen sat there, as graceful and beautiful as ever. She looked down on me in silent displeasure.

All the guards bowed low, and after them I bowed low and said quietly, "Your Majesty."

She looked at me with a sort of motherly disappointment. "That will be all, gentlemen."

"But, Your Majesty," said the guard who opened the door, "We have orders from Arnet that we are not to—"

"We'll be fine, thank you, Lucas," the queen said gently, but firm enough.

All the guards glanced at each other but bowed in respect and retreated the way we'd come, the gigantic doors echoing behind them.

I watched them as they left, wondering why the queen was putting her trust in me, when a lovely voice said, "It's been awhile, hasn't it, Galayne?"

I looked back at her still sitting on her throne of power, beautiful with the light shining behind her, a gentle smile on her face. Everyone loved her. Everyone respected her. But every time I looked at Aurora, I saw... *her*.

I gazed up at the queen with disguised annoyance and said, "Yes, Your Highness. It has."

She stood and began to slowly make her way down to me. Before I knew it, we were standing face to face. She smiled gently at me but noticed my blank expression. "I'm not angry, Galayne," she said, clasping her hands in front of her and beginning to walk to the side of the room, her chin held high in importance. "I called you here for another matter entirely."

No response, not a trace of acknowledgement came from me as I watched her.

She noticed my sour mood but was used to it. She went and sat on a sofa; the same sofa that I had been laid on all those years ago.

She motioned for me to sit next to her. I wanted to leave immediately, be far away from her presence which reminded me of a negative memory. But, knowing I couldn't refuse, I unwillingly went and sat next to her.

She took my hands gently and forced me to look into her pale green eyes. "Galayne," she began, "Arnet told me of what passed the night of the ball."

My heart dropped a little. I had hoped she wouldn't have found out about that, but I mean, what could I expect? She knew everything, *always*.

"I called you here to let you know that everything has settled down. No one else knows about it." She continued smiling gently.

Well, I thought, *maybe Arnet won't hate me as much now.*

Her voice and countenance seemed to drop then, "But I also called you here for a different reason."

I blinked, not sure why she suddenly became so serious.

She sighed. "I heard you found out about Vir."

My heart leaped at the sound of Blue's real name.

"Listen my dear, I have always thought of you as my daughter."

I felt a pang of hate at those words, though it wasn't entirely her fault. The unwanted memory I couldn't push from my mind was to blame.

"And I wish that we could always be absolutely honest with each other."

She paused, but I didn't say anything.

"I know he was a dear friend to you and that you were very close."

My heart ached.

She looked at my face apologetically, her voice as quiet as ever, "But it's true my love . . . I banished Vir about three months ago."

I could feel the surge of anger as I pulled my hands from hers. I asked, shaky and quiet, "What did he do wrong?"

She looked pained. She seemed to be hiding something as she said, "Galayne it doesn't matter. What matters is . . ."

I shot up from the sofa. "*What did he do?!*" I yelled as furious as could be. I was done. I needed answers.

She stood immediately, powerful eyes radiating, "Galayne!"

For a second, I swallowed at my foolish behavior. I needed answers, not more enemies. But, as usual, my anger fueled right back up. "He must've done something . . . and I want to know *what*," I glared.

She stared at me until I thought she would answer, but instead she called, "Guards!"

The guards quickly burst through the doors and made their way to us.

The queen began to walk back to her throne as the guards took their place around me. At the top of the podium, she turned and said rather emotionless, "Galayne . . . I had hoped that we would be able to discuss this reasonably as the close friends I know we are."

I bit my tongue in anger, my nostrils flaring.

"But I can see you're in no mood to do so. So, I will get straight to the point, as you seem to want." With no sympathy in her voice, "The truth is Blue did nothing wrong. As you have witnessed, he is completely changed. He is more dangerous than you yet realize." Her eyes were fierce. "I banished him in hopes of protecting the people of Umplidore, and in particular, *you.*"

The words weren't computing in my mind. Every word she said brought a new level of fury and frustration to me. When she finished, I actually charged her, but a guard on each side lashed out and got a firm grip on my arms.

FOR THE INTENDED

"Till next time, Galayne," she said indifferently, sitting down on her throne of authority.

The guards began to march me towards the door as I fought them, and just as we were going through it, I glanced back at the queen with a look of such loathing. She still sat there, on her large powerful throne, looking unsympathetic and tyrannical.

SECRETS

I got pushed and shoved all the way to my chamber. I pushed and shoved right back, but their fingers only dug further into my arms. I got thrust into the room and the door flung shut right behind me.

I seethed. I began to pace angrily back and forth, breathing deep, trying to keep it together. A new thought popped into my head and I froze. *Blue . . .* My breathing deepened as I thought of how hard it must've been for him, not just me. *The queen . . . when I get the chance I'm going to—*I snatched a small vase off the nightstand and hurled it at the wall, yelling in frustration.

It shattered along with my thoughts. I sunk against the wall; the setting sun's light washed over me from the window, everything about me becoming blank and colorless. Face went blank, emotions were blank, thoughts were blank, and my life had become blank. *This really could be the way I'll spend the rest of my life: Away from people, trapped in this room, never seeing any of my friends.* I swallowed with regret as I thought for the hundredth time about how I would never get to tell Blue that I understood everything, that it wasn't his fault.

While thinking over everything, I heard a light knock at the door. I didn't answer, but it didn't matter because the visitor came in anyway.

Arnet silently closed the door behind him.

"You!" I shouted, jumping to my feet.

"Before you say anything," he said hurriedly, "I'm here to help."

I didn't listen. "You," I snarled, jabbing a finger at him, "betrayed Blue."

"No, Galayne," he said calmly, "I saved him."

My mind didn't expect that answer, so my finger slowly lowered.

"Galayne," Arnet began again, "I am here to explain everything, and hopefully," he gestured around, "get you out of this room."

I crossed my arms and said with a sour face, "What do your buddies at the door think of that?"

"What, who, the guards? I sent them away so we could talk in private." I knew when he was lying. He wasn't then.

We just looked at each other until Arnet finally walked over and sat on the edge of the bed. He motioned for me to join him. I walked over and sat down next to him, my arms still crossed.

He seemed to think for a second before he said, "Galayne, I am sorry for the way things have turned out. I didn't mean for it to get to this point."

"You gave the orders!"

His voice grew a little, "You forced me to do such. I do not take back what I said in the orchard. Your attitude has been unacceptable of late." I tried to interrupt, but he held up his hand and said, "Let me finish. I understand your anger and frustration," he paused, "but the rules and orders I give are to protect you."

He looked sincere, so I began to listen.

"When I give an order, I am looking out for you. Protecting you from things you don't understand yet. And sometimes," he looked regretful, "I can't even control the orders I make. Sometimes, I have to make orders and carry out commands because those are *my* orders." He looked at me apologetically. He seemed to be getting at something.

Then I realized. "You were there when she banished him," I said in quiet shock.

He looked straight into my eyes and said, sadly, "Yes, I was."

"And you didn't try to stop her?" I asked. My voice broke a little at the end.

"Believe me, Galayne, I tried my best." His eyes were full of truth and apology. "I tried to get her to see that . . . that we could control him, face anything time threw at us. But she wouldn't hear it."

I stood. "You have to go back, you have to convince her!" I said desperately, beginning to walk to the door.

"Galayne, that's not all," he interrupted me.

I turned.

"I think it important that you know how fragile the situation is." His voice lowered slightly, "The queen didn't originally wish him to be banished."

I came and sat slowly. My heart felt like it sat at the top of a cliff, about to plunge off at the next bit of information.

He continued quietly, his voice as low as could be, "She ordered him to be executed . . ."

I backed up. *What?* I was horrified, "That's *murder*!"

He shook his head firmly, "No, Galayne. She didn't mean it. She did it in haste. I talked her out of it easily, and she quickly softened his sentence. She just . . . She's just trying to protect you."

I filled with fury.

He saw my face and said hurriedly, "I can assure you though that Vir is safe from harm. He—"

I stood abruptly, "What?! How can you even say that when you just gave orders to kill him if he comes back!"

"No, Galayne. I gave that order to appear as their commanding officer. Just like *you*, I must maintain my position. Afterwards, I went and spoke with Guardsen Gidd, giving secret instructions to disregard the last order I'd given." His voice lowered as he glanced at the floor, "The queen hasn't a clue."

I then saw an ally again. He had betrayed his queen for me, and not for the first time either—a deed I knew weighed heavily on his heart. He once again became Arnet, *my* Arnet. My arms uncrossed, and my face lightened.

He hugged me, and I let him—the first time in a while. Then he said enthusiastically, "Now, to get you out of this room. The process will be slow. We need to make sure everything is settled down. Everyone thinks you've gone away on a trip, and I think it must stay that way for a little while longer."

"Why?"

His enthusiasm left. He looked down. "Galayne, part of the reason you're still here is because . . . I think it's the safest place to be."

"Why?"

His eyes narrowed, "Prying eyes."

"Prying eyes? What do you mean," I asked skeptically.

"Since your unexpected power burst, some people have begun to ask questions. They are suspicious of the situation and would do anything to reveal the secrets we keep."

"What secrets?" It was a dumb question, but it slipped out.

"Galayne . . . you know we have always kept secrets. Only the most high in rankings, and a select few after that, know of your powers. Everyone knows you're The Summer Born, but they don't quite know what that means. They try to sneak in and see things, well . . . things they aren't ready to see. They don't know what you'll be able to do." He laughed, "In truth I'm not even entirely sure what you're capable of. But as suspicion rises, we must be more and more cautious." He tilted his head to the side, looking at the floor. "There might be people who'd be interested in a Summer Born."

I got his point. It's something I knew ever since I'd become the princess. I was an asset.

Despite the situation, I felt quite satisfied. My entire being seemed to relax. Everything would be okay. Slowly but surely, I would get out of that room. Everything would go back to normal . . . except for Blue. Blue wouldn't be there.

I couldn't figure Arnet out. His fear of Blue had been genuine, but he was telling the truth about trying to save him. The more I thought about it, the more I didn't understand his behavior.

We heard indistinct voices coming down the hall.

Arnet shifted. "The new guards are here," he whispered, but an encouraging smile spread across his face. "I'll be back when things have settled down enough. It shouldn't be long now."

With that he walked over to the door and opened it to see two eavesdropping guards immediately take a tense stance. They both looked embarrassed, and the one with the extra red face said, "Reporting for duty, sir."

"Yes, you are," Arnet said with a powerful voice, "and I expect the best. No interaction of any sort is to be permitted. No one but myself is allowed to enter or exit the princess's chambers without direct orders. Is that clear?"

I smiled at his complete transformation.

"Yes, sir," they nodded nervously.

"Very well, I'll leave you to it." With his chin held higher than normal, Arnet strode down the hall. The guards relaxed. One stepped forward to close my door but paused when he saw me.

I smiled as I thought, *Arnet did it all for me.* I couldn't believe it. I plopped down on the bed, leaning up against the pillows, eyes gleaming, my smile getting bigger.

With a creeped-out look on his face, the guard slowly closed the door.

I shimmied down into the suddenly extremely comfortable bed, enjoying the moonlight that poured from my two windows. The nightingale came back, and I actually liked to listen to it despite its usual annoyingness. As I absorbed the peace, I thought, *It's going to be ok. Everything is going to work out fine.* With that, I closed my eyes and had the best night of rest I'd had in a long while. I dreamt of green fields filled with flowers with a bright, golden sun above.

The next few days consisted of me anxiously watching the door, waiting for the long expected knock. I sat on my bed, knees pulled in, staring at the door—so ready to be out. I missed everyone, and I mean, there was only so much I could do to keep occupied. I stared out the window, trying to get a glimpse of anyone I knew, watching the ant-like people go about. Then I would pace back and forth, thinking of everything. After that I would go over and pick up the candle stand in my hand. I slumped against the wall and did tricks with it. I spun it one way, then around the other way, then flipped it in the air and caught it. After I got tired of doing it one day, I thought of how some people I knew passed their time counting things, so I decided I'd count the stones in my walls. *One ... Two ... Three ... forget it.*

Early in the afternoon, a week after Arnet's visit, I lay on my bed again. I tossed the silver candlestick in the air and caught it. My tricks were becoming more and more advanced, of course after quite a few painful knocks on the head. I threw it up, and while it was in midair I heard a knock on the door. I sat up. My attention stayed on the door as my hand instinctively snatched the candle stand from above my head before it gave me a nosebleed.

Arnet walked in promptly, and I immediately stood with a grin on my face. But before I could greet him, the guards came in behind him.

My heart dropped at first. I thought nothing had changed, but with the guards standing behind him, Arnet gave me an excited smile, letting me know everything had gone according to plan.

He turned, and with a commanding voice he said, "Her Highness is no longer in need of protection. I was wrong about the threat, she is safe," he finished conclusively.

The guards glanced at each other but said nothing. They seemed pretty skeptical.

"You may return to your posts." Arnet bowed his head in dismissal.

They bowed low in return, almost mockingly. Then they marched out the door, one of them bowing again as he closed the door behind him.

We heard the footsteps echo down the hall and disappear entirely. "Are we good?" I asked hopefully.

"Yes, I do believe so," he smiled, looking rather relieved.

"What about the queen?"

"Auror—the queen . . . has cooled off a bit." He looked at me and, realizing the hate I had for her, spoke up. He looked at me intently, "She isn't angry at you, Galayne. You must know that. And *you* mustn't be angry with her." He looked so serious, like what he said meant a lot to him. "She does so much for you . . . for everyone." He walked over silently and sat down on the bed. "All her life has been a constant struggle to protect the people, though most people never see it."

My eyes watched his face, amazed at his sincerity. "She's a monster," I exclaimed in shock of his defense for her.

He looked at me sadly, clearly disappointed with my view of her. He looked out the window and said, "In the past, the queen knew someday you would come. The Aedine Prophecy told us of you, though not when you'd arrive." He paused with a pained expression. "When signs came to us that you were coming, Aurora . . ." another painful pause, "Let's just say she wasn't ready for it.

"She lost herself with worry. She spent night after night, anxiously awaiting your arrival. She sent scouts throughout Edgeladine looking for you. But when a few years passed with no sign of you, she began to calm down." He smiled with a gleam in his eyes, "She became herself again."

I realized that he'd forgotten I was there.

His focus fell on me again, "Then you came to us. As the queen, she has a duty to keep The Summer Born safe, and it has filled much of her life. You can't blame her for her actions. She has lived a very confused and stressful life that no one should ever have to live." With that, he stood and walked to the door. He turned and said sincerely before closing the door behind him, "Remember that."

HAM SANDWICH

After thinking about everything he'd said, I remembered my long-awaited freedom was right out the door, and my grin returned to my face.

For the first time in . . . well . . . a longer time than I am willing to mention, I washed my hair. It felt awesome. I went to get dressed and realized I didn't have a change of clothes. I rang the bell and waited for Milly, excited that we could finally have a real conversation.

I sat on my bed, drying my hair, when I heard the quiet patter of feet quickly coming down the hall. I straightened up on the bed.

Milly flew through it. "Galayne!" She exclaimed happily, dropping my clothes all over the floor as she barreled towards me.

"Milly!" I cried excitedly. I stood up in time to receive a huge hug from her that almost knocked me over.

"Oh, Galayne! I'm so glad you can get out of here!"

I laughed, "Me too."

She grinned. Then, after a good long hug, she said, "Alright now, you best get ready. Everyone is waiting to see you."

She snatched up the clothes and handed them to me. She smiled the happiest smile I'd ever seen her have as she closed the door behind her.

FOR THE INTENDED

I had a crowd of people to surprise, so I quickly got changed. Milly had given me my riding pants, green vest, white blouse, and my favorite black boots. I shoved it all on.

I threw open the door and rushed down the hall with a whoop. I burst into the kitchen and shocked the maids preparing the lunch there. Without a word I snatched a ham and cheese sandwich from one of the plates and a binya and continued out the door to the outside. On the way out, I heard one of the servant's exclaim, "I didn't know she was back!"

I scarfed down the sandwich as I headed for the stables, hoping to see my friends there. It tasted great. I only stopped for a second to poke a hole in my orange and yellow binya. I held it above my head as sweet, purple liquid shot out of the exotic fruit right into my mouth. *Yum.*

I ran up to the door of the stables and peered in. Nobody seemed to be there. I ran to Pickadilly's stall, not surprised to see it empty since Tucker usually went out to herd the horses. I ran down to Minya's stall, Lily's horse, and found it empty as well. I ran a little farther down the aisle and found Dare's black horse, Treader, gone too. I was disappointed until I finally found Falna, Robert's cherry bay horse in his stall.

But before I went to look for him, I ran out of the stables. *Drayla.* I looked at the hundreds of horses in the pastures. They were particularly frisky that day. The weather looked rather dark and gloomy, the clouds thick and black, laying a shadowy blanket over everything. The wind blew a bit strong; not cold like the other night, but strange enough to excite the horses.

I reached for the whistle about my neck. I blew long and hard, the sound scattering in the wind. I waited for a minute. Nothing. I blew again, and searched hard with my eyes, Drayla nowhere to be seen.

"Drayla!" I yelled as loud as I could. I listened for a second, but no answer came. A slight fear began to creep into my mind. She hadn't stayed in the castle gates. I knew her too well. When she found out what had happened to me, she would have been furious. She would have tried to fight back, tried to get to me;

and they would have tried to catch her. She would have run far, far away. I blew the whistle halfheartedly, knowing it wouldn't help. Then I turned sadly, worry in my heart, to seek out Robert and catch up on everything I'd missed.

The blacksmith was a good place to start. I jogged through the courtyard, a slight drizzle beginning to fall. Servants were milling around, but none really seemed to notice me. When they did, though, you could tell. Some looked very surprised, but some seemed to talk quietly amongst each other, eying me suspiciously. Two men in particular gave me a creepy feeling when they talked in the shadows of a rundown shed, eyes on me.

I saw the smithy ahead, its front open to the old courtyard, the cracked sign swinging in the wind. Lakon looked up from his work in surprise when I bolted inside. "Hello, Galayne!" he exclaimed happily. "When did you get back? . . . Galayne?" He asked, confused, when I continued right past him into the back room.

"Hello, Lakon . . . I'm looking for Robert," I said as I peered into the back room and, finding it empty, continued, "Do you know where he is?"

He still seemed a bit confused but said, "He just left. He said he was going to lunch. Is there anything I can—" But I had already headed out into the pouring rain.

"Thanks, Lakon!" I yelled back, flipping on my hood, already halfway across the courtyard.

"Anytime!" He yelled with a smile.

I jogged into the kitchen and bumped into Robert, making him spill his four ham sandwiches on the sopping wet ground.

"Hey! Watch where your go—" he began angrily but then his voice dropped, "Galayne?" He asked with surprise.

I hugged him, "Robert, glad I found you."

"Galayne, where have you been?" he said with real concern, hugging me back despite my soaking wet clothes.

I stopped hugging him, grabbing his shoulders, "It's a long story. But actually," I said, glancing around ". . . Can we talk?"

"Yeah, absolutely." He said, his face still concerned and still a little bit shocked. "One sec . . ." he turned his head and shouted into the kitchen, "Hey, Joey, why don't you go on ahead, I'll be right there."

One of Robert's blacksmith pals called back, "But it's raining and lighting and stuff."

"I know, but just go ahead anyway."

"Why in the world should I just . . ." That's when he came to the door and saw me. His eyes widened as his mouth curled into a smirk, "Oh, I see . . . I'll just leave you two alone then." He slipped past us, smiling and taking a large bite of sandwich on his way.

Robert shook his head. He motioned me into the kitchen, "Come on."

We walked into the kitchen and I closed the door behind us and locked it. Robert walked over to the other door and bolted it as well. We both met at the picnic table.

"Are you okay?"

"Yeah, I'm good," I said, sliding onto the bench, "I didn't think I was for a while there, though." I smiled, but he still looked so serious.

"Where have you been?" His normal cheeriness had vanished.

"I've been in my room this whole time." I sighed, "Under guard." I didn't want to share all the details, so I skipped to the part where I fought with Aurora. An amused smile spread on my face, "I had a . . . falling out with the queen."

He sighed and rubbed his face, "Oh, Galayne," he murmured through his hands, "What'd you do?"

"Not much . . . I just kinda lost my patience with her."

He raised his head, "Galayne, you can't just *do* that with the queen."

I studied him. He seemed so different. Normally, he would be the one to crack a joke about the queen behind her back. Once he even played a terrible prank on her. He never thought of how dangerous that had been.

"I know . . . but at that moment, I didn't care." I crossed my arms, "She deserved it."

He sighed again.

Silence lingered for a few moments before I said, "So, what about you?"

His face lightened up a little bit, "Things have been going pretty good."

"Where is everyone?"

"Dare is out on a hunt. Lily and Tucker are out herding the horses into the lower pasture. Everyone else is just going about their normal stuff."

"Where is Elon? And Caspian?" I swallowed back my anxiousness, "And Drayla . . . where is she?"

"Elon, the last I heard, was delivering a message to Sinda. He should be fine though, he's just not back yet."

"And?"

He seemed hesitant, "Drayla . . . well . . . she wasn't too happy when I told her what happened. She tried to charge into the castle. I guess she was probably trying to get to you. But there was no way she was going to make it."

I knew where he was going.

He sighed, scratching the back of his head, "For being a horse, she was actually causing a lot of ruckus. They tried to catch her, but she got away and ran off into the forest . . . Caspian went with her."

"What?! Did you go after them?" I asked, concern flooding my voice. The varnants the other day gave me plenty to worry about.

"Yeah, I did, but I couldn't keep up with them. I lost them within the first few minutes," He said, seeming rather disappointed with himself.

He saw my discouraged face and said sincerely, "I did try, Galayne."

He had tried. I had to focus on that. "I know," I said, wiping the worry off my face. "I'm sure they'll be fine," I lied.

He nodded distractedly.

There was a pause before I said, "Hey listen . . . about the other night . . . in the glen—"

He interrupted me, "Why didn't you tell me?"

"What?" I asked, having no idea what he meant.

"About Vir? Why didn't you tell me?" He had gotten serious again.

I was confused, "I don't know what you—"

"Forget it," he said, hurriedly looking away.

I studied him again, extra confused. *He's different. So different.*

We had an awkward silence before I stood, "Well, it's great to see you again, Robert."

He stood, shaking himself from his thoughts, "Yeah, you too, Galayne."

I stepped around the table and gave him another hug.

He hugged me back pretty hard. Then he went over to get a ham sandwich. I unlocked the door, pausing a moment before stepping out in the rain.

"Hey, Galayne?"

I turned, "Yeah."

He was dead serious, "You're not nearly as careful as you should be."

I couldn't believe it was coming from him.

He made intense eye contact with me. "Be more careful."

I wanted to say something, but our conversation was broken by a happy exclamation.

"Galayne!" Lily shrieked with happiness as she ran at me, Tucker close on her tail.

"Hey, Lily!"

She threw herself at me, "Galayne, you're such a—" Her voice muffled into my shoulder as she hugged me with a death grip.

Tucker came around the other side of me and waited his turn.

Lily let go and Tucker moved in.

Lily spewed, "Galayne, are you okay? Where have you been?"

"Yeah, I'm good. I—"

"We thought we lost you," Tucker said, his hug much gentler but just as sincere.

He stepped back and they both stood there expectantly.

"It's a long story," I said as I glanced at Robert, who had his back to us as he fixed his sandwiches, putting five extra slices of meat on each one. "I'll tell you over lunch."

"Sorry, guys, can't stay for lunch, I gotta go," Robert smiled his normal enthusiastic smile. "But it's great to have you back again, Galayne. See you tonight," he called with his normal cheeriness over his shoulder as he ran out the door.

I watched him, baffled by his mood change. But my concentration broke as Lily led me to the table. She slid next to me. Tucker brought over a platter of sandwiches and sat down across from me and Lily.

I took a deep breath and told them everything. Well, almost everything. They listened without breathing a word, hardly eating anything—shocked most of the time, and horrified the rest.

When I finished, they didn't say anything. But finally Tucker asked, "What were you thinking?"

I didn't want to have the same conversation over again, so I simply said, "I don't know. I guess I just wasn't thinking straight."

"Don't do it again," Lily said, reaching her arm over me for a side hug. "I don't know what we'd do if we lost you."

Nothing, I thought, *you'd be dead. Well, eventually I guess.*

We heard the bells echo through the walls, and Tucker and Lily got up. They grabbed their stuff in a hurry. Lily paused and set her satchel on the table. "Will you be alright?"

"I'll be fine," I smiled assuredly.

She nodded her head, obviously still worried I'd disappear.

I stood, and Tucker gave me one last hug. "Please don't ever do that again."

FOR THE INTENDED

My heart fluttered at his sweetness. "I won't." I said, hugging him back.

He smiled, grabbed his stuff, and headed out the door with Lily. "See ya tonight," he called back as they both charged through the door into the downpour.

I walked to the door frame and leaned against it as I watched them run through the thick rain. The wind blew every few seconds, blowing the water sideways. Observing the weather, I noticed Robert's soggy sandwiches still lying on the ground. They brought a sad, depressing feeling, though I didn't know why. I kicked one over and saw that the mud had soaked into it. As I looked back up, I saw that Lily and Tucker had disappeared from my sight, and I felt that the sandwiches somehow resembled me. I never found out why.

"MUD"

The next few days after that, I watched, waited, and hoped for Drayla and Caspian to come home. I jumped back into the swing of things, doing my chores and stuff, but I remained distracted by their absence. Sometimes I would just stare at the front gate, wanting them to come bursting through.

Every once in a while, I would get in my mind that I should go after them. One night I even packed everything, and began to tiptoe down the hallway, before I thought better of it. *What if they come back while I'm gone . . . and then something could happen to me . . . and then of course they'd only go back out for me.* So, I painfully went back to my room, and of course had a fitful night of sleep.

Then another day, I and a few others were escorting some merchants by the forest. I didn't know if I could get away with it, but I started to slow my pace. Me being at the back of the pack, I thought no one would notice. And no one did. I eventually completely stopped and watched as the group headed up and over the next hill.

I almost darted into the trees right then, but I realized how stupid that would be. I didn't have anything with me and the other guards would notice sooner or later, so I simply took out my whistle. I blew long and hard once, just once, then gave up. They weren't coming.

FOR THE INTENDED

At least everything else wasn't that bad. I managed to avoid the queen easily. She seemed to be very busy by what I heard from Milly. She never left the throne room apparently. She filled her time by talking to important people, and occasionally, yelling could be heard seeping from the oaken doors. Arnet got summoned regularly; in fact, he took part in most of the discussions held in the throne room. One day, when we were alone in one of the chambers off the Great Hall, I asked him what was going on. He sighed anxiously and simply said, "It's just as I feared."

"What is?" I asked, oblivious.

He opened his mouth to answer, when a guard marched into the room and summoned him. Without a word, Arnet followed him quickly out of the room, leaving me confused and worried.

Finally, I got a break from my problems when Elon returned. I found him on accident while carrying an extra saddle—in desperate need of a cleaning—to the stables. I turned the corner and dropped the saddle in surprise when I saw a small brown bird. I knew him immediately by the way he fluffed his feathers as he talked to the man next to him. The man listened to Elon say something about the horses while he distractedly scrubbed a saddle with oil.

"Elon!" I called.

The bird jumped a little as he turned his head in my direction. He gave an excited chirp as he darted towards me, "Galayne!" He flew all around my head, chirping happily.

"Hello, Elon," I laughed. "Where ya been?"

"Oh, Galayne..." He said, finally landing in my hand, "I do apologize. I had no intention of leaving you all alone in that dreadful room. I meant to come back that very evening when I saw you, but my orders were changed most inconveniently. I was—"

"It's alright, Elon." I smiled. "It's not your fault."

He gave a contented peep as I rubbed his small head with my thumb. "I am so glad you're back," he said sweetly.

We both heard an irritated cough. I looked over to see the man who had been scrubbing the saddles had stopped. His arms were crossed.

"Do you mind?" he asked me.

I was confused until I saw him gesturing to the saddle I had dropped. I looked down and realized I had dropped it right into a mud puddle.

"Oh. Sorry." I said, lifting Elon to my shoulder. I bent over and pulled it out of the mud, and when I say *mud*, I mean I hoped it was mud.

It dripped in clumps as I brought it over to an empty saddle rack. Elon whispered to himself, "Ooh, that is nasty," which didn't really help.

I slung it over the rack and wiped some of the thick muck off. I turned to walk away when I saw the man's face. "I'll do this one for you," I smiled, as if I meant to do it all along.

He rolled his eyes and sighed irritably as he turned back to his work.

Elon jumped down and glided to the end of an empty rack next to me as I began to clean the saddle.

"Do you have time?" I asked hopefully.

"I have only a few minutes to talk. I have to go to the docks after this, and many places after that," Elon said regretfully.

I nodded and began to ask things that I thought were appropriate to ask while the man still stood there. I didn't know if he would listen in, or if he really cared, but I wouldn't risk talking about anything important. Elon seemed to understand and went along with it, answering my useless questions about the weather on his journey or about what he ate for breakfast or anything else I could come up with.

When the man finally stepped into the stable for a minute, we quickly had a discussion about Elon's travels to Sinda. He said everything had been pretty normal, except, on his way back, he saw Duke Lemly and his escort making their way to Umplidore.

"They should be here late this afternoon," he said worriedly, studying my face.

I looked back at the door, making sure the man hadn't returned yet, "I thought they might come."

He looked surprised.

"The queen has been having a lot of meetings with all the dukes and duchesses," I said quietly. "I think things aren't going good."

"Do you think anyone knows about—"

I interrupted him quickly in case anyone listened in, "I don't know. But I sure hope not." I tried not to sound as worried as I felt.

We both glanced at the door when we heard the man approaching. "Hurry up," he said gruffly, coming out and picking up a finished saddle. "It might rain again, and these need to be cleaned and stored before then." He then turned and strode back into the barn. The tack room was just around the corner so I knew I only had a moment.

I leaned over the rack, bringing my face closer to him, "You didn't see Drayla or Caspian, did you?"

"What? Are they gone?" He said a little too loud.

I held my finger to my mouth as a reminder, and then said, "Yes. And they have been for a while." I heard the man approaching, so I whispered quickly, "When you get the chance, please go look for them."

He looked shocked that they had left but nodded determinedly. The man came through the door then.

"Thank you, Elon," I said in a normal voice, standing back up, "That will be all."

I could feel the man eyeing us.

Elon bowed with a, "Milady," and took off in the direction of the docks.

I smiled after him.

"Alright, Your Highness." The man said impatiently, clearly not frightened by who he continued to order around, "Are you finished chatting?" Before I could answer, he said rudely,

"Good. Now can we please finish up here?" With that he picked up another saddle and trudged grumpily back inside.

    I sighed as I wiped one more clump of "mud" off, watching it plop into another puddle below. When it sparkled and shined, and didn't smell half as bad, I carried the saddle into the barn right as it began to sprinkle. After I helped a little more, I bounded out the door into the rain in the direction of the castle, the stableman glaring and grumbling at me.

LOST AND FOUND

I sat in the kitchen by myself that evening, the moon pouring into the room from the window and the open door. I listened to the patter of the heavy rain outside and saw the occasional flash of lightning as I waited for Elon. I had just finished dinner alone and knew I should probably be heading to bed soon, but Elon had promised he'd be there, so I waited. I tried not to be anxious, but I turned my mug around and around, tapping the table with my other hand with a nervous touch.

Taking one last sip of apple cider, about to leave, I heard a little flutter. Elon darted into the room, flinging water as he did.
"Oh, the weather is so dreadful this time of year!" He exclaimed as he landed on the table and shook the rain off his waterproof wings before pulling them in.
"Elon," I smiled, "Glad you could make it." I didn't waste time, "Did you see them?"
He looked just as sad as I did, "No. And I looked far and wide for a good hour before this storm started up again."
He saw my face and continued, "I'm sure they're alright."
I gave a little smile.
"I have never seen a finer horse than Drayla. She is strong and wise and can fend quite well for herself," he said, very sure of his words. "And don't forget she has Caspian with her." His

voice had some annoyance in it as he said, "That stubborn-headed wolf wouldn't let anything happen to either of them."

I gave a larger smile, "You're right, Elon." I concealed my real thoughts, "I have nothing to worry about. I'm sure they'll be back soon." But I had already decided to go after them.

"That's right, darling, they will. Now don't you worry anymore," he smiled. "If I'm not mistaken, you should be getting to bed now. Long day ahead of you tomorrow," he said it enthusiastically.

You have no idea, I thought as I smiled, "You're right. See you tomorrow." *If I'm still here.*

With one last smile, he nodded and flew out the door as I got up and brought the plate and mug to the counter.

Surprisingly, I went to bed that evening and had a wonderful night of sleep. I guessed it was because I knew I was finally going to do something about Drayla and Caspian.

I woke up a little bit earlier than usual and quickly packed a satchel. I put three changes of clothes in it and an extra pair of boots but made sure to leave a lot of room for the food I still needed to store in it.

I snuck down to the kitchen, pleased to find breakfast had already been served. No one had come yet, and I hoped nobody would until I managed to get out of there. I snatched handful after handful of fruit, quickly laying them inside my bag, and stuffed a few pieces of toast at the top of it. I didn't know how long they'd last, but it would have to do.

I had just finished securing the tie when I heard footsteps coming down the stairs. I only had a few seconds, so I scanned the room for a place to hide the satchel. I just had time to fling the bag into the back corner of an unused cabinet before a stablehand who I thought I'd seen before came in silently. He noticed me but didn't really seem to care about my presence. He grabbed a banana from the almost empty fruit bowl and headed out the door.

I reached for the cabinet door, about to make a run for it, when I realized the time wasn't right. If I left then, I wouldn't be there for sword practice, which Arnet taught. He would suspect that I'd left, and I would be found before the first hour. I had to wait until the afternoon. Everybody's work usually died down by that time, and I could sneak away easily.

So, I did. I did all my normal stuff and played everything cool. And I don't think anyone suspected anything, until of course I messed up at the last minute.

I headed back to the kitchen for my hidden satchel, horrified to see a maid holding it. She rummaged through it with a confused look on her face.

I, in a very panicked state, ran up and took it from her, "Thank you."

She looked surprised and asked quickly, "Is this yours?"

I swallowed, but quickly answered, "Yes, it is. Thank you for finding it. I lost it." I turned and began to walk away. *I lost it? What was I thinking?!*

I fought the urge to glance back, but I knew she watched me as I scurried away.

I had to hurry. She would tell someone, and I would only have minutes to get out of there before they found me. My pace quickened as I slung the satchel over my shoulder, trying to look as natural as possible. My heart beat a little faster every time someone glanced at me. I felt like everyone knew what I was doing as I made my way through the old courtyard.

"Hey, Galayne!" a happy voice exclaimed from my right, nearly giving me a heart attack. Lakon waved at me and grinned, "You're just in time! A sword in need of desperate repair has just arrived. I thought you might like to help me fix it."

Normally, any other day I would have been thrilled to hear that. I was excited for Lakon because I knew that was what he preferred to fix, and even more so because I loved to help fix them myself. But instead I simply said, "Sorry, Lakon, not today."

His face dropped as I quickly walked on by. That was bad. He had to know something was up. I took a second to peer behind me and quickly whirled my head back around when I saw him standing, looking after me.

I got closer to the front gate which was tall and menacing with two strong guards on either side. *Calm down*, I told myself. *They'll let you through. They have no idea what you're up to.*

But they weren't the main problem; they were still hundreds of feet away. My main problem was that Arnet appeared out of nowhere with guards on either side. He stepped out of an alleyway about twenty feet away on my left side and noticed me immediately.

I pretended not to notice him and kept walking down the slight decline to the front gate, past all the merchants selling different products. I could feel his eyes on me as I did, and I could feel my hands start to sweat. *If I do this, his trust will be broken again, and I could easily end up back in that room.* I took a moment to think it over, still heading down the hill at a steady pace; I could hear them starting to follow. *Nope*, I heard a voice in my head say, *you're going. Okay*, I thought, *then I gotta be quick.* I started to look for a way to slow my followers down. Then I had an idea. I began to sprint.

"After her!" I heard Arnet shout. The sound of pounding feet began to follow me down the hill.

An opportunity approached quickly on my right: A fruit cart. At the last second, I flipped my arm out and sent a hundred apples everywhere behind me. The ones that didn't get lodged against uneven stones in the road began to roll down the hill after me, slowly picking up speed. I glanced behind me and watched the guards having a hard time dodging them, looking very annoyed. I came upon a stand of crates, and those went everywhere too, some smashing against the road. I didn't worry about destroying other people's stuff because I knew Arnet would pay everyone back for everything.

All of the guards were so far behind me, having a harder time getting around the people in the busy street than me. I watched one trip on an apple and face plant into a pile of crates. I grinned; the plan was working way better than I thought. Then all of a sudden, an arm lashed out for me out of nowhere. It barely got a grip on my arm but lost it. I tripped for a second but kept running, the new guard right behind. Apparently, there were more people I had to worry about than I had previously thought. And the new guy was *fast*, and not as clumsy as the others. I flung more merchandise from the sidelines into his path but he jumped and dodged easily, right on my tail. Finally, he got so close I could hear him breathing. *No! Come on!* I thought. Then he latched onto my satchel and began to pull. I managed to let it slide off and kept sprinting, and the sudden lightness on what he was pulling sent him tumbling over. I knew it was foolish to leave it behind, but there was nothing to do about it then. I had my bow. I could hunt.

    I was approaching the gate and the guards in front of it, and I saw them eyeing me. I realized I wouldn't be able to get past them without some serious advantage. That's when I heard a neigh and saw my ride. A long-legged horse appeared. It was being led towards the gate by a villager not too far from me. I just had to reach them.

    They were fifteen feet away . . . ten feet away . . . five feet . . . I slammed into the villager, sending him to the ground. I immediately grabbed the horse's lead rope. The horse gave a frightened whinny, its ears pinned back as it eyed me. I continued running so that the horse immediately went into a nervous trot and then a canter. I reached my arm over his neck and tried to mount. After a few tries I managed to sling my leg over his saddleless back. I clung to his mane as he transitioned into a gallop, hoping he would go where I needed him to without a bridle.

    The guards behind me were still pursuing, yelling for people to get out of the way. I heard Arnet yell again, closer than I'd thought, "Don't let her *through that gate!*"

The guards at the gate began to walk towards me, their spears held high. *It's okay,* I thought determinedly, *they'll move. You'll make it.* I urged the horse faster.

The horse gave a small whinny of fear as we got closer, his whole body tense. I got the feeling the horse wasn't too fond of having big, sharp sticks pointed in his direction while he ran straight at them. But he kept moving since I pressed him forward constantly. When I just began to think we were going to make it, that's when the horse decided to do it. About ten feet away, he reared up so suddenly I had no time to think. I tried to clutch anything I could, but I tumbled off and painfully slammed into the ground. *Ouch.*

As fast as I could manage, I drew my sword. The guards were already beginning to surround me with their blades drawn, Arnet amongst them. We were at a standstill. No one knew what to do. The whole street seemed to be holding its breath, the villagers watching us intently. *I bet they don't see something like this every day.*

Guards on all sides began to slowly close in. I answered with a raised sword and a scowl. I could still, if I tried my hardest, get out of there. I tried looking for weaknesses, holes in their circle, any way that I could escape. I then saw what I had to do, but a sound echoed down the street, stopping my thoughts. A neigh I knew all too well broke the tense silence along with a furious, growling bark.

My heart leaped in my throat as Drayla and Caspian flew through the gate. They looked murderous as they charged right at us. "Drayla! Caspian!" I exclaimed, lowering my sword, completely forgetting the guards all around me. But Drayla and Caspian didn't seem as thrilled as I thought they'd be. My happy face died as I watched them barreling toward us.

Then all of a sudden, Drayla burst into the circle of guards, sending them toppling sideways. Arnet got flung and I saw him hit his head on the ground. Caspian came right after her. He lunged at a very surprised guard who yelled in terror as Caspian latched onto his back with his fangs. His bite only penetrated the armor, but it didn't make the guard any less frightened. The villagers screamed and ran into their shops and houses.

"Guys!" I yelled. "Stop it!"

But they weren't listening. Drayla barged into three more guards who thankfully got up unharmed and ran. Caspian let go, and that guard fled as well. After that, there were no guards between us and the gate. Drayla and Caspian stepped in between me and the guards, her rearing and stomping her hooves, him snarling and baring his teeth. Most of the guards were younger and were quite frightened.

"Guys stop! They're not—"

"Enough!" Drayla hissed to me. "Back up." She ordered sternly.

"No," I tried to say, "Everything is—"

But she wouldn't listen and began to step back towards me, swishing her tail angrily and pinning her ears back at the guards. Caspian raised his tail high as he began to do the same. They were forcing me back towards the gate. The guards' swords were all drawn, but their owners didn't advance. They watched us nervously.

I didn't know what to do. I knew Caspian and Drayla were just trying to protect me, but if they stole me away, all of us would be in huge trouble. I had to convince them that everything was alright. Still thinking over how I should do it, someone stepped out from behind the guards.

"Welcome back, Caspian, Lord of the Wolves. And Drayla, The Timeless," Arnet said loudly. Blood ran down the side of his head, but other than that he looked fine.

Drayla and Caspian watched him, suspicious.

"There seems to be a misunderstanding," Arnet said. He continued tactfully, "Galayne is safe."

Drayla and Caspian looked back at me for confirmation and I just nodded. They both looked rather surprised, and their tenseness dropped immediately.

Villagers were peeking out from their hiding places.

Arnet helped settle everyone down, "Everyone return to their posts! Everything is well here. This was a test." He feigned amusement, "Unfortunately, Princess Galayne failed." He grinned, "We'll have to keep practicing." It was a believable lie.

The people pretended to be amused too. The guards sheathed their swords, mumbling to each other, and began to walk up the hill. The gate guards returned to their original position.

When the guards were well enough away for them to feel safe, Drayla and Caspian attacked me with hugs and kisses and very enthusiastic greetings, knocking me to the ground. Too shocked at what had just passed and so happy about everything, I couldn't answer any of their questions.

Hugging Drayla's head and clasping my arm around Caspian, I made eye contact with Arnet. He still stood there, staring at me. He didn't look mad or anything. In fact, I couldn't tell what he thought. Drayla and Caspian didn't notice him as they still happily bounded around and snuggled with me. Arnet seemed to be trying to tell me something as he stared. He looked disappointed or aggravated or something. And then I finally understood. His trust *had* been lost. In his mind, I should have consulted him before I tried to do anything. He turned without a word and began to walk up the hill. He had already given me a second chance to follow his orders. And I knew from then on, our relationship would never be the same. And really, it never was.

FOR THE INTENDED

DRAYLA

Drayla and Caspian were pretty flustered and shaky, especially Drayla. They walked close to my side and were wary whenever we came near guard posts. I stroked Drayla's mane with my right hand and Caspian's head got rubbed with my left as we walked through the empty courtyard. I asked them how they knew I was at the front gate and they told me they didn't. They were attempting a rescue and were surprised to find me so fast. It was clear they didn't know exactly what had happened to me or where I had been.

When I thought we'd reached a place where no one would be able to listen in, we sat down. We all rested under the shade of a very old tree with boughs that threatened to break right through the wall behind it. Drayla tucked her legs underneath her as she lay down, asking quietly, "What happened?"
Caspian sat right next to me and nudged my arm. I wrapped it around him, thinking about the way Arnet had looked at me. "It's all one great big misunderstanding," I said to her as I reached for her head. She lowered it and I scratched between her eyes, which she closed contentedly.
I then proceeded to tell them all that had happened. Caspian lay down and rested his head in my lap as I stroked his soft, white hair. He listened intently, tensing up at all the parts that

made him angry. Drayla listened without a word, remaining motionless, appearing wise and in control.

I finished telling them everything, but they didn't speak. Caspian only lay there and kept his thoughts to himself, still snuggled up close. Drayla swished her tail anxiously as she thought in silence. The few years before she had been the same—always worried, always thinking over stuff, always contemplating to herself and never sharing her thoughts. She hadn't always been like that though. I thought back to the first time I saw her—the day she became my horse.

I was eight years old, traveling back to Umplidore from Dom with Arnet. We were plodding along, accompanied by an escort, through the thick forest on our horses. Everything seemed normal until the horses started to get restless. They neighed and shifted, and some began to rear. An unnaturally bright, golden light shone through the trees just ahead of us. Arnet grabbed the reins of my horse to keep it from bolting and stood up in his saddle trying to see better.

"What is it, sir?" A guard asked Arnet while trying to calm his own horse down.

"I'm not sure," Arnet said, handing my reins to him. "Stay here."

The guard nodded and gripped the reins to my small palomino pony tightly.

Arnet dismounted and began to lead his horse in the direction of the light while all of us watched nervously.

"Aye tuld yah thurr wurr unnaturrrral thengss en these wudds," a particularly anxious guard said to his comrades when Arnet had disappeared through the trees. "Munsterrs en creeturrs en turrerrs unured ove," he said shakily.

"Silence," the head guard barked, though even he sounded unsure, "There's nothing out there."

The timid guard quieted down, but they all seemed just as nervous as their horses. Then a sound rang out through the trees loud and clear, and everyone, horses and all, pricked their

FOR THE INTENDED

ears up and stared at the bright light. It was the sound of a horse, *my* horse. I didn't know how I knew, I just did.

I slid out of the saddle in a second and dashed into the glade ahead. "Your Highness! Stop!" The guardsen cried out in horror. I kept going, not listening to all the guards coming after me.

I burst through the trees right into the bright light. It poured from the center of the open space. Awe spread across my face as I stared at the black and white filly that stood in the middle of it, radiating pure power. I took a step forward, not believing the beauty.

Arnet stood on the other side of the glade, doing the same thing. He was admiring it all, but the moment he saw me his wonder-filled face broke. "Galayne, stay back!"

But I didn't listen, pretty normal for me as you've probably noticed, and I took another step closer. Arnet came charging after me, and that's when I bolted towards it. "No!" he yelled. The guards rushed into the scene on their horses with their swords drawn, but everyone froze when they saw what was happening.

I stood right in front of the filly, my arm outstretched. The horse looked at me, studying me, and then did something incredible that I only now understand the importance of. She touched me. She put her muzzle into my hand to the amazement of all who were standing there. The ground began to shake and rumble, the golden light turned bright, bright white and shone all around me and her. Somehow, I wasn't scared, even though the guards were shouting in alarm. I just stared into the silvery blue eyes that looked as if they'd seen things like no other.

Then, after a few seconds, the light got even brighter for a split second, then quickly faded. I heard a sound and looked down to see a beautiful symbol growing in the ground right under us. Silver took overtook the grass and shimmered magnificently.

The guardsen took off his helmet in shock, "That can't be..."

Arnet cut him off, "She is." He said in joyful wonder, "She is one of the Lyna... the Horses of Old."

The guards all stared in fascination.

Arnet bowed, "Welcome Drayla, the last of the Lyna."

All the guards immediately dismounted and did the same, their horses kneeling as well. But I just stared at Drayla because she smiled gently at me. She seemed far older than she looked. She appeared wise and powerful.

We both looked at Arnet when he stood and said, "Your arrival is most fortunate, and although it was predicted two centuries from now, is perfectly timed, Drayla The Timeless," he said, bowing his head one last time.

And from that day on Drayla was my horse. She provided advice when needed and was always there to defend me. She was more than a protective counselor though—she was one of my greatest friends.

FOR THE INTENDED

CASPIAN

I was pulled back into the moment when I heard a very satisfied sigh escape Caspian as he dreamed on my lap. He must have been really shaken by the whole thing, because he didn't care that Drayla saw him breaking from his normal warrior-like behavior. I ran my fingers through his long, white hair while Drayla got lost in her thoughts. While Drayla stared at the courtyard stones distantly, I remembered how Caspian entered my life.

It was a rather cold night, the stars brilliant in the dark sky. I was nine years old, again on the way back from the annual trip to Dom with Arnet. We and another lord's family were being escorted to Umplidore by at least thirty guards. We were all on horseback heading north.

Everything seemed calm and silent, except the horseshoes clacking down the road. Even though it felt a bit chilly, it was nice out. The wind hardly existed, and when it did, it barely disturbed anything except the tree leaves which swished and fell delicately. The ground was covered here and there with leaves from previous falls, and patches of dirt and sickly green grass spread throughout the forest because of the lack of water. Even some of the trees looked dry with dead leaves struggling to stay on their branches.

Where we were at on the old road, the sides were two steep banks and the trees were not as thick as usual, allowing the sky to be seen above the treetops. I was looking at the millions of stars spread above us, pulling my cloak closer around me, when I felt a hot breeze on my face. Drayla's head shot right up, ears flicking, eyes darting about.

Startled, I whispered, "What is it?"

She looked incredibly stressed, "I'm . . . not sure."

Just like when I met Drayla, the horses around us began to act up, whinnying and rearing. Arnet looked around quickly to see if he could find the culprit. His horse, being accustomed to chaos, calmly trotted up next to me and Drayla when Arnet asked him to.

"What is it?" Lord Drell asked as he pulled on his horse's reins.

No one breathed a word as they watched Arnet, looking to him for direction. Another hot wind blew by and I could feel Arnet's apprehension as he sat next to me. Like before, Arnet just said, "I'm not sure yet." He leaned side to side in his saddle, trying to see through the trees.

I tried to see it too, but something else in the sky caught my attention. The sky began to turn orange and the stars were veiled in black to the northwest. The orange slowly got closer and more intense, turning red. More hot wind blew; a faint crackling sound could be heard.

Being totally oblivious, I simply pointed up and asked innocently, "What's that?"

Everyone's eyes followed and Arnet immediately cried out loudly, "Fire!"

As if on cue, the fatal flickering orange flames came into sight, and the cracking of dead trees became sickeningly close and loud. The horses were in a terrified state, and the people on their backs weren't much better.

"We all know the way," Arnet cried out quickly, everyone listening with horror in their eyes, "If we get separated, we meet at the other side of the Narnstein. Now *move!*" Arnet yelled, and we all spurred our horses onward.

The horses flew into a frenzied gallop, thundering down the path, whinnying in fear every time an especially loud crack sounded. My heart rate increased. The heat intensified, and more fire could be seen in the east as we raced to the north.

One time, my heart stopped at the sound of screaming coming from a rider and his horse as they tried to dodge a huge tree falling into the road. The tree landed with a gigantic thud in front of them, causing the horse to rear and plunge into the forest. Another person's horse lost control of itself as well, and darted in the same direction, taking several others with it. Our group was breaking.

The smoke agitated everyone's eyes and nostrils as it closed in around us. The entire left side of the path danced with fire all the way around the next bend. Sometimes along the road, there would be a long bough that reached over the path and brushed the leaves on the other side, causing the other trees to catch fire.

The stars were no longer visible under the burning red sky. "Come on! We're almost there!" Arnet yelled over his shoulder. That's when I realized why we were still heading to the north. We needed to get to where the fire couldn't: across the river.

Something told me we were still about a mile away from the crossing, and I swallowed anxiously as I saw another burst of flames engulf a tree to my left. I looked with fear for assurance from Arnet that everything would be okay, but he didn't notice. His eyes were staring with frightful determination in the direction of the river.

I looked to my left to see Lord Drell's son, Tillen, galloping on his small, white pony next to me. He seemed at least two years younger than me, the fire reflecting in his wide eyes.

Being at the top left of the pack, I saw our refuge first. The river flowed peacefully from the north to the southeast, showing no concern as the fire raged on its shores. Large and welcoming, and not that far away anymore, we all got a burst of hope.

We were beating the fire in our race to the river, but it wasn't that far behind. We were all starting to breathe again, sure that everything would be alright, when everyone's stomachs flipped in unison. A howl burst through all the noise, coming from across the river. All the horses reared or dragged their feet to a shuddering halt.

"What now!?" someone asked for all of us.

I looked at Arnet in absolute panic, but he looked just as bad as he whispered, "The Arakin..." He looked all around, but not frantically. He looked confused and distracted, and absolutely petrified. His eyes rested on me, full of terror and horrible defeat. He looked completely broken.

"Arnet?" I asked, unsure, my voice breaking. Everyone listened with their hearts in their throats to the snapping of twigs and falling of trees not too far behind.

He seemed to wake up, shaking himself. "Onward!" he commanded, still trying to give hope and courage to those around him even though I could see he had none left.

Nobody believed we'd make it, but nobody argued. Some hope was better than none, so we all forced our horses onward. I could feel Drayla's apprehension as we did; I could practically see her mind going hundreds of miles a second as she pressed forward into a tense gallop.

The river was getting closer, and I leaned forward in the saddle as if it would help me be there sooner. Everyone else seemed to be doing the same thing. Everyone gasped when we heard another howl, closer than before, but thankfully the horses only neighed and snorted and continued even faster.

I looked over to see Tillen was even more frightened than before. I could hear him whimpering beside me as we galloped on. It looked like he needed to scream but was trying to hold it back for the cause of seeming brave. But it was a lost cause because every jolt of the saddle beneath him set loose a small gasp of fear.

FOR THE INTENDED

Everyone's eyes turned towards a creaking sound to our left. A massive tree set just along the path fell over due to the fact it had just been swallowed by flames. It took a few pieces of road with it and a lot of the dirt bank as it tumbled down the hill into a mass of blistering heat. The path suddenly had a large chunk missing which produced a steep cliff.

I was about to pull Drayla to the right to avoid the upcoming blemish in the road when I had one of the strangest experiences I've had yet. I heard an immensely loud cracking sound. I immediately felt as light as a feather as I heard the little boy shriek beside me. I saw black and bright orange swirl together as I flipped over, the screams of several people and the neighing of horses above me. Then I hit the ground hard, right smack on my back. The wind had been knocked out of me, as well as my bearings for a second. I lay there in total confusion as I saw orange and red stuff dance in the trees above me, bright burning dots flickering through the air. Finally, after what seemed quite a while but probably couldn't have been more than a few seconds, I felt someone shaking my arm desperately. They were saying my name over and over again though it sounded distant and faint. Then all of a sudden, I got sucked out of the drowsy void. All noise, heat, and vision flooded back in an instant as I sat up. Tillen knelt next to me, scrapes on his small face, frantically trying to get my attention.

"Galayne! Galayne! Please get up!" his high-pitched voice pleaded. "We have to get out of here!"

I looked around and saw that the tree that fell must have loosened the dirt all along the upper bank, and we must have set a small landslide in motion by our weight. We had tumbled all the way down the hill and the road could just be seen above us to our right. The air was filled with the faint crackling of the burning bark around us. Once or twice, I thought I heard my name being called, but it seemed so far away and blended in with the hot wind. We were the only ones that seemed to have fallen, besides our horses. *Our horses!* I looked around quickly and found Drayla lying at the base of a tree that hadn't caught fire yet. I bolted to her.

"Drayla!" I reached her side, "Drayla, are you okay?" The boy followed me over as Drayla moaned and gained consciousness.

Tillen sniffled, "Duke ran off." It took me a second before I realized he meant his pony.

"Galayne?" Drayla mumbled.

"Yes, Drayla," I said, turning back to her, totally relieved. "I'm here."

"What . . ." then she saw the fire and our frightened faces. She stood, grimacing in pain as she put weight on a seriously injured leg—hopefully not broken. "Get on," she commanded.

"No," I said firmly, "You can't carry us."

"I must," she said, aggravated and stubborn, "Now both of you *get on*."

"No, Drayla," I said, "You carry Tillen up the hill to the road. I can make it myself." I promised with my eyes.

She swished her tail, thinking it over, but then she saw we had no time to argue. "Very well. We must be quick if we are to reach the road before these trees give in to flames."

I hoisted Tillen up onto her quickly. I saw him swallow anxiously at Drayla's height since he had probably only ever ridden ponies. He looked up the large slope in hesitancy as Drayla said, "Hang on, little one." With that she began to make her way up the hill. She jumped upwards and pushed against the slippery dirt, trying hard to find a foothold here and there. I could see her shake with pain each time her wounded leg hit the ground.

I started to head up after her, when I felt something inside me. All sound faded again and I turned slowly to the north, burning ash floating through the air. It's hard to explain, but I would just get these feelings sometimes. It's like when I said I knew the river was a mile away, I knew it really was *exactly* a mile away. I didn't find out till later that the sensations were the early beginnings of my Summer Born powers. I knew in that moment that something wasn't right, and I don't just mean the fire. Someone needed help.

I looked back at Drayla as she climbed the second half of the hill. She didn't seem to notice me still in the burning glen as she determinedly struggled up the hill, needing to focus so she wouldn't tumble down again. A very large tree fell just behind her with a large pop, prompting her to go even faster.

I felt the feeling again, and I looked north, the hot wind making my hair dance softly. I felt an urge to plunge into the fiery forest to discover the origin of the call. I glanced one more time at Drayla who was almost at the road, and then I did something really foolish, but something I would always be thankful for. I darted to the burning north, ready to find who was calling me.

I bounded through openings in the trees, dodged falling branches, and tried to ignore the loud snapping and cracking sounds. I went to the left here, then to the right there, somehow avoiding direct contact with fire. Every once in a while, I heard the howl of a wolf, way too close to me. It felt hot, but amazingly not too hot for me. I later found out that perk came from my powers as well.

I kept a pretty good pace, until I stopped dead in my tracks to a small sound coming from my left. It sounded like a whimper, and then like a strangled, high-pitched, yapping sound. The feeling in my gut felt more like a pang of need. I immediately felt a connection to whatever cried out in the next circle of trees; I could feel its presence and how much it needed me.

I jumped over two large roots into the next glen and froze as I instantly saw a wolf. But not a scary wolf; in fact, it looked rather pathetic as it struggled to untangle itself from a twisted thorn bush, yelping madly. The wolf pup with silky white hair, a black nose, and golden yellow eyes looked at me. He had a black design in his fur that grew up on his left foreleg, letting me know immediately he was one of the Arakin. I stood and just looked at him. *Was I allowed to touch him?* I had no idea, but the sound of a tree crashing behind me decided for me. I ran over to him and immediately started untangling the puppy from its painful snare.

He stopped struggling when I did, and just stared at me. He didn't look frightened, he looked grateful. He seemed wiser than a puppy should with his golden eyes contrasting the blackened bark behind him.

I finally pulled the last vine of thorns off him, expecting him to bolt, but he didn't. He just stared at me. He stood and bowed, and I watched in wonder as the black markings on his shoulder and down his left leg began to radiate light. They shone like the sun, lovely and bright in the gloom of the forest. Then the light faded away and I saw that the markings did as well, fading from black to gray and then blending into the soft, white fur. The wolf looked up one more time, meeting my eyes, and I thought again how much older or wiser or something his eyes looked; they were so intense. Then I jumped when I watched him suddenly fall on his side, unconscious on the ground. I ran to him and scooped him up in my arms, relieved to feel his quick little heartbeat through his fur. I got him situated in my arms when another howl wound into our glade. And trust me, that one didn't sound like a cute, little puppy. I stood abruptly and became aware of how fast the fire continued to spread. Fire charged in all directions, burning in every tree. The smoke got unbearable, and my eyes stung as I tried to get my bearings. *Where's the river?* Luckily, the feeling came again, and told me which way it was. I turned and then sprinted, clutching the small creature to my chest.

Large branches were falling everywhere, and the noise became overwhelming. The smoke thickened, and I had to stop every once in a while to squat down and breathe a few deep breaths before running again. I covered the wolf's nose with the edge of my shirt as I ran on, hoping to shield him from some of the smoke. He woke up a few times, but only managed to look around weakly before passing out again. I didn't think about it too much then, for fear it would suddenly leave me, but I felt unusually brave. Darting here and there, I hardly thought of the fatal flames, the deathly thick smoke, or the head-crushing boughs tumbling from the trees. I had a goal; get to the river, and that's all that seemed to matter.

I began to get hopeful when I suddenly screamed as a large branch came down right on top of us. I tried to dodge it but slipped and dropped the pup as I did. After falling right on my back, the large branch landed painfully on my right arm, pinning it to the ground. I cried out, sure my arm had snapped. I tried to shove the wood off with my other free arm, but it wouldn't budge. It was a large branch and ran the length of my body, so I positioned myself just right and finally got my legs to push it off. I breathed a shaky, painful sigh of relief as it finally rolled away and I sat up. I didn't have time to look at my arm to see the damage, and quite frankly, I didn't want to. I immediately gathered the unconscious ball of fluff with my left arm and continued on.

Finally, I saw it. I could see the shining river just through the trees and I began to run all the faster, suddenly terribly frightened. Gasps of fear came with each breath I took, and my heart thudded in my ears. I began to stumble a little, barely catching myself sometimes. Then I actually did trip on a protruding root with a little yelp, but I managed to hold onto the wolf and immediately scramble back to my feet. Tears were beginning to run down my small, frightened face.

About to run out on the pebbly bank, I screamed again as a wall of fire burst up right in front of us. I couldn't see an alternative route; fire closed in on all sides. I breathed deep and concentrated, everything else blurring into the background except the river and the fire in front of it.

Then, I did it. I jumped through the huge fire wall with a strangled and absolutely terrified cry. It felt searing hot and excruciatingly painful as I did a headlong dive. I hit the bank with no control and started to tumble and roll down it, somehow managing to keep hold of the pup. Yeah, rolling down a hill of rocks isn't the most comfortable thing in the world, especially when parts of you are on fire. I slapped right down in the water, extinguishing the fires burning on my clothes. I burst into tears with everything that hurt, and the fear that refused to leave. I clung to the puppy in my arms and sloshed quickly across the shallow water. I reached the other side and kept running on and on, still gasping in terror as if the fire continued to follow us. Finally, I began to feel faint. I started to lose my footing, and after I had just run into a grassy glade, I collapsed.

    I rolled over onto my back and sobbed. I stroked the pup's long, soft hair with my sooty fingers, comforted by his presence as he lay on top of me. Various places all over my body felt like they were still on fire, and my right arm began turning purple and black with an extremely sore pain.

    After a while, my crying died down to shaky breaths. I listened to the wolf's calm breathing as he slept contently. Despite just being in a furnace-like heat, I felt freezing as the temperature returned to that of a cold, unaffected night. The quiet seemed odd after the intense noise of the fire that was too far away to hear anymore. The smoke was to the south of us as we lay together, but only took up a very small portion of the sky. The stars could be seen from my side of the river, and they were gorgeous in their multitude. Despite the pain and adrenaline, I began to calm down. I pulled the puppy up closer to my face and closed my eyes in comfort as his little breaths kissed my face. I was finally in control of myself, when my heart skipped a beat. I heard a howl.

    I sat up painfully, glancing around. Another howl, way too close, replied to the other. I heard rustling all around the glen, and the sound of many creatures, *large creatures*, running through the forest in my direction. It sounded like the hunt Arnet had taken me on the year before, with hundreds of hounds darting through the woods. I stood up in absolute terror, and the sounds suddenly stopped. The only sound became my quick breathing and pounding heart. The little white wolf didn't seem to notice, but he began to shake from the brisk night air. He curled up closer in my arms, wedged his nose underneath my arm, and then passed out again. As I peered through the trees, I wrapped him in the excess cloth at the end of my ruined shirt without hardly thinking.

Nothing happened for a few seconds. No sound, except for the light wind, and no movement. I tried to steady my breathing, and once I felt calm enough, I took a step forward to examine the last place I had heard movement. I nearly fell backwards when the bush moved. I started to back away, wanting to turn and run in the opposite direction, when a gigantic creature erupted from the foliage with a terrible snarl.

It was a brown wolf, but not the ordinary kind. He stood taller than normal wolves, which are already pretty big. He had a white design growing up his left foreleg, just like the puppy. I shrieked as I tripped over a small rock. I fell on my back, still clutching the white pup. He walked towards me slowly and menacingly, as if he were enjoying my fright. He didn't seem to notice the white puppy curled up in my left arm, still shielded by the edge of my shirt. I stared, unable to do anything as I lay frozen in the short grass. The wolf threatened to charge, when a creature just as horrific bounded into the scene.

"Enough, Daeod," a brown wolf with similar markings said. "We must wait for Lord Anoltan and Lady Demelaine."

The wolf in front of me rolled his eyes, baring his long fangs. "Come on, Solen," he said angrily, "the rat is *trespassing*." He said "trespassing" with a hissing snarl.

"No, Daeod. We must wait for them to arrive or—"

"Or what?" Daeod snapped, whirling on the other.

"Or I'll stop you . . ." Solen stepped forward threateningly. "Just like last time," he smirked.

Daeod charged him and stopped abruptly just a few feet away from Solen with his hair raised all down his back, "You didn't stop me last time. I just changed my mind."

"No, you didn't." Solen said in disbelief.

"Yes, I did."

"No, you didn't," Solen said, getting annoyed.

"Did."

"Didn't."

Daeod lunged, snapping down on Solen's shoulder, "*Did!*"

I blinked in absolute terror as they fought with a lot of ferocious noises. They didn't notice as two more creatures climbed to the top of a large pointy rock at the edge of the clearing. In fact, several new wolves appeared on the outer edges of the opening. A few voices among the wolves could be heard saying things like, "Ugh . . . it's the Kel brothers again," and "Really? Again?"

I gazed up at the two wolves at the top of the rock in awe. They were bigger than the others and were definitely a lot wiser-looking. One was black with a shiny silver design that crept up his left foreleg from his paw. The other wolf had similar markings, but they were bronze on red fur. They were both beautiful despite being totally terrifying.

They were looking down with annoyance on the pair of brothers who continued their bickering without a clue the others were watching. I looked back and forth between the pair on the rock and the pair snapping and rolling around, and couldn't decide what to do. No one seemed to be paying me any attention. *Could I just slip away?* I began to slowly stand, shaking. No one noticed. I began backing away when the red wolf spoke.

"Wrong," she called to the brothers below. Her voice sounded beautiful and wise, but still made me shudder at the sound of power that radiated from it. The brothers jumped to face the wolves on the rock, looking shocked and really embarrassed. "Your Ladyship," they bowed in unison.

She leapt down gracefully, and I swallowed at her stature. She walked slowly and silently, with her fur reflecting the moonlight, to the brothers who looked nervous and fidgety. "You are both wrong. *I* stopped you, Daeod," she said.

The black wolf jumped down and followed after her.

Daeod swallowed, "Yes, milady . . . you did."

FOR THE INTENDED

She smiled with authority, "And it seems I have done so again."

"Yes, Lady Demelaine." He swallowed again.

"Will this happen again?" she asked in a sweet but ever-so-threatening tone.

"No, milady," the brothers bowed anxiously.

"Very well," she said, lowering her head a little to let them know they were dismissed.

The brothers didn't waste a second and darted out of the clearing.

All eyes turned on me, and I thought I might have a heart attack. The black wolf came and stood next to the red and glared at me with deep, dark eyes. "Now who is this?" he asked gruffly, no friendliness to be heard. I couldn't decide if I should answer or not, but apparently it was a rhetorical question, because he continued, "Galayne, *Princess of Edgeladine*." He said it as a mockery, and some chuckling could be heard throughout the crowd. "What brings you to the realm of the Arakin?" He didn't sound very pleased to see me.

I got angry that he treated me like a joke. Frustrated, I went all high and mighty on him, despite the fact it was me against a whole pack of over-sized wolves. Fear left as my face shaded over with an angry pink. I answered with a snarky reply, "I think the question is: what are you doing in the realm of the Domians?"

The red and black wolf looked very surprised, and they raised their heads in agitation at being slighted by a child. The wolves all around the glen seemed to hold their breath, moving their tails side to side, unsure of what would happen. An edgy silence filled the space until Lady Demelaine broke it.

"We are moving farther to the south as winter draws near. It is our way, young one. This has been our home for far longer than Man's."

I felt bad when I actually thought about it. According to the Domian's legend, they claimed the land for themselves through an epic war with the Arakin. I realized that it had been the Arakin's land first, and I thought about how I would be pretty upset if someone stole my home away from me.

She continued, seeming to get more and more agitated each second, "They invaded our lands and drove us back with their swords and axes and fire, making it difficult to find food and shelter." Her voice had been rising in rage until her face broke with sudden remorse as she turned, staring blankly to the side, saying, "And pups." She whispered, "So many lost pups."

The black wolf, who by then I had guessed was Lord Anoltan, didn't say a word, but seemed to be thinking the same things as he glared at me. In fact, all of the wolves seemed to have an ancient abhorrence for mankind.

Lady Demelaine continued after her trance with new fury, her hazel eyes glowing with hate. She began to advance on me very slowly, and even though I was quite a few feet away, I began to back up. The other wolves began to close in on all sides, too, snarling and champing their teeth in anger.

I looked everywhere for a chance of escape with a small whimper in my throat.

"Your kind have all but destroyed our home," her voice grew with each word. "Why, this fire is probably those Domian's doing! Your kind have killed hundreds of ours . . . sparing not even the pups . . . the pups," she finished in a whisper again. I watched her in fascination as the terrible creature lost herself to an emotion almost human.

Suddenly, she woke from her second daze of depression with a terrible snap of her teeth, "We lost our son to your people . . ." She smiled a disgustingly evil smile as she said, "And now mankind will lose their princess to us." The wolves growled louder than before. I just stood petrified in the center, tears streaming on either side of my face.

The huge red wolf, with the black one just behind her, came at me, gaining speed with each step. I held my breath in complete disbelief as I saw Lady Demelaine coming in for a death strike.

FOR THE INTENDED

Then, I felt a small movement by my arm. The pup stretched his head upwards, making the shirt fall away. Everyone froze, the silence almost worse than the champing of sharp teeth. I barely breathed as I gazed at the looks of surprise. The puppy was still turned inward to my chest, hiding his face. I heard him give a small yawn before turning from the shelter of my arm to face the crowd.

I didn't think any of the wolves were breathing when they saw his golden eyes. The lord and lady gaped. The red wolf looked like she might pass out as she breathed, "Caspian?"

The puppy yapped a cheerful bark in reply.

"Caspian!" The red wolf exclaimed in emotional elation. The black wolf said nothing, but I could tell he felt the same as she did as he stared in disbelief. They began to advance slowly in relieved bliss.

The puppy began to squirm, wanting to be put down. I didn't know what else to do, so I bent down and put him softly on the ground. I saw Lady Demelaine's eyes widen in horrified sorrow as I did, stopping in her tracks. I heard Lord Anoltan whisper to himself, "No," looking as heartbroken as the red wolf.

The white puppy, whose name seemed to be Caspian, sat happily in front of me, licking his paws. Lady Demelaine breathed, her eyes glistening, "No . . ." her voice seemed to be breaking as she said, "My son."

Son? Uh oh.

Suddenly she thundered, "*Look at what you've done!*"

Caspian whimpered and ran for cover in between my legs.

"I'm sorry," I said quickly, my voice breaking. I was shaking so bad it was hard to stand, "I-I was j-just trying to save him."

Up till that point I thought she wanted to tear my throat out, but her voice washed over with confusion as she asked in a lowered voice, "You saved him?"

"Y-yes," I stuttered, still trembling, "f-from the fire."

Lord Anoltan's anger had been slowly rising until suddenly he burst out with a hiss, "This sneaky snake has taken our son from us!" Apparently "snake" was their worst insult. I had no idea what he meant, but I fell backwards to the ground in terror, Caspian jumping into my lap. I thought Lord Anoltan would rush at me when Lady Demelaine spoke up.

"No, Lord Anoltan . . . he gave himself up to her." She didn't seem as shaky anymore. She looked at her son in my lap with a new sort of distance. "He is old enough to follow his own path, whatever that may be. He bound himself to her by his own decision . . . and that decision we must respect." She was hurt and angry, but she hid it extremely well.

I had no idea what they were talking about until I finally got it. Caspian's black markings were no longer there. I remembered what Arnet had told me about the Arakin, and actually quite a few other distinguished animal species. The Arakin were a noble kingdom that had many ancient practices, one of them being their ability to Bond. According to Arnet, it was very, very, rare, and it only happened to the people that were held worthy by the wolves. In Bonding to the human, the wolf would give up his place in the pack and his connection to his ancestors. The Bond would last until the day either of them died. Shocked, I realized the puppy sitting in my lap had done just that. In giving up his black markings, he did way more.

The black wolf only got angrier, "Let's just kill the rat then!"

"No!" That time the red wolf actually put herself in between me and him. "The Bond is young. If you kill the youngling, you may shatter the Bond and kill them both." She paused, then with sadness flooding her voice, she whispered, "No, my love . . . we must let him go."

The black wolf breathed deep, glaring at me, and I saw his black eyes moisten as he turned and walked out of the clearing without a word. The other wolves were still holding their breath. No one had stirred as they all listened to the whole thing.

The red wolf shook herself from her depressing thoughts. She raised her muzzle to the sky and took a deep breath of the cold air, a large cloud billowing from her mouth. She declared, "We will go east to the edge of the forest, and then continue south from there." A gray wolf nodded to her, and then raised his head and howled. We heard a reply, and then as if that were their cue, all the wolves turned with excited barking and ran out of the glade to the east. I stood, watching them go, holding Caspian close to my pounding heart. All the shuffling in the woods finally disappeared.

A twig snapped, and I whirled around with a gasp to see that the large, red wolf was much closer than before. Only about four feet away from me, she looked at me intently. She had gorgeous eyes that spoke of nights long ago, a magnificent mane of glistening hair, and a look of extreme understanding. "Stay near him, young one. Nightlar Bonds are not to be taken lightly. You both have quite a journey before you," her eyes became distant, the stars reflecting in them, but she shook herself out of it and met my eyes again. "I cannot see it clearly, but I know before the end, you will have saved his life and he will have saved yours, many times."

I didn't know what to say, and I ended up just standing there with my mouth hanging open.

She glanced down at Caspian in my arms, and the sadness came again.

The pup's eyes met hers, a similar look rising in them.

She leaned down, closed her eyes, and nuzzled noses with him, "Farewell, my son."

He rubbed his face against hers, a trace of a whimper in his throat.

When they were done, she stepped closer to my face to emphasize her next words. Her voice came with a hiss as she whispered, "Do not waste my son's sacrifice." Then she left, and I didn't see her again for a long, long time.

I stood there, just breathing, trying to take everything in. I looked down at Caspian who gazed intently at my face with a look of understanding that a puppy that small shouldn't have had already. He began to squirm again, so I put him down.

"What is it?" I asked, not really expecting an answer.

He stood importantly, looking a little bigger than the moment before, and said while I listened in surprise, "You have saved my life." His golden eyes were amazing as he continued, "I make an oath now, to hold unto the ends of the world, that I should stay by your side until I have done the same for you and more." He bowed, swishing his tail. I just stared in amazement at the little wolf who had so much wisdom and heart.

He looked up, smiling gently. Despite seeming really content, he shook from the cold.

I beckoned him to me with a playful smile on my face. He came and bounded into my arms with a happy yap. In a childlike voice I laughed and said, "And I'm sure we'll be the best of friends."

He kissed my face in reply.

I laughed again and then wrapped him warmly in the edge of my shirt.

And from that moment on, he never left me. Well, I mean, *entirely* left me. He went out by himself occasionally, but he always returned soon afterwards. He became one of my trusted council, the warrior always by my side, and most importantly, my puppy dog.

I felt the tug in my gut, letting me know which way the river was. I hefted Caspian closer to me and trudged back the way I'd come.

I swallowed when I reached the bank, the fire still burning bright on the other side. I started to head along the shore to the east, hoping to find the stone bridge. About to turn the next bend, I heard something come in the wind. My name, soft and faint, reached my ears.

I began to run along the bank. I could see moving torchlight through the trees on the left side of the river. I reached the bridge and turned sharply. A handful of guards spotted me. The rest of the night was sort of a blur.

FOR THE INTENDED

A whole bunch of relieved grins greeted me as we walked into camp. They immediately took me to the medic who dressed my burns and tended to my arm which ended up being just severely bruised. I told them I wanted Arnet, but they had to send someone to get him since he was out searching for me. Amazingly, no one noticed Caspian still wrapped in my lap.

Done being examined, I went and sat on a secluded rock, observing all the people resting their horses. I saw Tillen across the glen next to his pony who had found his way back. Tillen had a few bandages where he had minor burns, but when he saw me his entire face lit up and he called to me happily, waving enthusiastically. I waved exhaustedly back. He tugged his father's sleeve excitedly while he tried to get his parents' attention as he said something indistinguishable. But I don't think either of them heard him as they hugged him, trying not to cry in front of their child as they embraced the son they almost lost. Even though I had had one of the worst nights of my life, I smiled gently as I saw them. They were my idea of what a family should look like—the family I'd never had.

Arnet galloped into the glen as I observed the reunited family. He saw me instantly and began to make his way over. He didn't look like I thought he would. He trotted his horse up in an abrupt manner. I looked up, confused, into his infuriated face as he reined his tired horse around. He dismounted and immediately grabbed my upper arm and led me up the path farther to the north, already scolding me. Nobody seemed to notice us leave, or at least pretended not to.

He led me to where some of the horses were tied up, and when we were out of hearing range, that's when things really heated up. I didn't really hear everything he said, but "What were you thinking!" and "You could've been killed!" and a whole bunch of other stuff poured from his mouth in a continuous stream.

Tears were rolling down my face one after the other until finally I blurted out that I was sorry and that I wouldn't do it again. He took a step back, realizing how harsh he was being, but his face hardened again as he ordered me to mount. I looked over to see the horse he meant and saw that it wasn't Drayla.

"Where's Drayla?" I asked, eyes wide and wet, sickeningly worried.

He didn't soften his words, "Drayla has been gravely wounded due to your actions and must stay behind with the medic until she can move."

I didn't have the strength to tell him that it wasn't my fault she got hurt, but I wouldn't have even got the chance because Arnet mounted his horse and rode up a small hill so everyone could see him. "We ride through the night!" he barked loudly. "Mount now!" Then he turned his horse round roughly and urged him into a quick canter, passing me without turning his head.

I thought about disobeying and going off to find Drayla, but I knew I'd be in so much trouble if I did. I also knew she would want me to listen to my orders, like she constantly advised. So, still sniffling, I mounted one of the extra horses we'd brought. I put Caspian in an empty saddlebag and watched as he curled up comfortably and went back to sleep.

I told my horse to walk forward, and he did in a sluggish manner, his hooves clopping gloomily down the path. I waited for the others to join me, and they all didn't look much better than I did. Even their horses seemed worn out and sorrowful due to the night's unhappy events. My head stayed low as I rode along slowly, and the other people quickly passed me on their horses.

We continued for a few minutes before one of the guards asked, "Where's Arnet?"

Nervous murmurs went through the crowd.

Despite being totally depressed, I began to think about how strange it was that we hadn't seen him yet, and since I rode at the side of the pack I volunteered quietly to look for him; anything to get away from other people for a second. I pulled off the road and cantered around the next few bends silently in the soundless grass. I turned the last corner and halted my horse in the shadows of a large tree when I spotted Arnet. He sat on top of a hill in the path, the large moon behind him. I didn't make a sound as I watched him, wondering why he had stopped.

He was hunched over in the saddle, his hands to his face. I didn't think too much of it, until I saw his back shaking horribly. I gaped as I heard him sobbing into his hands. I had never seen him like that. We heard a neigh from one of the other traveler's horses. Arnet immediately took deep, shaky breaths as he tried to steady himself, wiping large tears from his face. I saw him straighten himself up in the saddle and take one last breath, then continue to the north without ever seeing me.

That was one of the only times I ever saw him as what he really was. Not my commanding officer, not my guardian by law, but the person on the inside who cared for me more than I knew: My father.

SPONTANEOUS COMBUSTION

About three weeks after I had tried to leave the castle, everything settled down again. No one mentioned my trying to leave, and in fact, I don't think everybody knew about it. I saw Arnet every day. He wasn't openly mad at me, but I knew he still was by the way he acted. He talked to me and all that, but it was only the stuff he had to say, like chores and orders and stuff.

So yeah, everything went back to being normal and boring. I did chores, patrolled, ate, and slept—day in and day out. The only good part of those days were the long rides I would take with Drayla, Caspian, and Elon. With all of us thundering over the open plains, I got to escape—if only for a few hours.

The important meetings were still being held, and I got severely annoyed at not being invited to any of them. Normally, I would be called to listen in, and sometimes even give input—you know, being the princess and The Summer Born and all. But nah, sometimes officials wouldn't risk upsetting me for various reasons. It was usually to hide information they didn't think I was ready for, or to keep me safe.

FOR THE INTENDED

I found Robert returning to his normal self, to my great relief. His behavior lightened, and he returned to his pranks. Many times, while heading down the stairs to the kitchen, I heard his obnoxious laughter fill the room as he told jokes. He always smiled his cheeky smile at me when I passed, his eyes gleaming, before going straight back to his audience.

There had been no monster attacks, which to be honest, I hadn't expected. Those varnants had come so close to our borders, and what if they came closer next time? But there didn't seem like there would be a next time. Everything stayed calm and quiet as we neared the time for the beginning of fall. But I decided to remain attentive just in case.

One day, I started down the hall that the throne room opened on, when the large doors burst open. "That *imbecile!*" Arnet grumbled loudly to himself as he stormed past. "He will be the fall of the kingdom!" He turned down a separate corridor, leaving me standing alone, wondering.

I peeked into the large throne room doors that Arnet had accidently left open, and saw a meeting being held. A very large round table had been set up, and many important people were gathered around it.

The queen sat at the table, facing my direction. She sat in a large, beautiful oak chair that resembled a throne as she listened patiently to everyone bicker.

A councilman who I didn't recognize stood angrily and said, "You see! Arnet is a fool!" Everyone quieted down from their own arguments with one another to listen to him. "'Send out patrols' he says. How absurd! There hasn't been an attack by the Dark Landers in a long time!"

Some people said loudly, "Yes, he's right!" While others whispered amongst themselves disapprovingly.

The man continued on, "Peace is in our midst, and troublemakers like that Arnet are always looking to stick their nose where it doesn't belong. If you send scouts into the lands beyond our borders," he pointed to the south, "you will bring evil back into our lives. Let it be *as it is*." He finished, and everyone turned expectantly to the queen.

She had been sitting quietly, looking as fair as ever with the late sun behind her, pondering. She spoke shortly after he had finished, standing with her hands in a triangle before her, "And what if Arnet is right?" her voice light and beautiful, "What if there are monsters, Lord Wen?" Her voice darkened as her intense eyes watched him, "Monsters, growing in numbers and size, multiplying in the dark where the light does not touch and where we cannot see." Her eyes stared him down until he sat uncomfortably. Everyone was silenced. Her voice lightened a little, but remained firm, "My dear friend, Arnet, is wise and very well informed of the things that happen in this land, good or evil." She smiled, "So, in the future, Lord Wen, I think it would be wise if we at least let him finish what he has to say."

Lord Wen swallowed, clearly embarrassed. A few people could be heard suppressing their laughter, and he huffed and puffed as he struggled to hold his tongue.

"Now," the queen said, a bit more cheerfully, "Why don't we—Galayne!"

She had seen me peeking in and I choked a little as I took off down the hall. She looked pretty upset, like I shouldn't have heard all that. I pounded down the very long hallway and swung around the corner into an empty corridor breathing deep as I heard the huge doors close behind me.

Nobody talked to me about it as the day went on, and I didn't see Arnet til dinnertime. We were eating in the gardens to honor our old tradition. Since we were little, we ate as many meals as we could out there every summer.

Lily, Robert, Tucker, and Dare were gathered around the bonfire on logs. Lily and Tucker sat together, a bowl of soup in each of their laps, cracking up to a story Robert was telling. Robert waved his hands around to demonstrate, and occasionally made stupid noises to accompany it. Dare ate quietly on her own log, smiling slightly when she found something amusing. Arnet sat on the opposite side of the fire, completely by himself, staring distantly into the fire.

I walked into the small ring of light and headed to the cauldron sitting on a large decorative boulder. I lifted the lid to find the vegetable soup only halfway gone. I scooped two ladles into my bowl and went and sat next to Dare, tuning into the story. I slumped next to her, falling into the gloom we both seemed to be in, when something Robert said made me choke on my soup with laughter. I don't even remember it, but it must've been pretty good because Lily and Tucker were having a hard time staying upright as they gasped for air, and even Dare tried to stifle her quiet laughter. Robert grinned as he looked around at us, very pleased by our reactions. We were all still going, when a guard ran frantically towards the fire, crying out, "Arnet! Sir!"

Arnet came out of his trance, searching the darkness for the voice.

The guard came gasping into the light, "Sir, we're under attack! Varnants have been spotted in the forests to the south!"

Arnet stood immediately, surprise on his face. We all gaped at the guard. The warmth of the fire and close friends left, and the night felt chilly as the wind blew through. "How many?" he asked, determined.

"Several dozen *at least*, sir." Arnet thought for a few seconds, before the guard asked in panic, "What are your orders, sir?"

"Get everyone inside the castle gates..." he picked up his sword, which rested against the log, then made firm eye contact with him, "Make sure no one leaves!"

"Yes, sir!" And the guard scrambled off.

"All of you, with me," Arnet commanded, and all of us leaped to our feet grabbing our swords. I also grabbed my bow and slung my quiver on my back, happy I'd just come from archery practice. Then we all followed him quickly from the gardens.

"So, what's the plan?" Robert asked as we threw tack on our horses.

"The *plan*, Robert," Arnet said as he put his saddle on his horse, "is to keep them as far away from the castle as possible. These are varnants, quick and agile. They are on the wiser side of the beastly creatures, so if we can push them back far enough, we may not even have to defeat them. If they see that they are beat, they will return to their foul nests." We all mounted quickly and rode to the front gate.

We halted our horses when we got there, and found the front gate abandoned by its guards. The street emptied, and not a single candle remained lit in the windows of the houses lining it. Other fighters were lining up behind us, several more groups coming down the road from the stables.

We were all rolling our shoulders, swinging our swords, or whatever we needed to do to feel ready for a battle when Arnet said, "We do not know the number we are going up against, so try to stay together as much as possible. And do not venture too far into the woods, or it is likely we will not find you again."

Good pep talk, Arnet, I thought sarcastically as we all peered out anxiously from underneath the tall arch. The night felt dark, cold, and windy. Storm clouds blocked out the stars, and the moon only seeped out occasionally. I could just hear the horrible screeches faintly on the wind.

It wasn't my first battle without him, but I always disliked when Blue wasn't around to help. In the past, we had almost always fought side by side. Over time, we developed unique maneuvers where each of us played a different part in taking down the enemy. But the more I thought about his absence, the more I realized those days were over . . .

We all took a few deep breaths before Arnet commanded, "Onward!" And we all jumped into a gallop, thundering down the road. When we reached the bottom of the hill, we turned off the road towards the woods.

FOR THE INTENDED

The forest started a few miles to the southwest and looked ominous as we got closer. A flash of lightning lit up the trees for miles and gave them a frightening appearance. As rain began to drizzle, it stung our faces and made us shiver as we went on.

Drayla snorted underneath me, her large hooves pounding powerfully into the ground. I hadn't needed to tell her what was going on. She somehow already knew or had guessed by the screeches, and I found her stamping her feet anxiously at the pasture gate.

As we were riding over the plains, I wished Caspian were with us. After two weeks of hardly ever leaving my side, he had been requested as a scout. About a week earlier, he said his farewells and disappeared to the south, promising he'd be back within the week. He should've been home by then, but he must've been delayed.

The shrieking was getting louder, and the old trees grew taller as we neared them. Once or twice, I thought I saw something large and black illuminate in the flash of lightning, flying above the trees. Then, with the ominous canopies above us, we plunged into the woods.

The forest grew thick, even at its outer edge. The trees were ancient and massive, and there were no saplings to be seen. So, even though everyone entered only a few feet from each other, our group was quickly separated. And soon, I could only hear Drayla's breathing and the sound of her steps thudding against the moist, mossy ground.

The quiet began to feel unnerving, and the trees seemed too close. The rain hadn't made it through the tops of the trees yet, and only one or two drops fell here and there. It felt disturbingly warm as we slowed down to a canter. I looked around and tried to hear the rustling of a varnant but heard nothing. No sound. Finally, after a few minutes, I thought I heard yells and thumping sounds, but they were so seriously muted I couldn't tell if I'd actually heard them or not. But then, I heard a small ruffle above me.

"Hold on a second," I told Drayla, who slowed down to a halt, her ears constantly searching for our next opponent. I reached back for an arrow, comforted by the soft, feather fletching on the end. I pulled it out gently and nocked it. I opened my hand and then closed it softly around the bow, readying myself. The moon shone suddenly and burst its way through the darkness in small beams. It made hundreds of leaves illuminate and reflect the light, giving the forest a bright green tint that made it feel spookier than before. My arrow head flashed as it reflected the moonlight, and that's probably what gave my position away.

I breathed in sharply as a creature squawked just above me, and I instantly aimed upwards and let my arrow fly. A huge, full grown varnant tumbled to the ground, an arrow sticking from its chest. I heard more varnants screaming not too far away, slowly getting closer. My bow strung again in an instant, I said, "Go."

Drayla lunged into a quick canter, turning here and there. My plan was to keep moving so they wouldn't be able to attack all at once. I could handle one or two, but all of them at once and I'd be a goner. I shot another varnant who hid in the bough of a tree, and then one that charged from the shadows.

We reached a small opening and I didn't even need to tell Drayla to stop, she did so herself. We were sheltered in shadows, listening to rustlings and faint stampings. Then I breathed in deep as I raised my bow calmly and aimed at a tall tree on the other side of the glen. My arrow flew with a quiet whistle and hit its hidden mark. A varnant toppled down from where I shot with a strangled cry.

Drayla immediately thrust herself into a canter again and asked playfully, glancing back at me for a brief moment, "How ever did you get so good?"

She turned back around, a proud smile crossing my face.

We were riding with no interruptions for a little too long. I raised my hand and said, "Wait." I thought I heard a screech, but it sounded far away and came with the wind.

FOR THE INTENDED

"Never mind, Drayla, I—" I gasped as a black form shot from a large bush to my right, knocking me from Drayla's back and my bow from my hand. I hit the ground hard and several arrows spilled from the quiver on my back. Drayla staggered from the blow with anger and surprise as I clawed for my bow which had fallen a little farther than I had. But I didn't have time to get it before the varnant charged me. I grabbed for anything to put between me and him as he plunged towards me, his sharp beak pointed at my chest. My fingers grasped something behind me that felt like, and I hoped was, one of my arrows. I thrust it upwards just in time. He died on top of me, his grimy black feathers engulfing me.

"*Galayne!*" Drayla called frantically, running to me.

I shoved off the disgusting creature and tried to bring down my adrenaline, steadying myself. Drayla breathed in relief when she saw me uninjured.

I began to get up and she asked, "Are you alright?"

"Yeah, I'm good . . ." I heard another screech, "but I think we should probably start heading back."

We cantered back north, I shooting every once in a while when I spotted something. After a few minutes though, there were less and less flying monsters, and more and more quiet, until eventually I began to think Drayla and I were the only ones in the forest. We went on for a while until Drayla slowed down to a steady walk. As I rocked back and forth in the saddle, I tried to listen for anything dangerous. Wind, trees rustling, maybe the faint sound of a small creek, but nothing else really. I began to think we'd won when I heard a very quiet cry for help.

"Lily!" I yelled. I drew my sword and we charged to her aid.

We were getting closer to where the fight really seemed to be, the sounds of swords and the cries of terrible animals surrounding us. We burst into a large glade, the rain thick, to find Robert and Lily fighting on opposite sides of it. Varnants were circling in the sky, trying to find an opening to strike either of them, or threatening to charge from the ground. Lily looked worn out as she slashed the air, trying to keep them away from her. Robert's face filled with fury as he sliced and bashed his victims, definitely doing well for being completely surrounded.

I went to join the fight when I heard Lily give a little scream. I turned to see her trip on a rock and try to scramble to her feet. The varnants around her had landed and were forcing her back into the forest, grinning wickedly. I knew I needed to help her, but I also couldn't leave Robert alone. Even though he had the upper hand, if he messed up even one stroke, he'd be bird food.

I quickly slid from Drayla's back and yelled over my shoulder as I ran to Robert, "Go help Lily!"

She didn't argue, and immediately galloped to the other side of the glen.

I jumped into the fight with a powerful slice, and then let my mind flood with years of training. I slashed, deflected, rolled, plunged, and overall kicked some monster butt.

After a while I realized we were back in the dark forest, the battle pushing us into it. We finally killed off our last attackers, and we lowered our swords, panting—relieved and worn out. Quiet returned except for the sound of a small brook a few feet from us.

"Well, that was fun," Robert smiled, wiping sweat from his brow.

I laughed nervously, "Yeah."

He smiled even bigger at my laugh and stood up to say something else when a straggler darted from the trees above him.

"Watch out!" I yelled.

He whirled around, swinging his sword just in time to deflect the huge animal from skewering him. I tried to help, when I gave a small gasp as another varnant charged me. They seemed older, and much more experienced. They knew the strokes we would make and knew how to make some pretty successful ones themselves.

FOR THE INTENDED

Robert and I were fighting in opposite directions, trying to force the varnants back. We were slowly getting farther and farther from each other, which I didn't like, but I didn't know what we were supposed to do about it. The fight lasted a little too long and my arms were getting tired, and my energy was wearing out. Finally, I saw my chance, and I thrust forward with one last exhausted blow, silencing the creature.

I bent over for a second, trying to catch my breath. I could hear Robert yelling in one glen over, and I was preparing myself to go help him when I noticed something. The tree in front of me glowed with a faint orange. I stared at it, confused, when I noticed the grass around me became cloaked in the light orange color as well, and my black shadow appeared very distinct in front of me. I whirled around in terror when I realized. I looked up in the sky to see fire dancing in the treetops—the trees that were where I'd heard Robert last.

"Robert!" I screamed in horror, having flashbacks of events that occurred in the same forest. As I scrambled in that direction, desperate to get him out of there, I could almost feel the fire on my skin again.

I darted into the glen and froze stiff, petrified as I stared at Robert. Robert had just made a triumphant sound as he brought his blade down on the vicious varnant, ending the battle. But fear still gripped me since Robert was clothed in *fire*.

"Robert!" I yelled in absolute panic, running towards him, "*You're on fire!*"

He turned around, surprised to hear me squeak like that, but then realized. He spurted, "No! No!" he held up his hand to signal me to stop, "Galayne . . . it's okay."

I gaped as I watched flames dancing all over him without doing any harm. Arnet and the others poured into the glen, coming to help fight, and all of them froze with wide eyes as well.

Robert moved his hand in an arc and all of the fire in the glen died instantly. With a stupid grin on his face he proudly announced, "It's my power."

NAETERA

We were all sitting back around the bonfire. We had defeated the varnants and met up at the castle gate a few hours after we'd left. The rain disappeared, but the dark shadowy clouds didn't. We all stared into the fire, a tired depression falling around us. It felt late and I really wanted to get to bed. I didn't want to be a part of the conversation that was about to happen. I hoped that with everyone so tired, we would put it off until the next day.

    The garden was empty besides us and only the sound of the fire filled the silence. I blinked the sleep out of my eyes, resting my chin in my hand. I tried listening to every crack and splitting of the wood, when all our attention turned to Arnet as he spoke.
"You have all seen what Robert can do," he said plainly.
Robert stared into the fire dejectedly, as even he seemed to be worn out, the happy smile of earlier gone. I think he finally understood from everyone's reactions, that his powers meant more than he thought. It wasn't all fun and games, and it needed to be treated seriously. As if to emphasize what Arnet said, he moved his hand sideways in front of the fire without seeming to care about how awesomely cool it was that it roared up several feet higher for a second. Everyone stared, still not able to comprehend what they were seeing.

FOR THE INTENDED

Arnet glanced at him. "Yes, thank you, Robert."

Robert gave a small smile.

"I have been expecting this for quite some time now, and was waiting for the perfect time to tell you all." He sighed, "I had hoped it wouldn't have come so soon . . . but I suppose now will have to do."

Everyone listened, eyes wide and fixed on him.

He took a deep breath and said, "Have you ever wondered why you have been put through more training, and more intense training at that, than the others?" By "others" he meant the other students in his class. "Why I require you to be the very best? Well, it's because you must be."

The gears in their heads were turning. I couldn't believe what he was getting ready to say.

"I am sorry I couldn't tell you this before, for fear you weren't ready for it." He looked around at all of us with a small, proud smile, "But now I think you are."

Everyone held their breath, leaning forward in anticipation.

"The truth is . . . you are all Naetera . . ."

I expected an up rise of angry or surprised cries, but none came. They all looked shocked out of their minds. No one said anything until Tucker spoke up quietly.

"You mean . . . we have powers . . ." he actually pointed at me, "like Galayne?"

"Yes. It was hard to tell at first. One of the most common ways to identify a Naetera is to look for black markings. Markings like Galayne has on her hand."

I shrunk a little. My mark had shown up in the past few years. As best we could tell, it was silver because I was bonded to Winlit Cordial. Otherwise, it would have grown in black like every other Naetera in history.

He continued, "Unfortunately, the markings don't show up in a Naetera until adolescence, so I couldn't depend on that method. I found out about you all when you were young, but I saw other signs that let me know you were of the Naetera. One of the signs was that you all were orphans that had been picked up in the woods. All of your guardians said you had no memory of where you came from before they found you, but they didn't know that meant you could be Naetera. As you have probably noticed, most information about Naetera has been kept from the public, so they thought the memory loss came from the poor condition they found you in. But just like Galayne, you are all from another world—*The Outside*. None of you have memories of the time before your arrival in Edgeladine, which is quite normal for Naetera."

I bit my lip.

Everybody went blank with shock.

Nobody said anything, but I saw Lily shift and I knew why. Lily was an orphan too, but she had been born in Edgeladine.

Arnet turned to her, "While all of this isn't true for you, Lily, you are still a Naetera. It is extremely rare for a Naetera to be born in Edgeladine, but it has happened once before in the past." He smiled gently, "So don't worry, I'm sure you are one."

She smiled back.

"Anyway, as I said, there were other signs that confirmed you all were Naetera. So, I consulted with a few select and very trustworthy scholars and brought you here for training. Of course, I couldn't tell your guardians, so they just believe you were selected to be part of the prestigious school here. As I said, your powers were not clear at first, and I wasn't able to discover any of your domains at the time. But now I know which one each of you belong to."

Everyone looked back at the fire, some with confusion and some with a mild case of terror.

"Robert," Arnet said, turning to him, "You are of the Filma, or more commonly called, Fall Born. Your powers are just now developing, and it is hard to tell what they will be exactly, but you may have fire abilities, wind capabilities, and of course the ability to change the trees' leaves to the color of your preference." He smiled amusedly at the end.

Robert thought it over as Arnet continued, "Dare."

Her eyes met his intensely.

"You are of the Dimdra, or Night Born. You may have storm capabilities, but I'm not sure. Each domain has many powers, but not all are present in every Naetera. But every Night Born can move silently and blend into their surroundings with ease. Shadows are your friend."

I didn't doubt that for a second.

"Lily, Tucker," they both looked at him with wide, childlike eyes, "You are both of the Lenac, the Spring Born." He smiled gently, "More common among the Naetera, but no less important. You may have healing powers, a knack for gardening, and amazing connections with creatures." They seemed to absorb it as best they could.

"And Galayne," I looked at him, "You have all known hers for a while. She is The Summer Born, the rarest of all." I tried, but I couldn't enjoy the awe that escaped him as he said, "She is a mixture of Aedena (Day) Born and Vitaela (Summer) Born. This means she has various strong connections with nature and can shoot pure white energy. Without her, Edgeladine would fail and fall into darkness, quite literally. She has been expected for centuries."

Wow, way to say it, Arnet, I thought. I hoped none of the others would think my powers were better than theirs or something, because they totally weren't. I didn't want them to be jealous. But I was reassured when I looked around and saw that they didn't seem to care about what Arnet said about me. They were just focused on themselves.

Silence took over for a few minutes while Arnet let us process it all, until he began less excitedly, "Now . . . to talk about the varnants." I felt a pang of guilt for not telling him about the attack I'd had in the woods all those weeks ago. "I don't have to tell you the danger is growing. You have seen it. The Dark Landers seem to be pushing back against our borders. Not only that, but there are whispers and rumors in the castle—our enemies are not as far away as we think they are. They are everywhere, even in the gates of Umplidore." The wind blew through then with a small howl. He paused, questioning if he should continue, but decided it would solidify his point. "Naetera are very rare. If more Naetera start showing up, it means something big is coming. Your powers, while they are amazing, shouldn't distract you from the message they bring. Something is not right in Edgeladine. We need to be careful now, more so than ever. Your training will intensify, and you must commit yourself to it, for you never know when it will save your life."

And so we did. We trained twice as hard and twice as much. We woke up earlier, and training didn't end til late at night. We learned new fighting techniques, survival skills, and even did more studying.

A month after the varnants in the wood, my powers really started developing, and so did everyone else's. I actually got a little scared, because they became somewhat hard to control. Sometimes when I got angry, which happened a lot, I would hurl something at my wall. But because of my uncontrollable powers, it would be clothed in white energy; Yeah, not good. At least it wasn't hot enough to melt the stonewall.

Also, my connection with nature or whatever you want to call it, became unbearable for a time. All of the sudden, in the middle of me doing something, I would get a splitting headache, and my stomach got sickeningly tight. It felt as if my body were accounting for everything around me all at once. I could feel the Narnstein and Lake Lunadine in my gut, both of which were miles away. I could feel every animal moving and sense the sun above me. I couldn't control it at all, but at least Arnet predicted each thing, giving me some small preparation. He said that, after a while, I should be able to control and summon the powers at will. The pain would go away he said, but it would take time. It was so great to be me.

Sometimes, I would get to see the others training. Robert could shoot these amazing fireballs; not like my balls of energy, but actual fire. His markings showed up fast—three downward triangles on his bicep. I spotted Lily and Tucker once standing in front of some wilted flowers. I couldn't hear what Arnet said to them, but he moved his hands to demonstrate. They both reached over the plants and did the same motion. Their faces lit up as the flowers sprung back to life and grew new buds, turning into full-grown plants with beautiful vibrant petals in seconds. Five black dots appeared on Tucker's right-hand fingers, one on each fingertip. A beautiful black vine grew on Lily's left ear. And Dare, well I witnessed Dare's skill firsthand. One second she was there, the next she wasn't. She could disappear right into shadows it seemed. Almost overnight, a thick black "v" appeared on her neck.

All of us participated in sword practice, archery practice, and other practices whether we wanted to or not. We still had our preferences though. I my bow, Robert his sword, Dare her daggers, and Lily and Tucker didn't really care for any of them in particular, so they stuck with their swords.

Drayla, Caspian, and Elon helped me get through everything, and we still continued our normal rides, no matter how late in the day we had to take them.

One night, after a long day of training, I started getting ready for bed. I had just told Milly goodnight and blew out the candles, when I heard a small whooshing sound come from the open window. I looked over skeptically. There hadn't been the slightest trace of wind that day, but cold air turned several pages of an open book on the windowsill.

I walked over slowly, trying to peer through it, when I suddenly got knocked over by a big hunk of soft, black feathers. *Varnant!* I scrambled for my sword, which I finally found still at my side. But before I could draw it . . .

"Ouch," the thing said, standing up, brushing himself off. "They should make the windows bigger."

I couldn't believe it, "Blue?" I asked, stunned, still lying on my back.

He looked at me with his light blue eyes, "Well, who'd ya think it was?" He smiled that great smile.

I charged him with a bear hug, managing to avoid his large wings, "I can't believe you're here!" I grinned. My heart thudded. I hadn't stopped thinking about him. There were days I thought about running away again, just to find him. Just to tell him.

He hugged me back, "Of course. I wasn't going to leave just because the head of all the guards in the castle told me to."

My smile grew, and then dropped immediately as I stopped hugging him, pushing him away, "You have to get out of here! If anyone finds you, they'll—"

"They'll what? In case you've forgotten," he crossed his arms and became slightly more serious than the moment before, "I can totally take care of myself. And besides they won't find me," he finished with a smile.

I pointed to the snowflakes falling from the ceiling, "Ahem."

He looked up. "Oh. Sorry," he moved his hand in an arc like I saw Robert do, and the snowflakes dropped to the ground instantly and melted. "I've gotten so used to it." I spotted new black markings on his hand—a small triangle at the base of each of his fingers, all of them right on the knuckle.

"Wait . . ." I said as I noticed the wind leaving, and the snow and icicles melting, "You can control it now?"

"Yeah. It took a while, but now it only does stuff when I want it to." I opened my mouth to say something, when he finished mildly annoyed, "Except the snow, I have to keep manually turning that off."

I gave a small laugh at his face and he smiled at me again. Besides it being a little chillier than normal, he controlled his powers well enough, and I knew he could stay hidden. I began to relax until we were chatting about everything just like we used to. I felt seven years old again, and we talked and laughed for hours.

I didn't ask him where he'd been; I didn't want to spoil the moment. He looked so happy and relaxed, telling stories and occasional jokes. He didn't mention it either, and I felt content to leave the subject alone. I trusted him and his decisions, and I figured it didn't matter where he'd been, as long as he was finally with me. There was one thing I wanted him to know though.

"Blue?" I hadn't meant to, but I had interrupted him.

He turned, a little concerned by my tone.

"The queen told me."

He looked down. He paused before saying, "Well. What's done is done." He forced his depression away with the snow that had started again, and he continued his story less energetically.

We talked until we saw the dim light of the rising sun and Blue said he had to go. He left, but not for long. The visit put in motion a continuous routine, and I saw him almost every night. Naetera training and Blue's visits continued on for about nine months, right through spring, until my world got even more shaken than I ever thought possible. It happened on the first day of summer . . .

Haven Berg

HAPPY BIRTHDAY

Milly burst enthusiastically into my room, way too early in the morning, "Happy Birthday, Galayne!"

"Wha?" I said, lifting my head slightly off the pillow, my eyes still blurred with sleepiness.

"What do you mean 'what?' It's your birthday, young missy!" She brought a tray over excitedly and set it in front of me as I sat up. My eyes widened when she did, and a smile spread across my face when I saw what was on it. "I made your favorite," she grinned as she straightened the fork next to my breakfast.

"Wow! Thanks, Milly!" I took the fork and plunged into cheesy eggs and ham; more ham and cheese than eggs of course. Then I took a huge gulp of iced sweet tea.

"That's right, my fifteen-year-old! You're going to have special treatment all day long!" She went over to the nightstand and prepared the wash station.

"But what about Arnet? I thought—"

"Unh, unh, ah. There will be no 'ifs,' 'buts,' or 'when's,' today," she said, setting a washcloth down.

I grinned and took an extra-large bite of ham.

She finished pouring water into the basin and said, "Now, you enjoy your breakfast in bed, and then take as long of a bath as you want, and come downstairs whenever you're ready. Okay?"

FOR THE INTENDED

"Thanks, Mill," I said, a huge, appreciative smile on my face as she walked to the door.

She nodded happily and closed the door behind her.

I sat there. *Wow. Today is going to be awesome.* I finished up my breakfast, enjoying the "no rush" feeling. Then I took a warm bath, again taking my sweet time. I put on my most comfortable set of clothes; my tan riding pants, white blouse, green vest, and of course my favorite black boots. I strolled down the stairs leisurely until a collection of servants reminded me just how unrelaxed my day was going to be.

"Good morning, Your Highness!" Some of them looked disgusted with my outfit, but didn't dare say anything. "Many happy returns of the day!"

"Yes, thank you," I managed, trying to back down the hall.

They continued on their way, but as I continued on mine, dozens more greeted me.

I heard "happy birthdays" and "many happy returns" every few seconds as people appeared out of nowhere. There were people everywhere doing a lot of different stuff. Some were setting up tables, hanging tapestries, putting vases of flowers in every crevice they could find. White and light blue decorations were everywhere. The smell of glorious food poured from the kitchen as I walked past its large doors.

Finally, after the fiftieth person congratulated me on another year of living, I thanked them and then ran off to find my friends that were hopefully somewhere among all these people. I bounded down the stairs into the small room where I and my friends normally ate, and immediately bumped into Lily.

"Hey, birthday girl!" She hugged me tight with that sweet smile on her face. "Where you been?" Robert, Tucker and Dare took notice of me as well.

"Hey, what up?" Robert called enthusiastically, "Congratulations for making it another year with your crazy, idiotic, annoying friends," he grinned, toasting his bacon to me before taking a huge bite out of it.

"Galayne!" Tucker called happily, his mouth full of banana, "Happy Birthday!"

"Congrats," Dare managed, a small but sincere smile on her face as she leaned against the counter.

"Thanks, guys," I smiled, glad to have them in my life. I looked around, "Where's Arnet? It's the big day and all, so I might have a thousand chores."

"What?" Robert said in a whiny tone, "Ditching us for the old guy? Come on!" I smiled as Arnet came in from behind him right in the middle of Robert's speech. "You would rather hang out with that old, grouchy, stingy, smelly—"

Everyone tried to suppress laughter.

"What?" Robert asked, unaware.

Arnet coughed, and everyone burst into laughter as Robert turned to look into his face. "You were saying, Robert?" he said, crossing his arms.

"Oh hi, Arnet!" Robert exclaimed happily. "We were just talking about my grandmother." He put his hand on his heart, his voice becoming tinny as he took a distinguished accent. "*Lovely* old soul. Though sometimes she can be a bit grouchy without her coffee, and can smell like a dusty bag filled with old prunes left at the bottom of the ocean then dried in the sun then . . ." Everyone snickered, trying their hardest not to laugh as Robert continued, ". . . then left in a musty cave for two years then soaked in lemon juice, and then thrown into horse manure—"

"Are you quite finished, Robert?" Arnet asked impatiently.

Robert took a deep breath and then a long pause. Arnet tried to say something before Robert finished quickly, "And then mixed with moldy cheese and eaten and regurgitated by a Molda."

Tucker snorted out orange juice and everyone finally let go, laughter filling the room.

Even Arnet couldn't help but crack a smile. Robert took a sip from his mug as if he hadn't said anything unusual, but he couldn't hold up his act as a smile broke through on his face.

FOR THE INTENDED

We laughed until Arnet said, "Now that *that's* over," he looked at Robert who munched contentedly on a sausage, before finishing, "It's time for business. Galayne, if you please?" Arnet gestured for me to step outside with him.

"Awh," everyone groaned.

"Don't you worry," Arnet said as I walked over to him, "You'll see her tonight." Then he grinned and closed the door behind us. We began walking across the grassy courtyard, the hot sun radiating above us. I took my place next to him, shocked as he slipped his arm through mine. We walked on, arm in arm. I stared straight ahead, not sure what to expect.

"Now," Arnet said, putting his hand on mine, "How is my birthday girl?"

"I'm good." It came out blunt, just like most of my replies had been of late.

He continued talking, trying to make conversation. "Fifteen years old," he said in disbelief. "Wow, did the time fly!"

I remained silent. At first I thought he was going to lay some chores on me, or tell me about any rituals I needed to perform as a fifteen-year-old princess, so I can tell you, I was shocked. The birds sang, the wind blew nice whirls of cool air by my face, and the flowers were beautiful as they colorized the landscape.

I got pulled back into the conversation when I heard Arnet laugh a little, saying. "Why, I remember when you were only seven years old in the forest. Blonde hair tangled in a heap on your head!" He laughed again.

I smiled, enjoying the pleasure of the memory on his face.

We walked on a few more steps when his face darkened, and his voice lowered as he said, "I'm sorry I haven't been there for you, Galayne." He stared straight ahead, "I know we've both been so busy of late . . . and we don't have time like we used to . . ." He silenced for a while as we walked on, and the subject seemed to have been dropped. Despite the birds and the children laughing and playing in the sun, I could hear his deep breathing next to me.

I blinked. Part of me wanted to tell him it was okay, that it wasn't his fault, but I didn't know how to word it.

Then after a few minutes of walking through the courtyard in the sunshine, he stopped under the shade of a large apple tree to look me in the face. He grabbed both my hands, still to my surprise, and said, "I know you're not a child anymore, Galayne . . . but I want you to know I will always have your back. I will always be there to catch you. And you will always be my little princess." Just then, from underneath his vest, he pulled out a rinlin.

I took a step back.

He handed the white flower with the blue pistils to me, and I felt like it was my ninth birthday all over again. I took it in shock and didn't have time to react before he leaned over and kissed the top of my head. "Happy Birthday," he whispered into my hair. Then he turned without a word and walked away to attend to his duties.

I could only stare after him.

He called over his shoulder with a smile, "I'll see you tonight." Then he disappeared from my sight and left me standing alone under the tree.

Too confused and moved to think, I sat down under the tree, the cool breezes tossing my hair occasionally. It was so weird to see Arnet like that. He hadn't treated me that way, since, well, I was nine.

The memory from my tenth year starts in the early morning. I woke up before dawn, snuck downstairs, and sat alone in the kitchen. I swung my legs and could hardly hold still with excitement. I mean, after all, turning ten is supposed to be like entering a new world, right? Double digits and all.

I thought that Arnet would surprise me like he had done for my birthday the year before. He had made me my favorite breakfast, and let me eat cake with it. Then he had secretly stored backpacks full of ham sandwiches and sweet tea in the cabinets, not to mention a new seashell necklace. He told me we were going to have all sorts of adventures that day. But that had been my ninth birthday.

I had to resist every urge not to peek in the cabinets to see what surprises he had for me. I patted the table, rolled an apple back and forth, and sang quietly to myself, trying to pass the time faster.

Finally, I heard Arnet's footsteps pounding down the stone steps, and I knocked my feet together in anticipation. My smile broke as soon as he turned the corner into the kitchen.

"What are you doing?" He asked angrily. "You're supposed to be by the docks by now!"

I looked at him, very surprised. After a second, I tried not to smile at his teasing.

He stared at me incredulously because I didn't immediately run to the docks. "Go on! You're skipping breakfast, we have to hurry!" He grabbed my shoulder and started to push me towards the door, saying harshly, "You aren't a little kid, Galayne. We're not playing games anymore. You're ten years old now, and I expect you to act like it!"

And that was it. I never ever had a true birthday after that. Like I mean sure the whole kingdom celebrated it every year, but not Arnet. Not really. Most of the time he was just concerned about whether or not I looked presentable and made sure I seemed worthy of my title to all the officials.

Why should my fifteenth birthday be any different? Nothing out of the usual had happened of late. In fact, I thought the situation had gotten worse. Arnet only ever spoke to me when he had to, and when he did, he always seemed aggravated and impatient.

I fingered the white petals and smiled. I didn't care. I got my Arnet back, even if for only a moment. I carefully stored it in my pocket, making sure not to break it, then headed to the castle for my birthday preparations with a much more positive outlook on the day.

Yeah, despite it being my birthday, the first day of summer really stunk. The whole castle spent the day preparing for the

Summer Ball, or my birthday party. Actually, it functioned as both. For hundreds of years the Summer Ball happened on the first day of summer. Then, when I showed up as a seven-year-old, it celebrated my coming into the world, *their world.* Not mine.

What I am about to tell you, I couldn't have told anyone else, at least not back then. I knew since seven years old that I wasn't from Edgeladine, no matter what my caretakers told me. When I got older, Arnet finally agreed with me and told me I was right—I was from a place called *The Outside*—but I couldn't tell anyone. The public wasn't to know about it, and I could only speak about it in front of the few officials who already knew of its existence. I didn't know why, but I complied. But I knew Edgeladine wasn't my home. I also knew my birthday wasn't on the first day of summer . . . Actually, ironically, I was born on December 25th.

I remember Christmas in *The Outside*—sitting next to a large pine tree in my living room, on my *real* dad's lap. The memory felt like looking through fog. I'd pulled my hair out and screamed in rage many times trying to remember, but I could only muster a few words and two blurred faces.

As I told you, I sat on my dad's lap. I knew it was him not only because of what he said, but I just felt it. His charming, brown-blue eyes broke through the haze as he said lovingly, "You know something?"

"Yes, Daddy?" I replied. I could tell that I was just five years old.

He pointed to the angel at the top of the tree and said, "Do you know what that reminds me of?"

I looked up, studied it a moment, then turned to him, "No, Daddy."

His warm smile came into focus. "It reminds me of you."

I beamed.

"Five years ago, on this very day, something very special came to Mommy and Daddy."

FOR THE INTENDED

I gave a high-pitched giggle when he said "special," because he poked me playfully in the stomach at the same time. Then I asked, "What? What was it, Daddy?" even though I had heard the answer a million times.

He swung me into a cradle-like position with me giggling, and waited till I stopped to say, "It was you. Our little angel." He smiled again.

I smiled back at him. We didn't say anything for a moment, before he widened his eyes and got a crazy look on his face. I tried to get away, "Wait no! Daddy! Wait—" but burst into laughter as he tickled me and made munching noises, pretending to eat me.

We were still going when a blurry object appeared in a doorway beyond us. We heard an irritated cough, and the fun stopped immediately. A tall, elegant woman stood there in a sleek black dress, sporting a sparkly handbag. "Come on, dear!" She said with a lovely voice that made my face feel hot. "We're going to be late if we don't get going."

"Alright, dear," he replied, lowering me to the floor.

"No, Daddy! Don't go!" I whined, desperately trying to stop him.

"No, no, baby. Come on. We talked about this, remember?" He pulled my arms from around his legs. "We'll be home in no time. Okay, baby? And we'll have all sorts of fun tomorrow. Right?" He backed up to the door.

I gave up my efforts to stop him, slumping on the floor, staring at them. My dad looked back at me with hesitancy and asked the lady next to him, "Are you sure she'll be alright?"

"*Come on*, darling," the woman had a flirtatious giggle in her voice as she pulled on his arm, leading him in the direction of the door. "The babysitter just called—she'll be here in five minutes. We've got to get going or we'll miss our reservation. She'll be fine." By that time, the memory revealed that she was my mother.

He looked at her and decided she was right. He began walking down the hall with her towards the front door.

"Oh wait!" The lady exclaimed, "I forgot my earrings! You go ahead and warm up the car, I'll be right there," she said with that beautiful voice.

My dad continued out the door as my mom rushed back into the living room. She hardly noticed me glaring at her as she strutted on past to the mantel. She gave a happy exclamation when she spotted her jewelry. She put them on quickly and began to walk back to the door. About to step out of the living room, she paused and turned to face me.

It was Aurora, the queen. Or . . . at least . . . it looked almost exactly like her; strawberry blonde curls, pale, yet intense green eyes, and that aura of gracefulness. "Make sure you're in bed by nine, alright, honey?" She seemed sincere enough when she lovingly addressed me, but I still hated her. Well, I guess I didn't hate her. I was just mad that they were going out on my birthday. It wasn't the only time I had been neglected, and she was always the one to talk my dad into leaving me behind. At least . . . I thought so. I didn't have any memories to back up that accusation—just a feeling that came from the five-year-old in my mind.

Then she walked off through the door into the snow, closing the door behind her, leaving me all alone in the empty house. And that's it. That's the end of my memory. I had nothing to tell me where I lived, what my actual name was, or how I even got to Edgeladine. Nothing, nothing at all.

So, I know what you're thinking: "Wow! You've had a lot of horrible birthdays, haven't you?" And the answer is yes, yes, I have. And I am about to add another one to the list.

FOR THE INTENDED

BLUE

The day passed smoothly, actually, despite the usual birthday chaos. I had fewer chores but had to meet with various officials throughout the day. And of course, before I could even be seen in front of them, I had to get ready. And not just look nice, but look *really* nice—all day long. It meant I had to do dress fitting... twice! One gown to wear all day to chat, mingle, and have meetings with the officials, and one for the actual ball that evening.

At least the first dress fitting didn't take too long, and I actually ended up liking the finished product. It was light blue and silver of course, showing off the castle's colors, but wasn't as flashy or extravagant as I knew my evening dress would be. The tailors chose a thin fabric, so I wouldn't have to worry about sweating buckets in the hot summer sun. It didn't feel too heavy, and I could move fairly well in it. And, the best part? The shoes that came with it felt so comfortable. Let's just say, I was happy enough.

Milly got to be the one to bring my crown in. The tailors were packing up their stuff as she placed it carefully on my perfectly-styled hair (a small bun at the top with some long curls tumbling down from underneath it—one of the better hairstyles, trust me). She smiled when she finished and held out her hand, a piece of my favorite blue candy in it.

"Awh . . . thanks, Mill," I said appreciatively, popping it in my mouth.

When the first dress fitting ended around noon, I met up with Arnet and we headed off to the docks where we were to meet our first important guests. The Duke and Duchess of Cumberia weren't as bad as they could've been. They were polite and didn't seem so high and mighty like the rest usually were. After we said our hellos and told them where they'd be staying, we had a friendly chat about their home Cumberia and how their trip was. They said the trip was very long, but the ocean was friendly. Then they finished the conversation by saying they were very tired but extremely happy to be in Umplidore for the crowning of the princess. They smiled and bowed to us, and we did the same before they walked off to find their chamber.

Oh, and don't get too excited about the "crowning of the princess" thing—it didn't really have any special meaning. In fact, I had a coronation every year. It was a lot like New Year's Day—new beginnings, a fresh start. It was like a symbol of continuous reign, and it was also to show respect to me or something. It sounds weird, but everyone took it very seriously. Trust me, if you knew the history of Edgeladine, you'd know why. Anyway, a couple of officials down, a few dozen more to go.

We talked to so many people for hours. I liked to examine all of their different mannerisms and I especially loved talking to the pompous ones. They would wave their hands around in great exaggeration, widening their eyes to tell the awful trip they'd had and the incompetence of Umplidore's guards. They'd puff their chests out, chins to the sky as Arnet tried to apologize for any inconvenience they may have had, but both of us were stifling our laughter. Then, Arnet and I would bid them a good day and tell them we'd see them that evening, and turn and walk away without another word. Normally they'd turn to their spouse and say something like, "And to think we came all this way to be treated thusly. Why I never in my life . . ." then their voices would fade into the distance as Arnet and I left, amused grins on our faces.

And so the day passed. About a half hour before dress fitting session number two, Arnet left me alone in the ballroom to wait for the tailors. A servant would come into the room every so often to lay down some plates for the feast on the large marble tables covered in light blue cloth, add a few flowers here and there, or light a candle that had been forgotten (which wouldn't be hard to forget because of the hundreds that filled the room). *They really outdid themselves this year*, I thought as I took in the splendor. The ballroom looked completely different from the last ball, except the colors of course, and the room shined brilliantly under the silver chandeliers that had been commissioned just for that evening's display.

I was still basking in the glow of the candles when I jumped to the sound of a voice.

"Your Majesty?"

"Jack! Oh," I laughed, "You startled me." I suddenly realized the ballroom was empty and I didn't need to act like an airy princess—we could drop formalities.

He didn't notice our solitude—he stood there, stiff and serious as ever. "It's been awhile, Your Majesty." It was true, I hadn't seen him since my captivity.

"Come on, Jack, no one's here. You can call me Galayne."

He blinked, "Your Majesty, may I speak freely?"

I sighed, a smile growing on my face, "Please do, *Mister Lerran*."

He didn't catch the playful jab. "I would like to apologize."

I was surprised. "For what?"

He swallowed, looking for the best way to approach the subject. "Awhile back . . . during your confinement to your room . . . I noticed it did not seem to be . . . of your own will." He turned pale. It was way out of line. He was basically, in a roundabout way, questioning Arnet's orders. He spoke up quickly, "I do not regret the extra protection it provided you! I just . . . I feel it is only fair to let you know, I was your guard for a good portion of the time."

So, that's why I hadn't seen him since then—he was probably avoiding me. I smiled. The kid was so honorable—he couldn't hide anything from his princess. "I might've guessed. They would've been fools to use their best guard for anything else . . . At least now I know why I haven't seen you in awhile."

His face actually flushed from the compliment, but his eyes widened, "Yes, Your Majesty, I must admit I was hesitant to confront you. But I never strayed from my duties. You remained in my protection all along."

I nodded, "I know, Jack. Thank you."

He bowed, "Thank *you*, Your Majesty, for understanding." He didn't make eye contact again as he quickly marched from the room.

I sighed. He seemed to get more formal with age.

I walked out onto the balcony and leaned against the rail, gazing at the moonlit sea and the caravels coming into the port. I undid my bun, and let the tightly pulled hair flow free. I could hear the buzz of talking and laughter and could see torches moving below by the docks and on the road as people made their way to the castle to attend the ball. The noise and the sight of thousands of people coming to my birthday party made my stomach churn a little. I wasn't really nervous or anything. I mean, I'd been through the process so many times, how nervous could I be? But I definitely wasn't myself as I looked down on them.

I sighed as the chilly wind tossed my hair—a nice change from the hot gusts of earlier. I couldn't believe it had been almost a year since I'd found out about Blue. *Blue*, I thought, with another unhappy sigh. I hadn't seen him at all that day and I really needed his calming presence right about then.

I pulled the rinlin from a hidden pocket in my dress. (I'd tapped on one of the tailors shoulders earlier and asked her if she could make me a pocket just for the purpose of keeping my flower there. She said it wouldn't be that hard for her.) I twirled it around slowly in my hands, disappointed to see it already beginning to wilt. I pinched the stem between my fingers and began to concentrate on it really hard. Starting only about a week before, I'd discovered a new power of mine. Arnet told me I was made of energy or something like that, right? Well, I found out that I could transfer my energy to other living things. I realized I could do it when I grabbed a flower pot from the courtyard and helped move it to the royal gardens. Before I knew it, the pot shook like crazy and the flower began to shine with white light. Then it exploded, splattering all over my face. Needless to say, I went to help out somewhere else.

Anyway, I looked at my rinlin, focusing as hard as I could on it. I didn't know what I needed to do to get my powers to work, but whatever I kept doing must've been right because the things I tried my powers on either exploded or were teeming with energy by the time I was done. I smiled triumphantly as a wispy cloud of white energy curled up the stem from my fingertips, the flower perking up until it looked as if it'd just been picked. *Okay, that'll do*, I thought to myself, but the white wisp only thickened. *Alright, that's enough*, I told my powers hurriedly. I thought rare flower shards might decorate my face again, when suddenly the extra energy got sucked back into my fingertips. "Thank you," I said to them.

I observed the flower a little longer, trying to forget the night ahead, before carefully returning it to my pocket. I straightened up and took an extra deep breath, looking at the moon. I had to be ready. The ball was coming whether I wanted it to or not.

After standing there for a while, I looked to the west and saw the wall and a few trees of the castle's gardens. I could see a few people in the torchlight sprinkled here and there. They were laughing and talking, waiting for the ball to start, and I realized my friends could be there as well. I mean, that's where they normally hung out, and maybe they were having ball jitters as well.

After deciding I had a little bit more time, I went to find my friends. I peeked around the ballroom to make sure no one noticed me leaving, and then quickly made my way down a few long staircases and halls to get to the gardens.

The gardens were huge, and I only bumped into a few groups of people as I made my way down the path that wound all the way around the large garden. They bowed to me as I walked by, and I to them, but they didn't try to make conversation—to my appreciation.

Whoever lit up the gardens that year did a pretty bad job—only one lantern hung in every ten trees or so. But I didn't mind. I hoped it would shelter me from some unwanted eyes. As I walked along, the moon came out every once in a while and lit up all the flowers, making them glow. I stopped to enjoy it for a moment but moved on since the night was colder down in the gardens.

After a few minutes without spotting anyone I knew, I thought I might as well head back to the castle; I didn't want to be late and make everyone go into a frenzied panic. I had just turned around and taken a few steps, when I heard the unmistakable angry tone of Robert coming from a side trail.

"Robert?" I called into the tunnel-like path.

Nothing for a moment, but then his voice came through again.

I picked up the edge of my skirt and quickly made my way down the dark path, "Robert?"

No answer. I took a step closer to hear better, and then I thought I heard Dare's exasperated voice.

"Dare? Come on, guys. I—" I turned the corner into a small opening and froze in the shadows before jumping behind the nearest tree. I peeked from behind it. Robert yelled in Dare's face about how she did this or didn't do that, and Dare looked murderous as she shouted things right back at him. I could see why they didn't notice me.

FOR THE INTENDED

"You're always going off by yourself! And when I suggest we do something together, you don't even listen to me!" Robert shouted.

Dare yelled right back, "That's because I'm *busy*, Robert! And *me*? You think *I* don't listen!"

They both burst right into a rant about the other's faults, with me watching in horror. I had no idea that was what went on while I didn't see them. I mean, I knew they had started dating in secret a few months earlier, but I had thought they broke up a long time ago. At least I knew why Dare and Robert had seemed so tense the days before.

Robert finished his rant with a particularly loud yell. It made me more anxious than when I thought about the ball, because trust me, it wasn't your normal couple's fight. These were practically trained assassins, and I knew if the fight went too far, only one of them would come out of it. They were both dressed for the ball, but I didn't know if both of them would live long enough to attend.

Robert seethed as he listened in infuriated silence to Dare's ongoing monologue. But Robert's face changed a little, going from rage to something of sad shock, like he just realized he'd blown up in her face and hadn't meant to. Dare continued her vent when Robert did the unthinkable. I gasped in horrified disgust as Robert quickly grabbed Dare and kissed her.

Dare just stood there in shock, her mouth hanging open. Then her face came over with a look of incredible rage. Robert just cringed in anticipation of his punishment but seemed to think he deserved it.

I quickly stepped out from behind the tree to stop a murder from happening, before dashing back to my hiding spot. Dare had rushed forward in what looked like a death strike, but I couldn't believe my eyes. She kissed him back. Then all anger seemed to leave as if that action settled their argument. But I was not settled. I left quietly, resisting the urge to run.

As soon as I felt far enough away from them, I took a side path and went to sit on a marble bench in a different opening. I finally started to have some normal, complete thoughts, when I heard someone coming my way. I jumped up and hid behind another tree and watched as the two newcomers came.

They were talking softly as they walked a few inches apart from each other. They both laughed awkwardly when their hand accidentally brushed the other's. They went and sat down on the bench before looking up at the sky.

Lily brushed her skirt down as Tucker said, "Hey, Lily?"

She looked up with her gorgeous blue eyes, "Yes, Tucker?"

He didn't say anything as he offered something in his hand to her.

Lily gasped in admiration but didn't take it, "Oh, Tucker, it's so beautiful! I couldn't possibly—"

"I want you to have it," he said with an affirming smile, and then took a finely crafted hair pin and put it above her right ear. "After all, I made it for you," he finished with a warm smile.

Lily blushed while she watched him place it in her hair.

When he finished he said, "There," and with a happy smile, "Perfect."

Then Lily burst forth with a smile and gave him a hug, "Thank you, Tucker!"

He hugged her back. Then after a while, Tucker coughed awkwardly and said, "We should probably get to the ball." He stood, "It should be starting soon."

He started to walk away and made the same surprised face as me when Lily grabbed his hand with a smile and said nonchalantly, "Yes, I suppose we should be getting back."

Tucker's face turned bright pink, but he seemed happier than ever as they strode hand in hand towards the castle while I stared in disbelief. As soon as they were out of hearing range, I took off to get as far away as possible.

I ran toward a corner of the garden that I knew would be empty since most of the plants there had been dead for a while. Finally, I made it to the abandoned section of the garden and I slowed down to a walk. I went over everything that had happened in the last five minutes. *Robert and Dare? A successful couple?! And then Tucker and Lily?! Okay granted, but I mean really?!* I had never expected them to get anywhere, being so shy and awkward, but I guess their mutual adorableness made up for that. For them, hugging and holding hands was just as bad as kissing was for Robert and Dare. I couldn't believe it. My friends were losing their minds.

After a few more minutes of thinking it over, I stopped and looked around. The garden was definitely in need of some care. There were no working fountains, the vines climbing the walls were black and flowerless, and the trees looked dry with most of their branches completely dead.

The moon crept higher in the sky, and with a sigh I realized I should be getting back. I had taken a few steps down the path when I heard someone behind me, "Hey, Green."

While whirling around, I grabbed the nearest weapon, which happened to be an old tree branch that snapped off with ease, and thrust it towards my opponent's neck.

"Um. Wow. You've gotten faster," Blue observed as he glanced down at the spear-like tip centimeters away from his throat.

"What are you doing here?!" I hissed.

He grinned playfully, "Well, I had to give my best friend her birthday present."

I blinked in disbelief, but I couldn't stop a smile. "You know what they'll do to you if you get caught?" I said, tossing the branch aside and beginning to walk towards the castle as if I was too busy to chat.

"Galayne, we've been over this," he said, stepping in front of me and walking backwards, trying to keep up with my pace, "I won't get caught."

"Mmhhm," I said with a smile and a raise of my eyebrow.

"Yep. Wouldn't even see me if I walked right in front of them."

I gave a small, sarcastic laugh, "Oh, really? How so?"

"Yep. I've been practicing."

I stopped walking, "Practicing what?"

He gave a smile, as if he enjoyed knowing something I didn't, and turned around and kept walking. "You'll see." Then he turned back around, "Now do you want to see your birthday present, or not?"

I walked up to him and sighed, "Go ahead. Show me." I finished quickly, "But it better not be like last time."

He laughed, "No. Not this time. This time it's much better. But you've got to close your eyes."

"Wait what? What's going on?" I eyed him.

He laughed again, "No, I promise you'll love it, but it takes a second to make."

"Wait, you make it? What is—" but he grabbed my hands and put them over my eyes, and I was thankful he had learned to control his powers; his hands were only the normal kind of cold.

I heard a faint crackling sound and began to wonder, "Blue? What in the world are you doing? What can you possibly make in—"

"Okay, done!" He exclaimed.

I pulled my hands from my face, not expecting to see anything particularly cool, but I was amazed.

"Ta-da!" He held out his hand proudly, and in it, a flower grew from his palm. But not your ordinary flower shop flower . . . it was made entirely of frost.

"Blue." I stared at it. "How did you—"

"Do you like it? It took me awhile to figure out, but now I can do almost anything. And I am proud to say, you have gotten the first flower I've ever made," he grinned.

It wasn't completely formed yet, and I watched as it bloomed in his palm. He twiddled his fingers and the growing slowly ceased, an icy flower floating in his hand.

I didn't know what to say.

"Come on. Take it. I made it for you," he winked.

I reached out slowly, still totally amazed. But I barely got to pinch the stem between my fingers, before I gasped as the whole thing exploded into tiny droplets of water, splattering the sidewalk with small, dark puddles.

Blue laughed, but I was disappointed. "Yeah, I guess I didn't think about that," he said looking down at the remains of the flower. "Well, anyway . . . Ta-da!" He gestured to the soaked pavement, "Happy Birthday, Galayne!"

I laughed, "Thank you. It was pretty cool."

He smiled proudly.

I waited a moment before saying, "Now what was it you've been practicing?"

"Oh yeah! Watch this!" He slowly backed up into the shadows of the trees, and then I could've sworn he vanished right into the air—right in front of my eyes.

"Uhh . . . Blue?"

"Yes, Galayne?" His voice came from where he had been standing before.

"Where did you go?" I asked, peering into the shadows.

"I'm still here, but I blend in with the shadows. It's another one of my gifts. I'm not completely hidden though. Trust me, that's been tested."

I smiled, guessing a funny story hid behind that comment.

"But I can also move without a sound. It's pretty weird. Like if I try as hard as I can to make noise, I can't snap twigs, I can't make things rustle, and I can't even breathe loud. It's really awesome though, because I can just jump tree to tree and stuff, and no one would even know I was there."

"Wow, that's seriously cool."

Just then the sound of bells came from the castle.

My smile left. "I still have to do dress fitting!" I picked up the edge of my skirt and started running down the path.

"Hey! Chill!" Blue called after me, trying to catch up, "It's going to be fine!" Then I heard him mumble to himself, "Just like it always is."

"Actually, *Blue*," I said, taking a second to look behind my shoulder while continuing down the path, "It's not always 'fine'. You remember my eleventh birthday?"

I heard him laugh behind me, "Oh, yeah, that was a good one."

I grumbled.

"Oh, come on, Galayne, it's going to be great. Have fun with it. After all, a person's birthday is supposed to one of the best days of their year."

We were slowly getting closer to the castle.

"Yeah, well not for me." Then I had a thought. "Ugh! I forgot about the speech!" I had spent all day trying to forget it, but at that point I should've been rehearsing it. Added nervousness made me run faster.

There was silence for a second before Blue said, "Galayne, hold up a sec. I have to tell you something."

I don't know why, but I slowed down to a stop. I asked a little too impatiently, "What, Blue?" I turned, confused to find an empty path. I gave an aggravated growl before whirling back around. I gave a small gasp as I immediately came face to face with Blue, who of course hung upside down from the tree above me.

With an amused smile on his face he said, "Despite being the most stubborn and cranky person I've ever met . . ."

I crossed my arms and looked away in an irritated manner, but my face lightened up with each word as he finished his statement.

". . . you are also the funniest, smartest, and most courageous person I have ever met, and if anyone can brave her fifteenth birthday . . ." He grabbed my chin forcing me to look into his eyes which were suddenly filled with sincerity, "it's you."

I breathed a small laugh. Then with an appreciative smile I said, "Thanks, Blue."

He smiled back. He waited a second before saying with a goofy voice that sounded like a bad impersonation of one of my least favorite mentors, "*Now hurry up, Your Highness. Don't want to be late for the ball!*"

"Ugh!" I exclaimed in fake annoyance, but a large smile spread across my face. I pushed his upside-down-self out of my way before quickly running off towards the castle.

"Hey!" I heard his laughter-filled voice exclaim as he tried to regain his balance.

But I continued running with a smile on my face, feeling at least somewhat better about the ball.

When I got back, it didn't seem as if I'd been missed. After a few minutes of waiting back on the balcony, Milly came and got me, leading me off to the dressing room. I stood up on the podium in front of the three sided mirror and held out my arms for the tailors without a word. I noticed there were more of them than usual, and I saw a few new faces. They excitedly gathered around me, and were chatting and laughing, and having so much fun as they worked on my new gown. They seemed extremely honored to be doing my birthday dress, and I felt happy for them, but I couldn't join in their joy and humor as I stared into the mirror unhappily. I wished I could be anywhere else but there. Anywhere.

I began to not feel so good. Extra not so good. I knew why too. The speech I always had to give filled me with anxiety every time. But I also knew I'd be alright. I would get kind of nervous, feel like hurling, then as soon as I climbed up the stairs to stand in front of the throne, the butterflies in my stomach would fly away and I would be fine. I just had to get up in front of the people to realize it.

I took a deep breath and woke up from my trance to see an almost finished dress reflecting in the mirror. *Wow, they're fast!* But then I saw the moon and realized my thoughts had prevented me from noticing the time passing. The outfit came together, and amazement grew on my face. The light blue skirt puffed out far with the large petticoat beneath it, coming up to the waist to find a silvery blue corset with a sweetheart neckline. It had a shimmery, transparent fabric attached at the waist that veiled the silky blue cloth, and together they felt extremely light and breathable. It had no sleeves, but one of the tailors handed me something like arm warmers. They were made from sparkling, blue, transparent cloth that went up to my elbows, and allowed my fingers to stick out the bottom. The shoes, despite being heels again, were one of the most comfortable pairs I had ever worn. So pretty much, for an outfit I thought I would hate, I ended up liking it.

    The tailors were putting scissors and needles away and rolling up extra cloth when the makeup specialists, hairdressers, and jewelers came in. Everyone still chatted away, and the giggling never ended. Some of them worked on making sure my fingernails were clean, others worked on my hair, some of them rubbed stuff on my face, and still others were working on finding the perfect set of jewelry. I closed my eyes when needed and stuck out my lips when asked as they wiped makeup everywhere. They used the light pink nectar from the flower of Ora for my lips, and patted the pink pollen of the wen flowers on my cheeks. Then they used a light shade of blue powder from crushed juggajigs for my eyes. To make my eyelashes look longer, they brushed black paint made from blackberries and other thickening stuff on them. One of them without a word grabbed my mouth suddenly and forced it open to check for anything stuck in my teeth, and then she went back to making sure everything else claimed perfection.

Um ... thanks ...

    Milly called to me excitedly, "Galayne?"

    I turned, the makeup people continuing to work on me, and said, "Yes, Milly?"

    She stood next to a tall man who made her look even shorter. "This is Mister Barmly ... he's the one who made your Birth Cape this year."

    She gestured to him, and he did a low and very exaggerated bow. "Your Majesty," he greeted with an honored tone.

    Great, a groveler, I thought, but instead said with a curtsy and a small smile, "Sir."

    "Allow me to show you my work ..." he said, motioning for his servants to open one of the doors, "I hope you will be pleased." Another servant came in holding a large bundle of shining silver cloth. Mister Barmly took it in his arms, smiling at it with father-like pride before presenting it to me, "Only the finest silk was used, and that would be silver from the Dunster Mines woven into it," he said with admiration, as if he wished he could keep it and stare at it all day long.

At first, I thought he said Dumpster Mines, and I had to suppress a smile as I took it and pretended to critique it like I actually knew or cared about what I said. "Hhhmm, seems light and soft, very fine silk indeed, and the silver shines brilliantly. Well done, sir," I said with another curtsy and a smile, handing the cape to an expecting maid to my left. Milly looked so relieved by my response. Apparently, I didn't normally act that way on Ball Day.

"Your Majesty," Barmly bowed, a very satisfied smile on his face, before strutting out the door flanked by his servants.

You're probably wondering what the Birth Cape was. Every year on my birthday it was the thing I had to wear when entering the throne room for the first time. Every time, the room would fall dead silent when I appeared in the large doorway, and neither a breath was heard, nor a smile seen. Everyone would turn toward me in reverence and watch as I made my way to the podium. Even the queen got up from her throne and watched with a smile as I made my way towards it. As soon as I reached the bottom of the stairs, I'd stop moving and wait and watch as the queen made her way down to me. She'd then kiss my head to indicate her blessing or whatever, and then she'd step aside and allow me to continue up to the throne. But right as I stepped on the first step of the staircase, my Birth Cape, which by the way stretched thirty feet behind me, would fall off, and it would be left there for the remainder of the night.

Anyway, it sounds kind of weird, right? But let me tell you, it was no joke. Again, Edgeladine's history coming into play. The Birth Cape, when it fell off, symbolized a new reign and rebirth. It meant that every year that passed, I remained just as able to rule. When I reached the top of the podium, towering above the people, it symbolized just how important my role in protecting Edgeladine was. Everyone was expected to show absolute respect, including the queen. Honestly, I would have rather skipped the ceremony. I didn't like demanding all that attention. And it's not just that . . . everyone feared me. They feared what I might do. Just like the last time they had a Nateara as their ruler . . .

The maids put the cape on, and while they were busy straightening each lump out of it, the hair people finished, and Milly said to me, "Oh . . . Galayne . . ." Her eyes gleamed as she stared up at me, "You look absolutely lovely."

"What?" I said, turning to look in the mirror, the cape straighteners grumbling in annoyance as I did.

"You look five years older!" Milly exclaimed excitedly, "Just wait until I put your crown on! You'll look like a fallen star!" She then ran off to get the new crown.

I hardly noticed what she said as I stared into the mirror. I really did look older, and more majestic than I felt. I finally realized that the hair style got most of the credit. They had tied it up in an intricate bun but left a curl on either side of my face to dangle. It added maturity and grace.

Everyone jumped to attention when someone walked into the room and rang a bell. It was the signal that the ceremony would start soon, and it made my heart flutter. Everyone began to talk more, if possible. The jitters seemed to be a hold of everyone, but none like me. The jitters had practically eaten me.

Everyone began packing up but froze as Milly walked into the room with the marble box. They all watched as Milly made her way to me, opened the box, and pulled the crown from its velvety cushion. As soon as she placed it on my head, the room erupted with excited applause; their job was done, and they seemed happy with the outcome.

Various compliments came from around the room, "Happy Birthday, Your Highness!" and "You look absolutely stunning!" and a few others. Milly hadn't noticed that they were watching and jumped when they responded to the placing of the crown. But she said nothing as she looked up at me, proud tears brimming in her eyes. I smiled back down at her with appreciation, hoping she knew how much I loved her.

Then everyone quickly finished picking up their stuff and left within the minute, leaving me and Milly alone. We were still just looking at each other, until I jumped down suddenly and hugged her tightly.

"I love you, Mildrid..."

I could almost see her face breaking as she said with a sniffle, "I love you too, Galayne."

We just stood there hugging in silence, until she said, "I remember the first time I saw you... your little, seven-year-old self." She gave a small laugh, "You were so cute with your tangled hair, your pouty lip thing you used to do, and your face always covered in dirt." She laughed as she said, "You remember how that one time you fell into the pig pen?"

Still hugging I said with a smile, "Yeah, I remember."

"Oh, I've never laughed so hard in my life..." she laughed, until I heard it break into a cry.

"Milly, what's wrong?" I asked, concerned, hugging her tighter.

"Oh, I'm sorry, Galayne... it's just... you've grown so much." She backed up and put her hand under my chin, looking up into my eyes. "You're practically grown," she gave a sad smile. She seemed to forget that she was only five years older than me, but then again, she was always more of a mom than a friend. "You hardly need me anymore." A happy sort of sorrow filled her face, like she felt excited to see me like that, but teary that I'd grown so much.

I hugged her again and laughed, "Oh, come on, Milly... No matter how old I get, I'll always need you."

I didn't think she could possibly hug me any harder. We were standing there for a while until we were disturbed by a mumbled announcement from next door, "Everyone please make your way into the throne room! Thank you! Thank you! The ceremony will begin shortly!"

Milly stopped hugging me abruptly and her face filled with anxiousness, "Oh, the ceremony! It starts any minute now!" She snatched the crown off my head without a word and put it back on its velvety cushion in the marble box as fast as she could. Then she ran back over to me and started checking my hair to make sure there were no loose strands, even though I knew there couldn't possibly be any with it pulled so tight. She also started to smooth down my dress of some unseen wrinkles, and pull up my arm warmers even though they were already as pulled up as could be. "Oh! There's no time left! You still have to make it to the throne room doors, and we have to make sure your cape is in position, and—"

"Hey, hey . . ." I said, grabbing her by the shoulders so she could focus and look me in the eyes, "Everything is going to fine. In fact, it's going to be perfect . . . just like it always is," I finished with an assuring smile, just like Blue had.

She sighed and gave a small smile, "You're right. I'm worrying about nothing." Then after a moment she said with an encouraging voice, "Come on. Let's not be late." She stepped behind me and started pushing me towards the doors. Something of a happy smile spread on my face—happy because she was with me.

We were almost there when a side door opened and a servant's head peered around it, "Mildrid?" He spotted her. "We need you in the throne room. They said they need you to bring the crown as well."

Milly froze and her smile stopped for a second, "Thanks for telling me. I'll be right there."

The servant nodded and left.

Milly seemed nervous again. We both looked at each other and thought the same thing. Usually, Milly would stay with me up to the very moment when I went through the throne room doors.

FOR THE INTENDED

Milly looked at me in hesitancy before running over and grabbing the marble box and then scrambling over to the side door, I watching, growing sicker by the second. She opened the door, but paused before dashing through it. She mustered every bit of motivational comfort she could for me and said, "You're going to do great." She put on one more reassuring smile for me.

I knew she felt terrible about leaving me, so I put a large, fake smile on, "You betcha."

She smiled one last small smile before closing the door behind her. I could hear her racing down the hall for a few seconds before her footsteps disappeared.

All alone in the large empty room, I listened to the festive music in the next. Since the celebration had been going strong for a few hours by then, the laughter and talking started getting louder as everyone grew comfortable with each other.

I sighed uncomfortably, trying to balance myself, before I walked confidently over to the large doors. I took one more deep breath before opening the door into the hallway. A couple of servants were waiting expectantly on the other side.

"Milady," one said, gesturing for me to step outside the door. I did in silence, and he and the other one ran and gathered up my cape before running back and closing the door behind us. Then we continued down the hall to the throne room doors. My stomach did acrobatic flips as we stopped in front of them, the noise on the other side making its way through. I knew I only had a few seconds of preparation left before they would open.

While the servants straightened out my cape down the hall behind me, I tried to motivate myself in the last few seconds. I tried to fill my mind with things Milly would normally say at that point. *Okay, you've got this. Smile, don't stutter, and speak loud enough for everyone to hear...*

I heard a servant behind me say to the doormen, "Okay, I think we're good to go."

"Alright, Your Majesty," one of the doormen said to me as a heads-up, "I'm going to let the announcer go in ahead of you, and then it'll be time for us to open the doors, okay?"

It was nice of him to warn me, but it only made me feel sicker. I gave a small nod, but I barely breathed.

The announcer went in, but I couldn't hear him above my heartbeat.

Everyone around me gave a thumbs-up and a smile as the doormen grabbed the handles, but my vision blurred momentarily, and I couldn't see anything as the doors opened and golden light flooded over me.

FOR THE INTENDED

ASSERTIVE ASSASSIN

Silence. I could feel the tension. I thought I might pass out. It always felt so much worse than I remembered it. I started to take my first slow steps down the carpet in the middle of the room, hands folded gracefully in front of me. I refused to look at anyone, but occasionally failed as a face made its way into my peripheral vision. They were all scared—wide eyes, voices caught in their throats, not daring to look away from me for a second to make sure they didn't show disrespect. And some made my skin crawl from their angry glares—angry that their ranks and social reputation demanded *extra* respect from them. But even they were nervous.

    I mean of course there were some smiles mixed into the crowd, and some people who seemed to at least be breathing normally. But those were only the ones who knew me, who saw me day to day. The others in the room, some of whom were new officials who had never seen me before, had to respect a princess they didn't even know.
    I swallowed. *Halfway there.* I took a deep breath as I noticed the queen. She sat there, glowing in the candlelight. She wore a long draping dress, silver and light blue like mine, and a small white crown rested on her head. Her beautiful smile spread across her face as her gentle-seeming eyes looked down on me.

I reached the bottom of the stairs and exhaled sharply through my nose as I stopped. I stared straight ahead, heart pounding, my eyes refusing to look anywhere else for fear the world would collapse in front of them. *Keep your focus, it's almost over,* I told myself.

But the queen's movement distracted me, and I couldn't help but look at her. She stood up in front of her throne and paused a moment before her descent. Planted firmly in her place of authority, she radiated grace and power. I was grudgingly aware of how out of place I felt in comparison to her.

With a never-faltering smile that brought a sort of warmth to others that I no longer felt, she took her first few steps down to my level. I returned my gaze to straight ahead of me. It was the first time I had been that close to her since she'd revealed her shocking decisions concerning Blue, and I couldn't stand it. I wanted to bolt. I was disgusted with the thought of being so near her, much less letting her kiss my forehead. I didn't want her blessing . . . I didn't want anything to do with her.

I bit my cheek as she took her last step down and stood face to face with me. I looked ahead indifferently, pretending she didn't exist. She didn't notice though, and put her hands on both my shoulders, looking at me with a twinkle in her eyes. Though no one else could tell, I knew it was just for show, to make herself look good. She leaned over slowly, closed her eyes, and kissed my hair gently. My nostrils flared in suppressed loathing.

Then she sidestepped with a small bow, folding her hands in front of her. I pushed my hateful thoughts from my mind as I resumed my anxiety. *Okay here is the big moment,* I thought to myself. *Here is your time to shine, Capey.* I lifted my first leg up, *Please fall off, please fall off,* I pleaded with the cape. The cape was nice enough to do its part, and I breathed when it slid off my back to the ground. I continued my ascent with a little more confidence than before. *I can do this.*

FOR THE INTENDED

I made it to the top. I took a long, deep breath, closing my eyes . . . I turned.

There they all were, looking back up at me, a huge group of people I had to impress. My hands were still clenched in front of me, pressed so hard together that my knuckles were white and my palms were sweaty. I saw Lily and Tucker smiling up at me. I saw Robert and Dare up at the front—Robert's arm around Dare and a grin on his face when we made eye contact. I saw Lakon standing with his arms crossed, a large smile on his face. I saw Arnet leaning against a door frame to my right, inspecting me, hoping I would do everything right. I saw Milly with her hands clasped together under her chin, looking at me with two happy tears in her eyes.

I would usually relax by then. I would normally see my friends or people I knew smiling up at me and get the courage I needed from them—but not that time. That time I felt extra uneasy, a premonition falling over me.

I didn't smile. I couldn't. It wouldn't happen. I had the awful feeling that I needed to get out of there, and not for the normal reasons. I actually felt like I was in danger.

The Royal Crowner handed Edral Arshine to me, which I grabbed with my right hand with an unintentionally jerky movement. I swallowed again as I forced my eyes to look straight ahead at the large oak doors at the other end of the room. I felt safer with the sword in my hand. He delicately wrapped Winlit Cordial around my neck and then clasped the ends (I had only taken it off a few minutes before the ceremony, just so he could do that). The cold metal against my chest made me feel worse, and the symbol on my hand began to ache. Then came the crown. I bowed slightly, and tilted my head forward as he placed it on my head. Unlike most of my other crowns, that one looked plain and simple. With just one mountain-like point coming up in the front, it was hardly anything to look at, as the rest of the silver metal just curved around my head for a secure hold. There was nothing extraordinary about it except the reason behind its design. It was out of great respect for the past; our ancestors, our history ... The Kerastine Kingdom.

    I then held out my left hand, palm facing upwards, holding nothing. The open hand symbolized my connection to the people, and the peace and prosperity I would bring to Edgeladine. Winlit Cordial symbolized how the Selta chose me—that my reign was no accident. In an old book, it was said that Winlit Cordial was meant for The Summer Born, but it implied that it could've been for any Naetera. It was a source of power that anyone from any domain could tap into, but once they did, Winlit Cordial would tie into their life force. So, since I was seven, when Arnet bonded Winlit Cordial to me to save my life, we could never part. If I hadn't been a Naetera though, it would've killed me ... Anyway, the people viewed Winlit Cordial as more of a showy piece of jewelry than an essential power provider, and that's just how Arnet and my advisors wanted it. Its consequence wasn't totally understood, but Arnet made me promise never to take it off because he was that sure of its gravity. He was proven right when I lost it as a kid. Yeah, it was bound to happen ... Well, anyway, after a few hours without it, I stayed deathly sick for weeks, and so I learned to be extra careful after that. But the whole incident was kept under wraps, because obviously, I had enemies. Better they didn't know that I was a princess who was *extra* attached to her jewelry ...

    Edral Arshine also reminded them of my right to reign, but on a lesser note. It mainly symbolized my strong, unyielding hand, which (supposedly) wouldn't falter.

    When the crown had been placed, and the Royal Crowner stepped back and bellowed a few lines in the Eraldine Language, the room erupted into forced applause.

    Robert hooted and made sure his clapping was the loudest. Dare shook her head disapprovingly at him but clapped for me with a smile anyway. "Long live, Galayne!" Lily and Tucker shouted, as if they had rehearsed it. Lakon smiled and mouthed, "Happy Birthday, kid." Milly's happy cry rose above the clamor as she clapped excitedly, standing amongst all her maid friends, beaming with joy. The others in the room that could manage it, smiled uneasily, but all made sure that their applause seemed enthusiastic.

    Through all the movement happening in the room, I saw Arnet's still form in the doorway. I tried to hide it from the crowd, but I turned my head ever so slightly to look at him from the corner of my eye. A knot formed in my stomach. He wasn't clapping. In fact, he wasn't even looking at me at all. He glanced around the room, hand on his sword hilt. Being that far from him, I still saw him swallow somewhat anxiously as he shifted his feet. We made eye contact for a brief moment, and I read his eyes. Trouble. My eyes snapped forward again. I don't know how I missed it before, but there were guards everywhere, scattered throughout the room, mixed in with the crowd. They were all looking around uneasily, occasionally signalling to each other with discreet gestures. I saw Jack make his way to Arnet and whisper something, and that was almost enough to confirm my fears. But then I thought, *If something is wrong, Lakon would know about it.* I looked back at him and my blood chilled. A guard whispered something in Lakon's ear and Lakon's face washed over with concern. He turned and walked with the guard through the crowd until I lost sight of them.

    I went into a fearful trance, trying to decide what to do. Arnet had practically brought an army to my birthday party. I woke up when the Royal Crowner tried to take my sword. I suddenly yanked back on it without thinking. "No, I want to keep it," I barely whispered to him. He kept a firm grasp on it, and quickly replied, "It would send the wrong message to the people, milady." I licked my lips in apprehension, letting go. He walked away with my one means of protection if anything happened, and the room suddenly felt cold. A shiver ran down my back as a new thought came. *There are people here; innocent people.* My friends were there as well. They could get hurt, and I doubted any of them had brought weapons . . .

Suddenly, from nowhere, just as the Royal Crowner hit the bottom step, the encouraging voice that I had been waiting on came, *Stop it, Galayne! Nothing is going to happen. The guards won't let it happen, and neither will you.* I stood taller.

I clasped my hands in front of me like earlier, but much looser and out of comfort rather than stress. "Greetings one and all!" My voice rang out proud, bouncing off the polished white stone. "Welcome to the Summer Ball, and my coronation," I exclaimed, gesturing around the room and putting on the largest, friendliest smile I could muster. Applause again and a few friendly hoots. I waited for them to settle. "Thank you all for coming." I took a moment to think, but the pause seemed natural, "I see some new faces today, and I'm so glad. My birthday ball wouldn't be complete without each and every one of you." The officials I had never seen before seemed to appreciate that comment.

The whole room erupted, "*Happy Birthday*!" More hoots and hollering and clapping.

I nodded in thanks. I hoped I could convince them that I felt no better than them, which would hopefully bring us to a friendlier level. A few faces had changed to my relief.

I continued, "I know some of you have traveled a great distance to be here, and I want you to know that it is greatly appreciated and doesn't go unnoticed." A few grumblings were heard from the incautious, but a few light whispers could be heard that sounded like approval. "For this is the time when our kingdom is totally connected—united by our love for Edgeladine and our common history." The word "history" moved through the crowd like a death summon, and all the previous things I'd said to make them like me faded from their minds as they stared up in fear again.

I swallowed. Wrong thing to say. But I wasn't going to back down; I just had to fix it. Then an idea came. I began to stroll down the stairs.

A few small gasps escaped some of the officials before they clamped their mouths shut. Shock filled everyone as I continued down... After I ascended, I was never supposed to come down to their level for the remainder of the ceremony. From the corner of my eye, I saw Arnet shift again, clutching the pommel of his sword tighter, watching my every move—Jack replicated his movements.

When I reached the bottom of the staircase, Milly stood only a few feet away from me. Her face went pale when our eyes met, and it seemed like they were screaming it was the wrong thing to do. She knew of all the rules in the book, and knew it was a pretty bad one to be breaking. I looked away from her, convincing myself that maybe it'd be worth it. I concealed a deep breath and said, "There," a large, gentle smile on my face, "Now we can get to know each other better." I saw my friends, smiles no longer on their faces. I saw some elderly scholars in the room puffing, clearly showing by their expressions what they thought of my disrespect for the olden rules. I looked to see what the queen thought, but my heart jumped when I saw her being escorted quietly out of the room by multiple guards. Something was *officially* up. I had to remain calm though.

I took a sigh that I didn't mind if the people heard, before looking to the side in self-reproach, "I am sorry for the way things have been, my friends. It was by no intent that we should have grown so far apart. If we are all honest, hardly any of you know me. And at a far greater crime, I do not know you."

I felt Arnet's quizzical eyes boring into me.

"I know our ancestors put rules and regulations in place for our safety, and also so that we do not repeat the past," the scholars looked pleased that I remembered. "But I do not think they meant for it to be like this." The scholars took on pondering faces, seeming open to at least hearing me out.

"Though it may not seem like it, and though I pretended to think differently earlier, we are a torn kingdom. There is unity only because it is demanded. There is order, only because it is forced." I gave a small laugh as I said, "I mean, you follow me because of a set of rules that were put in place centuries ago!" I let them think that over for a second. My friends began to smile a little, pride growing in their eyes.

"All I'm saying is, I don't think this is the way it is supposed to be." I spoke a little louder now, in an excited tone, "That is why I am declaring that meetings will be held every month, in Umplidore, until their use has run out, which I hope will never happen. Only those who can find time to attend may come, and only at their greatest convenience. It will be a time of friendly conversation, a time to discuss issues between us, and to overall help unite the provinces. The need for the meetings is great in this time, as my reign is young, and our kingdom weak. And it is my highest desire that through reconstruction and time, I may not only be the best ruler I can be for you, but the greatest friend you will ever have."

Silence filled the space. I felt totally defeated as I looked into the motionless crowd. I desperately thought of what to do next, when the room exploded with applause. And that time, it felt sincere.

My heart fluttered with relief. I'd done it. My friends clapped hard and gave me approving looks, including Milly, which also brought a new level of comfort to me. The scholars whispered amongst themselves, but no anger seemed to be there. A grin on my face, I turned to see Arnet's reaction. He still leaned against the wall, rubbing his fingers together, but his expression remained unreadable as he looked at me. Jack whispered something to him again.

The clapping began to die down when my heart jolted to the menacing exclamation, "*Lies!*" that boomed out from its owner.

My eyes snapped to the center of the crowd where the voice had come from. It came again, the crowd parting without question to let the speaker through. "Deceit!" He came into view as he pushed two people aside, snarling, "Murderer!" He looked gruff and burly, nearly as tall as Lakon. Dressed in all black, his clothes were torn and worn as if he'd been on a long, rough journey. He had an odd-shaped sword strapped to his belt, and I barely managed to glimpse the ruby studded hilt of a dagger concealed behind the fold of a short, weather stained cape. He had scraggly and matted black hair that fell uncared for at his shoulders. Due to a pair of filthy and freshly scarred hands and several slanted tears in his shirt that looked like they came from a large claw, I had a feeling he'd been doing some unusual things lately.

He made his way towards me, heavy black boots trampling the Birth Cape on the floor, no one daring to oppose. I let him come, wondering what to do, but maintained a calm mindset. He came closer, jabbed a dirty finger in my direction, and repeated, "*Murderer.*" He stopped only four feet away—not nearly far enough. His eyes were wild and dark, and he brought an unsettling mood with him.

"I'm sorry, sir, I do not know—" I began before being cut off abruptly.

He whirled around to face the crowd and belted, "People of Edgeladine!" His voice filled every crevice of the room. "Do not be deceived by this treachery! These are sweet lies whispered to you by a cunning snake," he spat, obviously referring to me. He said the next line of his speech incredulously, as if he couldn't believe the people had fallen for it, "Umplidore seeks no friendship with its provinces, and its . . . *royalty*," he said, full of contempt and mockery, "Are no better than *Del Mendor*!!" The vile insult rolled off his tongue with slick hatred for its intended recipient—me.

Shocked and offended gasps came from the crowd along with agitated mumblings. I just stood there, not knowing what to do. *What are the guards doing?* I thought anxiously. I searched around for them, but only a few were in my sight, and even they disappeared into the crowd . . . in the opposite direction of the insulter.

The intruder wasn't finished though, "While this *child* pretends to have the people's best interest in mind, and seems to want a united, free kingdom, it could be no farther from the truth. All she seeks is an enslaved nation, under one hideously evil monarch. And she and her manipulative allies will do anything and everything to see it done.

"I have been on a journey," he began to walk down the aisle slowly, making eye contact with different people, "I have fought hard, and suffered many long months to bring you the truths that I have found and am about to share."

No one doubted it.

The man paused, seeming to think over whether he should reveal his next bit of information, but then said boldly, "I have been to the Dark Lands beyond The Wood, and have seen Mulkar with my own eyes."

Cries of disapproval came. A man near the aisle stepped out into it and exclaimed loudly, "You're mad! No one has dared to go there since . . ." his voice faded. Uncomfortable whispers dispersed throughout the room. Even I couldn't believe it.

"It was necessary, I'm afraid. Through many different failed attempts to reveal Umplidore's secrets, I pressed on, and now have been satisfied by the results of my efforts. When our princess goes on her quest, Kileana Mur, she goes as far as our borders will let her and stops on the threshold of evil—The Dark Lands. The purpose of that quest is to keep evil in check, and make sure we still have the upper hand. Yet, she has seen evil growing and spreading there from the mountain's view and does not share her newfound information." The people latched onto every word. "In the harsh caves of the mountains, I found monsters brooding and growing in numbers. It would be impossible to miss."

What? I thought. *That's not true! I didn't see anything in the mountains. Nothing! . . . I suppose I saw the varnants . . . but that's different . . . it wasn't on my quest, and I knew I could handle it. I was obligated to share nothing.*

"But what's worse is this. At the end of my long journey only a few days ago, I was ambushed by lagione and barely escaped with my life." I guessed that was where the tears in his clothes came from. "In the hands of the ferocious leader I had the displeasure to meet, was this," he had been rummaging around under his cloak until he thrust his hand into the air holding a piece of parchment scribbled on with black ink, bearing a red seal that made my stomach churn. He threw it at the ground in disgust and pointed at it, "Orders from Umplidore to have a shipment of our finest weapons sent to our enemies. Bearing the seal of the princess!!"

Horror and disruptive noises filled the room as people glanced back at me with newfound fear and distrust.

I could only whisper to myself in disbelief, "But I never... I never signed that..." I looked down at it and my stomach tightened. It *was* my seal, next to my very own signature. Someone, *someone in Umplidore*, had access to not only my seal, but a talented forger. But I couldn't think about that right then, because the man in black wasn't finished yet.

"And you!" he turned savagely, thrusting his finger at me again, "What else have you done? What else has not yet been revealed?"

I gaped. I didn't know what to say and I realized he expected me to answer. My brain scrambled as it decided what to do. I glanced quickly to where Arnet and Jack had stood, looking for an answer, and my heart leaped into my throat as I saw an empty door frame. *Where'd they go?!*

I tried to hide my shakiness and took a deep breath, looking away from the man to the audience beyond, pretending he didn't exist. "My dear friends, surely you do not believe these lies. I have been to the mountains, and I have seen no such things. The mountains were as bare and abandoned as ever."

The man seethed in silence, not taking his fury-filled eyes off me.

I proceeded, hoping they would listen, "Anything I saw I reported in The Records, which is available to the public. I have no desire to hide anything from you, and I have not the slightest urge to tyrannize your provinces. Such action would make the kingdom even more unstable, and I trust you all to take fine care of your homeland."

People looked back and forth between me and the man, not sure who to listen to. But relief came as I saw some of their faces change, losing their fear and worry, clearly supporting my side. I guess I looked a little more together than he did. The pleased mumblings throughout the crowd made the man stare at me with even more loathing, if possible. One person asked him, "Yeah, why should we believe the things you say?"

The man turned back around, desperately trying to convince them, "I have seen them myself, and I have fought many dangers to bring you this news." His voice broke through with a small trace of despair as he finished, "Look at her own seal!!"

"Ever heard of forgers?" Some mocking laughter ran through the crowd.

He looked around in disbelief, "Please don't tell me it was all a waste!"

But it was too late. The people had chosen to side with me, evident by the discussions and their happy faces. "Nothing is wrong," "Everything is fine," "The princess is our friend," and a few other things were said throughout the crowd like, "Who's going to believe the loon?" I knew doubts still existed, but people were already consulting with other officials and the scholars and my side grew bigger as they were convinced.

The man said a few things more, trying to prove himself, but he was talking to a wall. The people had full-fledged conversations going on by then, and he couldn't get their attention. He turned on me with a face of complete defeat. And that's when I did something stupid. I smiled triumphantly, a smug expression on my face.

Ignoring his growing rage, I looked past him at the people and said, silencing them, "Now that *that* is settled, why don't we proceed with the ball. I heard that the feast is going to be—"

My sentence got cut off by a horrible bellow as the man lunged for me, dagger drawn in an instant, crazed eyes fixed. Screams escaped in the brief moment from the crowd, but I couldn't move. Everything happened so fast. Guards appeared from nowhere, pushing out of the crowd from all sides. In a blink of an eye the man's left arm smacked the crown from my head, and then everything slowed as his right arm swung towards me, a terrible blade in it. In the slowed down time, my mind screamed for me to move, but my movements were slowed as well, and I could only stare with wide eyes. The screams of terror faded, the only sounds becoming my heartbeat and a long exhale as I saw the steel point brush just under my chin, barely missing my throat.

Then everything else happened in an instant. I got snatched from behind, a strong arm wrapping around my waist and dragging me backwards towards a door. Guards had secured the assassin who struggled and shouted in rage as they overcame him. Arnet had appeared again and shouted ferociously, "Hold him! *Don't let him up!*" A few others in the room seemed to have accompanied the man in black, and they were fighting some of the guards to get to their overwhelmed comrade.

I saw a guard raise a club to strike the man. "No!" I shouted. Too late. With anger boiling inside me, I saw the large man clothed in black fall to the ground unconscious before I was pulled out of the room. It all happened in a matter of seconds, too fast to contemplate.

Just then, the person dragging me tripped in the doorway, sending us both toppling to the ground on the other side of the door. Still lying on his back on the floor, the person immediately angled himself and kicked the door shut with a thud, the large bolt falling securely in place.

UNCONVENTIONAL

I scrambled to a standing position, painfully aware, *once again,* that my sword was not at my side. In a split second I decided that one of the torches hanging on the wall would suffice. I started to dart to the wall to get one, when the flash of a silvery symbol on the stranger's tunic made me pause. Umplidore's emblem—a large star that symbolized Umplidore surrounded by many smaller stars that represented the other provinces—shimmered proudly on his shirt.

The boy, who seemed about my age, calmly got up and brushed himself off. His dark curly hair temporarily concealed his face, leaving me to guess his identity. "Well, that sure didn't go as planned," he said, looking up after one last good pat that sent dust billowing in the air. His skin was a deep tan, and his eyes were dark, but not unfriendly. He had a few inches on me, and I realized a year or two as well. He had a disciplined air about him, and he looked like the kind of person who knew how to use the sword strapped to his belt. His hand rested firmly on its hilt, but it looked like a habit rather than a threat. I realized he looked really familiar, but I couldn't decide where I'd seen him before.

"Sorry about that," he said, white teeth glowing orange in the firelight, "I didn't mean to catch you by surprise. But if I may say so, you would've been in pieces by now if I hadn't done something."

"Yeah, no don't worry about it." I said, "Actually, thanks."

"No prob," he said, finally smiling. "I'm Lucas. You may have seen me in Arnet's sword practice."

Lucas. That's where I knew him from. I had seen him training in one of Arnet's many classes, but that's not what made the memory click. He was the one who the queen called to bring me back to my room that day. He had a savage grip. "Galayne," I muttered, a little less friendly.

Remembering protocol, he bowed and I curtsied. Then an angry shout broke through the thick doors. "Well then, milady, now that we're acquainted," he said, pulling a torch off the wall, "we should probably keep moving."

As he led the way down the hallway in silence, it gave me time to notice our surroundings which were dark and surprisingly dusty. A torch filled with reddish-orange fire sat in an old holster on the wall every few feet. After the grand extravagance of the ball, the deserted hall looked out of place. It amazed me how unfamiliar and untraveled the hallway was despite being so close to the throne room. "Wow, it's like I've never even seen this hall," I commented.

"Yeah, a lot of the halls aren't used anymore. We're assuming that's how they snuck into the party."

I realized he was right. The castle was massive, and there were so many parts of it I'd never seen. It would be easy to miss the hall.

When we had reached our destination—a door with light pouring out from under it—Lucas stopped and turned to face me. His head lowered though, and he fingered his sword's pommel. "Hey. Sorry about the other day. I was just following orders. Plus I didn't know you were—"

I cut in solemnly as I guessed, "What? A decent person?"

He looked up with a small smile, "Well . . . yeah."

I nodded, disappointed that I already knew the answer, but then I smiled. "That's okay. We're even. You forced me into my room, and I gave you quite a few bruises along the way."

That seemed to break the tension, and he laughed. "Yeah, you sure did. And some of them are still healing," he said jokingly.

I smiled again, and he opened the door.

We were in the ballroom—a completely empty ballroom. The candlelight seemed blindingly intense after the dark, cramped hallway. We both stepped in, Lucas returning the torch to an empty holster in the dim hallway before he bolted the door behind us. As soon as he did, one of the doors a few feet across from us opened, and Lucas's hand instinctively shot to his sword. We both relaxed as Arnet, Milly, Jack, and one of the higher-ranking guards came into the room, the guard bolting the door behind them.

"Galayne!" Milly cried, running to me, throwing her arms about my neck. "You're alright!" I saw her red face and puffy eyes—two of their tears still drying on her cheeks.

"Yes, Milly, I'm fine," I said distractedly, hugging her tight.

Jack looked devastated that he had, once again, failed to protect his royal, but his relief outdid his disappointment at the moment. Arnet and the guard remained uptight though, refusing to relax.

Arnet and the guard walked over, hands on hilts, and Lucas snapped to attention. I stopped hugging Milly, "What happened?" I asked, directed to Arnet.

"We will discuss it in a minute. First . . . Lucas." Arnet turned to him.

"Yes, sir," Lucas answered in a serious voice.

"You disobeyed my orders. You were *not* where you were supposed to be. You broke from the strategic position in the crowd I gave you, and therefore, we had a *hole* in our formation. *Three of them* got away thanks to you!"

I wanted to interrupt him, but I knew from previous experiences that that would only make it worse for Lucas.

Lucas had clearly been thinking the same thing and had been trying to hold his tongue, but it slipped and he blurted, "But, sir, I—"

"*Let me finish,*" Arnet barked, and Lucas fell silent, gripping his hilt in anger and embarrassment.

Milly looked down in pity for him.

Jack stared straight ahead, but I saw him questioning again.

Arnet continued, "You were disobedient, thoughtless, and *foolish* to disregard the plan. And for that I must say . . ."

Lucas cringed slightly but maintained eye contact.

". . . well done." Arnet broke into a grin.

Everyone looked at him in shock.

"In your realization that the plan was ill-timed, and that Guardsen Dessal wouldn't make it to his position, you saved the princess's life." He bowed to Lucas, "You have my thanks."

Lucas blinked in astonishment.

Arnet smiled, "A *promotion* might be in order. What do you think, Guardsen Dessal?"

"Yes, sir." The guardsen smiled at Lucas, but it looked fake and hateful, probably because Lucas had stolen his praise. "You are promoted to the fourth rank, Lucas Renal. You are well on your way to becoming a guardsen, despite your age, and I see the Royal Guard in your future. I expect to see you bright and early in the morning at the barracks."

"Y-yes sir. It's an honor, sir."

"Very well, you are dismissed. Jack, help him get situated."

Jack bowed, "Of course, sir."

Lucas and Jack bowed to Arnet and Guardsen Dessal, then to Milly which made me happy because I knew they didn't have to, then to me, one saying, "Milady." and the other, "Your Majesty." Then they walked to a side door, and just before they went through, Jack shook Lucas's hand, "Welcome to the fourth rank. You can bunk in the empty room across from mine."

Arnet turned, "Guardsen Dessal."

The guardsen tensed, "Yes, sir."

"You are dismissed." The guardsen bowed and began to walk away before Arnet's arm caught his, "And don't forget about tomorrow's meeting."

"Of course." Then he bowed again to both of us, excluding Milly, and strode out of the room with his chin angled upwards.

With the strangers out of the room, Milly erupted, "Oh, Galayne! Are you really alright?"

I hugged her tight, realizing I'd ignored her, "Yes, Milly, I'm really alright." But the truth was, I didn't know. I felt confused, angry, upset, and relieved all at the same time. "I need to—" I began, but Arnet interrupted.

"Mildrid. You are to prepare a room for Galayne in the western side of the castle on level four. Pick any that you wish." He said it nicely, but firm enough.

"But I . . ." she began.

"There's no time I'm afraid. Galayne is still in danger; we don't know how many others are after her. And if I'm correct, the spies in our castle know almost everything about Galayne. They will know where her chamber is, and we need to move it as quickly as possible. But don't touch Galayne's old chamber, leave everything exactly the way it is. We might have the upper hand if they think she still sleeps there. If they plan to ambush it tonight, we will have a surprise of our own for them. But hurry, promptness is most important tonight."

Milly's protest dropped immediately, overcome by determination. She bowed to Arnet and squeezed my hand hard, letting me know we'd talk later on. I smiled gently at her to let her know I really was fine, and her hand slipped from mine as she rushed off to fill her orders.

I turned to Arnet. "Now what?"

"*Now*," he said, walking over to a small side door that opened into another torchlit hall, "we keep moving."

Arnet's behavior surprised me. Normally, in that kind of predicament, he would have practically lost his mind. He would be angry and frustrated, especially with my decision to join the people during my speech, as he frantically tried to fix everything. But he wasn't like that at all. He remained quiet and actually seemed somewhat calm. His stride was steady, but again, it seemed too slow for his normal rush. I guessed that he felt relaxed because he felt prepared. He had anticipated the attack and therefore handled it with ease. He didn't need to panic because he had it all under control. And maybe, it was because he had me beside him again . . . Before Lucas pulled me from the room, I had seen Arnet's look of panic, because I had been *that* close to death. But once he had me safe and protected again, he could be the leader he was known to be.

We were walking silently down the hall for a few minutes before he said, "I'm taking you to the gardens. I consulted with some of the lookouts, and they say they doubt the traitors will look for you there; they're mainly occupied searching inside the castle walls for you. Although you won't have the guards, I think it is actually the safest place to be. Just stay low."

I clenched my teeth together and squinted my eyes as I followed him down the hall, staring at his back. I didn't like how he called them traitors. I mean, they *were* traitors, but some form of understanding welled up in me for the man in black, and I had a flashback to the club sending him to the floor.

"Why did you do that?"

He turned for a second, confused, but continued walking, "Do what?"

"The man in black . . . why did you do that?"

He sighed sadly, but didn't turn around or stop. "Galayne, sometimes in life, you have to do things you don't want to do. Things you know are right. If I hadn't done that, he might still be free. He was not only a threat to you, but to everyone in that room. My job was to protect my queen, you, and my kingdom. That is what I did."

I thought about it a moment, and the only sound was our feet padding against the stone floor. He did seem to be in the right despite the feeling of injustice in me. I couldn't place why

I felt the way I did, until it finally came to me. It was the man's eyes, wild and desperate. He truly believed the things he said. He thought I really did all those things, and braved treason to let the public know, to protect them. In a way, it was no less than what Arnet did.

But I knew I couldn't convince Arnet that their causes were equally important, so I just muttered, "Yeah, maybe ... but you didn't need to hit him."

He sighed again, a little impatiently, "Galayne, you know perfectly well why that was necessary. That man was obviously not a dimwit; he knew how to use that dagger. I was just making sure he didn't get to use it any further. Plus, Galayne, he didn't seem in his right mind. The Dark Lands will do that to you." His voice dropped at the end, having an edge of something I couldn't detect. Disappointment? Anger? Sorrow ... ?

I let the subject drop to the sound of our rhythmic step, pondering everything. I surprised myself. Like I said, I felt angry and frustrated, yet so indifferent with the night at the same time. I thought I should be angry with Arnet for not warning me, for knocking the man in black unconscious, for his speech about how his actions were just. Instead, I felt calm, and if anything, tired. I was done with everything for the time being. I continued slugging along when an idea popped into my head. The accusations the man in black had made— "liar" and "keeping secrets to myself"—brought one of my worst fears to the surface, and a secret long suppressed with it. My stomach churned, and I swallowed with uncertainty.

Not another word was said until we reached a small side door that opened into the dark gardens. Arnet paused, holding the door open for me, and sighed for the last time, but it sounded tired and apologetic, "The truth is, Galayne, it was not my intent for the day to turn out like this. And if I could have, I would have avoided the path I took entirely." A little cold wind wound its way into the doorway, refreshing and freeing after the musty hall.

I smiled slightly. "It's okay. I think what you did was right. Although it wasn't ideal, you served your purpose." It was half true at least.

He smiled, seeming more pleased with my words than I thought he would. "You know something, Galayne? I've truly underestimated you. Your idea to break the rules was dangerous, and I doubted it at first, but then you proved to me how strategic a move it was. You're ready to make some choices on your own now." He winked, "You have my trust back."

My spirits lifted. *Wow.* Between that statement and our walk that morning, I felt like our old relationship wasn't out of reach anymore. I also couldn't believe that he had let the breaking of rules slide, once for me and once more for Lucas. It showed me that I didn't know Arnet as well as I thought.

He hadn't felt so approachable in months, and it gave me the courage to say what had been haunting me . . .

He had started to say with a gentle smile, "Now go. Your friends are waiting for you. Wait there for my signal to—"

Suddenly I couldn't hold it in, "I'm going to tell them."

He blinked, "Tell them what?"

I swallowed, "Well . . . the man wasn't totally wrong. I do keep secrets . . ."

His face dropped, knowing immediately what I was talking about, "Galayne, I do not think that would be—"

"Oh, come on, Arnet . . . they're bound to start asking some questions sooner or later." He looked like he wanted to intervene, so I said quietly, "Arnet . . . they need to know."

He still didn't look convinced.

"You just said that you trusted me to make my own decisions. And I am making this one, for it is mine to make. Is it not?" I said it quickly, one part of me hoping he wouldn't oppose, but the other desperate that he would.

He looked down in a pondering state, rubbing his fingers together just as he had earlier. Then, reluctantly, he said, "Yes, Galayne, it is yours to make. It has always been yours ever since you discovered the portals. Without you, I would never have-" His eye twitched when a quiet clang echoed down the hall. We both stared into the darkness in the direction the sound came from but couldn't see more than a little ways down the hall since it turned a bend.

All the fear I expected to see jumped in his eyes. He stepped closer to me and whispered "I think we're being spied on. Hurry into the gardens. I will meet you later."

He pushed me from behind, and I just had time to turn around and say before he closed the door behind him, "But Arnet, what about . . ." I let my voice trail off on purpose.

He breathed in deep and said, "That is for you to decide." Another sound clattered down the hall, a little louder than before. He grasped the door harder, "But be careful who you choose to tell, and remember . . ." he mouthed the last part but it was easy enough to read, "the walls have ears." Then he closed the door.

I took a deep breath, trying to calm myself. I could tell my friends. Right? I mean, they were my most trusted companions, and I could tell them everything. I mean . . . right?

The sound of a voice came from a ways away and I could see the campfire burning through the trees. Looking at the flickering orange through the brush, I thought I made out a few people sitting about it, and I looked down. I knew my friends were there, gathered around it, wondering where I was and if I was okay.

I realized I kept wringing my hands. The thing I wanted to tell them could've been so life changing. They could've hated my guts for keeping it from them—they could've thought I was a liar. They could've . . . left. A lump formed in my throat. Because when I say "they could've left," I mean I could've never seen them again.

I actually shook, partially from the chilly night, and partially because I felt panicked. I had always planned to tell them one day, but that night's events made it almost unavoidable. I *was* a liar. I *did* have a secret . . . But I needed to

FOR THE INTENDED

stop freaking out. I was making it way too big, probably just because I had thought about it so long.

The voices were brought with the slight wind again, and I looked determinedly at their owners. It didn't matter. Despite what Arnet said, it wasn't mine to keep. They deserved to know. I took quite a few long breaths, forcing the lump in my throat down, before striding towards them ... no going back.

FAMILY

I don't know if I breathed all the way there. When I broke into the circle of light, I stood there, undetected. They were all huddled in a circle of discussion, exchanging whispers, their voices merging with the crackling flames in the center.

I was seriously reconsidering the whole thing. My memory from *The Outside* swirled in my mind, and I suddenly realized something. What if they had memories from *The Outside* too? They already knew that Naetera came from *The Outside*—but that's not what I was worried about. They couldn't get to *The Outside*, so they could disregard any memories from *The Outside* as weird dreams. But if I shared that there was a way to get there, they might decide that *The Outside* was their real home—I could lose them forever.

I could still leave; they hadn't seen me yet. I started to back away, pretending I'd never considered it, when Robert saw me.

They were trying to keep their voices down, and they seemed anxious, each of them glancing around in turn. Robert stood in the middle of them saying something when he saw me and stood up immediately, "Galayne?" All eyes followed his with gasps and relieved expressions. Even Dare seemed to relax as if she'd genuinely been worried as well.

I still stood there and swallowed hard as Robert strode over to me. "Galayne?" he said again, putting his hands on my shoulders. The others were right behind him, surrounding me with questions concerning the night's events—was I okay, and how did I escape, etc. Their words were all so jumbled together, though, that I could only focus on Robert's eyes that met mine intensely. They were full of true concern, huge relief, and questions. Then his face became determined as he read my thoughts—thoughts I couldn't hide. I knew he knew there was something I had to say. I also knew that I had to tell them... he wouldn't let me not tell them.

Through some unknown language between me and Robert that we'd had for a long time, he asked me with his eyes, *"What, Galayne?"*

Tucker hugged me, but I still maintained eye contact with Robert and had my eyes say back, *"I... need to..."*

His eyes squinted slightly as he realized how important my secret was, and our conversation ended.

Lily hugging me tight, and Tucker still spewing questions, Robert surprised them with, "Let's sit down. Then Galayne can share everything."

They all paused a second before going over and situating themselves on the logs. I took a deep breath, starting to walk to one, when Robert put one of his hands on my shoulder again, and walked me there. I sat down and he sat right next to me, his back facing the others. His eyes said one thing: *"Spill it... all of it."*

I panicked before I remembered my secret wasn't what the others wanted; they just wanted to know what had happened since the man in black attacked me. Maybe I could trick Robert into thinking that was all that my unusual behavior was from—that my "secret" was the uneasy feeling I had gotten from it all. But then again... I would never have behaved like that if that was all that had happened, and I began to realize that Robert would see me holding back. But before I let that scare me, I shared the answers to everyone else's questions.

I told them about how I had escaped the room with the help of Lucas. It didn't take long, and I finished by letting them know I was supposed to stay in the gardens until Arnet got back.

When I finished, a moment of silence passed. I gazed into the fire, all too aware of Robert's eyes studying me as he leaned on his hand. I became so uncomfortable that I said, without hardly thinking, "So, what about you guys?" And thankfully, Robert turned to face her when Lily spoke up.

She sat up straighter, "Well, when Cath drew his sword, several—"

She had hardly gotten a few words out, when I interjected inquisitively, momentarily forgetting my problem at hand, "Wait, what? Cath?"

She blinked, and after looking around and seeing that no one else knew him either, she explained quickly, "Gen Cath. I knew him a long time ago. He's from my old village near Gilden. He had a wife and two little kids that I used to play with. Well, when I say little, they were my age, so I suppose they're about fifteen now. Anyway, he used to be so nice . . . and very well respected there." She finished with a trace of sadness.

I felt worse knowing the man in black's name, and knowing he had a life before I'd met him. I also felt strange that I had never heard about him from Lily. I mean, I knew she came from a small village near Gilden, but she never shared much from her past. I became aware of how much I didn't know about her. Like how I didn't even know her village's name.

She paused for a second, before continuing, "Anyway, when Cath drew his sword, several others in the crowd did as well."

Tucker joined in, "It was chaos, Galayne. People running everywhere."

Dare even spoke up to say, still holding her dagger's hilt tightly, "There was no way we were going to get to you." Her eyes met Robert's as she said, "Robert was close, but he was intercepted by two of Gen's henchmen."

I couldn't see Robert's face, but I saw his back tense, and his knuckles were sickly white as he clutched his sword's pommel.

FOR THE INTENDED

She had paused a second before concluding, "By the time we had defeated most of them, we lost sight of you. We were instructed by Guardsen Dessal to make our way to the gardens, saying we would find you here. When we didn't see you, we were formulating a plan to search you out. That's what we were in the middle of when you showed up."

I nodded, thoroughly impressed. That was the biggest speech I'd ever heard Dare make. Normally I would've said Robert was rubbing off on her, but it was hard to tell at that moment since Robert had remained silent the entire time.

I thought about how panicked they must've been when they couldn't find me and wondered what I would have done in their place, when Robert turned back to face me. I could feel his pale blue eyes on me. I slowly looked up to meet them and knew I hadn't convinced him. His stare had turned into a glare, and I swallowed.

The extremely welcomed voice in my head that had come earlier to encourage me spoke again, but that time I hated what it had to say. It whispered comfortingly, *It's time, Galayne. They deserve to know . . . you've already decided that. You trust them, don't you?*

I straightened myself out, breaking my eyes from Robert's, realizing there was no choice to make. I took a calming breath of the warm night air that smelled of the comforting campfire smoke. But of course, it only reminded me of the past, with my eight-year-old friends and I gathered around the fire as Arnet told stories. It made me more uncomfortable than before, if that were possible. I shut the memories out. I would just deliver my secret and leave them to choose their own way . . . Quick and simple . . . right to the point.

I forced my mind to go temporarily blank. I would just focus on one bit of information at a time. I would pretend I was just talking to the fire in front of me, and surprisingly it worked. My friends blurred from my vision, and all I saw was the fire wavering. Just the fire and me, I began to voice my fear to the night air.

"You guys remember the tale of Bentur . . . the secret one we aren't allowed to repeat?" I asked the individual flames suddenly.

No one answered, but I could feel my friend's confused gazes despite my refusal to meet them.

I knew they did, but to get to the point, I thought I had better remind them.

I then told the campfire the tale the way I had memorized it—the way I heard the thing recited in my nightmares. "A long time ago, during the reign of King Bentur, it was said that a *Door* to *The Outside* had been found.

"Around that time, Naetera were not as rare as they are now. King Bentur, one of the strongest Naetera, was crowned because of his vast knowledge and power. Some say he was too knowledgeable, and that's where the idea came from that he had found portals to . . ."

I was startled from my trance-like conversation with the fire as Robert suddenly finished my sentence, "another world, the origin of Naetera." He finished gently, "We remember."

I looked at him briefly, before I snatched my eyes back to the fire, knowing I wouldn't be able to continue if I didn't. "According to the tale, only the king knew where the portals were, and no one else ever discovered them. They soon were forgotten, and now they are considered fairytales—something for people to fantasize about." I felt like their eyes were boring holes into me. *Don't look. Don't look!* I thought. *Just get it out!* Before I argued with my thoughts again, I added quickly, "But they're not."

My heart might as well have left my chest. I heard a voice but I couldn't make out whose, and it asked carefully, "What do you mean?"

I swallowed, my dry tongue scraping the top of my mouth. "I've used them."

Gasps. Then stunned silence.

"Look, guys," I blurted, breaking from my straightforward gaze to meet their disbelieving faces, "I never meant to keep it from you! I didn't . . . I mean . . ." I couldn't keep going—my voice had already broken twice. I took a deep breath, trying to be Galayne, not the frightened stranger.

My eyes stung, my face felt so hot, and I did everything I could to conceal it. Nobody moved. Everyone fell into shock. I had a hard time breathing, wanting to run, when I froze. Robert suddenly wrapped his large, muscular arms around me in a warm embrace. Only a second passed before I felt more arms encircle me. I stiffened. I didn't give many hugs and didn't receive too many either.

We all just sat there while I slowly stopped shuddering. They broke away, but seated themselves a few inches from me, giving me a safe bubble of comfort. We had been friends since I could remember, and I had forgotten how well each of them knew me.

Robert still sat on the log next to me when he said, "It's okay, Galayne. No one blames you for keeping this from us. Truth be told, if I was in your position, I would have too." He grinned, "We're pretty reckless sometimes. You just waited til you thought we were ready."

The others nodded their heads in agreement, and Lily who knelt by my feet smiled gently and gave my knee a squeeze for reassurance.

"We will always trust you, because we always have, and you've never broken our trust." His voice sounded so sincere. "And you can always trust us, cuz trust me, we're not leaving anytime soon." He smiled, amused, clearly proud of how many times he had worked the word "trust" into his speech, and I couldn't help but smile. They were truly the greatest friends ever. I paused a moment, before thinking, *No, not friends . . . family—**my family**.*

Haven Berg

MISUNDERSTANDING

After that, sharing wasn't hard. In fact, I practically threw up all that I knew about *The Outside* from the few short-lived trips I had taken there after I discovered the portals. It felt so good to get it out. Over the course of several nights, with my friends gathered around the campfire, I told them everything. I told them as much as I could about how the people got around there, what they ate, what they did for fun, how they talked, and the animals they had there. I wasn't an expert by any means, but I did know more than anyone in Edgeladine. They were mesmerized, asking questions every few seconds. If they did have memories of Earth, they never mentioned them, and I certainly wasn't going to ask about them. My plan had been to tell them about *The Outside and* the locations of the portals, but nobody pressed for the latter, so I held it back. They knew about my hesitations and respected me enough to be satisfied with whatever I was willing to share.

I spoke freely on those nights, without worrying about unwanted ears. Around the fire pit, laughing and joking around, we would seem of no interest—nothing suspicious or concerning going on. The only time when I felt a twinge of apprehension was when I let Arnet know the secret was out.

FOR THE INTENDED

We didn't say anything, but a brief moment of eye contact was all it took. He looked surprised for a second, as if he had thought I wouldn't actually do it, but then his face hardened and he left without a word.

While the week was one of the best of my life, it was also one of the most stressful. It turned out that the attack at my birthday party was a short assault that ended quickly. Most of the "traitors," as Arnet continued to call them, escaped. I didn't hear any more about my enemy in black, but I was afraid to ask.

Everything stayed on the chaotic side. The people were, of course, afraid and confused, and the officials were even more so with a greater level of anger than the rest. One of the things that brought the panic in the kingdom down was the meeting the queen took with the different dukes and duchesses of the provinces. I have no idea what she told them, but the next day everyone, and I mean *everyone*, packed for the trip home. And by the third day, not a trace remained of the Summer Ball, and all its guests never existed.

I suppose she must've wanted to separate everyone—to prevent them from building their fears off one another—and it seemed to work. The people were frightened, but they were constantly reminded of their security via announcements that occurred throughout Umplidore each day. And I could only assume the same announcements were being proclaimed in all of the provinces.

And me? What did I do during that time? Nothing. Laid low. Stayed unnoticed and unquestioned. I just hung out with my friends, and stayed in the castle walls where only the occasional servant or guard would see me—and we weren't too concerned about them. But . . . I have to admit, I felt like some of them were watching me. A glance here and whisperings there got me pretty on edge, and I stopped whatever I was doing and left the room a few times when I felt certain I was being spied on. I didn't tell Arnet, though. I mean, I had no proof. But that didn't make me any less careful.

At least I finally had time to spend with my friends. Not all of them though. With the heightened security, Blue hadn't been able to sneak in the past few nights. I hoped he'd find a way soon, but until then, I made the most of my time with the others.

"So, wait. Explain cars again," Robert said one night at the campfire. He absorbed my words, trying to imagine the object I described as he munched on a drumstick.

"Okay, they're like this," I said. "They're shaped like a rectangular box and really big," I saw a large bush at the edge of the cobblestones and pointed, "like that." After my friends took in the size of cars, I continued, "They have chairs that you sit on inside of it, and glass for windows. The windows go all around the thing, so you can see from anywhere inside it."

Robert absentmindedly took a bite from his chicken as he stared into his imagination.

"To turn it on, you . . ."

Tucker interrupted for everyone, "What do mean, 'turn it on'?"

Oh. Hadn't thought of that. "Um . . . say it's dead. You um . . . put this key in the keyhole by the wheel and then it comes to life."

There was a wave of "Ohh"s, before Dare asked, "Which wheel?"

"Well, the . . ." then I paused, realizing they were thinking of some sort of wagon thing, which in a way cars are I suppose, but I should have thought to explain that differently too. "Oh, actually it's the wheel inside the car. You use it to steer the thing."

More confused understanding.

"You'd really just have to see it," I said before I thought twice, and I bit my tongue hard when it fell out.

But Robert just said, "Sure wish I could. Sounds *amazing*," before finishing off the last strings of chicken on the bone.

"Same here," Tucker said in the same wonder, probably thinking from an inventor's point of view.

FOR THE INTENDED

Lily and Dare said nothing, both in a distant world of thought.

I was reminded of how great my friends were constantly. It amazed me that they never, not once, even hinted that they wished to know where the portals to *The Outside* were. They never pushed for the secrets to finding them or made me feel guilty for not revealing them. Which, the more I thought about it, only made me feel guiltier. I almost shared several times, but I was hoping that all the excitement about *The Outside* would eventually fade and we would never bring it up again. Mentioning the portals would rekindle the flame.

I thought about re-describing the gas pedal, when Lily said with a surprisingly steely voice, "Well, I think it sounds dangerous." And I couldn't really tell, but it seemed as if she were glaring at Tucker as she said, "I bet there are plenty of accidents, aren't there?"

I studied her. *Wow! She is glaring at Tucker.*

Tucker wouldn't look back at her as he picked at his pile of peas. It was the first time that evening that I realized they hadn't sat together or said a single word to each other.

"Well . . . yeah," I said as I recalled hearing two men discussing it at a diner once. One was reading a newspaper and commented on the number of car accidents that year. But after detecting some sort of jab at Tucker and not understanding why yet, I simply said, "Yeah, I suppose so."

Her eyes narrowed, her sharp gaze still on Tucker. "And the animals there? What are they like?"

I didn't know why she was so curious all of the sudden but I considered it. *The Outside's* animals were pretty much like Edgeladine's, with a few species missing in each world. "Well, they're—" I began before she cut me off.

"Vicious, right?" I noticed for the first time her food remained untouched.

Why is she being like this? I said the next sentence slowly, "Yes, I . . . guess some of them are."

"And the people there?"

I thought about it. I had seen a lot of nice people, but unfortunately one time the portal had dropped me off at a bad place. It was a filthy city, with foreboding buildings that seemed tall as mountains which later I found out were skyscrapers. The sky looked clouded and colorless with thick gray smoke, and trash lay everywhere. The people were cold and hostile, and one night in a dark alleyway, I got into a fight that I don't like to recall, and I certainly wasn't going to then lest Tucker lose the argument. "They're just like us, besides their clothes and technology." After a brief moment of her breaking her stare to look at me, I realized that didn't answer her question. "Some are mean, some are nice. It depends on where you go," I said indifferently.

That sentence seemed to anger her, returning her piercing glare to Tucker, "Hmm . . . Well if you ask me, *The Outside* sounds like a perfectly horrid place. Full of dangers and things we don't know about. Edgeladine is certainly safer, wouldn't you say?" She asked it fast and airy.

Tucker rubbed his temples and closed his eyes, hunching over on his elbows. I knew then that it really was the aftermath of some big argument between them. I didn't want to make it worse for him, but I couldn't resist the urge to build off of Lily's perfect foundation. I'd been telling them about all the incredible things *The Outside* had, but she had just given me a chance to make it seem like an undesirable destination . . . something that had been in the back of my mind the whole time. "Definitely. While it seems pretty cool, there is plenty I don't know about it. Edgeladine's a *way* safer choice."

Again, my tongue slipped. *Why did I say the word* **choice?**

But it didn't matter because Lily stood abruptly, "You see? Anyone with any *logic* could see that." And then she stormed out of the clearing in the direction of the castle, brushing past Tucker in a cloud of anger.

Tucker just sighed, letting a glop of mashed potatoes fall from his upside-down fork.

There was an awkward silence until Robert couldn't take it anymore. "Well, I don't know about you guys, but I'm going to bed." Robert and Dare, who had been sitting together, stood at the same time, Robert saying, "I think Arnet's making some schedule changes, and I think it involves an early morning. So, I guess we'll see you guys tomorrow. Night, Galayne." He turned to Tucker who was still slumped on a boulder, "Night, Tuck."

Robert's back was to me, but he must've made some sort of face at Tucker or mouthed a word, because Tucker's face went from an exhausted smile as he looked up at Robert, to an annoyed glare.

Robert faced me for a second as he grabbed his sword, an amused grin on his face. I had a feeling the two were also sharing in some conversation of earlier, and Robert was making fun of something that had been said. "Okay, guys," he half laughed, "See ya."

"Night, guys." I said simply.

Then he and Dare left, leaving me and Tucker alone.

It had been a few minutes already and Tucker hadn't stirred, and I wondered if maybe I should just go to bed too when he spoke up, "I guess I messed up, didn't I?"

I smiled a little, "Yeah, I suppose you did. What happened between you two?"

"I don't know. We were talking and then," he stabbed a piece of steak, "just like that, she's mad at me." He sounded tired, as if he'd tried to make it up several times, but his partner wouldn't hear it.

After a minute I asked, "What were you guys talking about?" I realized that could've been really rude and imposing, but I mean, Tucker and I having the relationship we had, it didn't feel like it.

To my surprise, his eyes narrowed slightly, and his grip on his fork tightened.

Whoa.

He pretended to think a second and said in his normal voice, his eyes softening, "I don't remember. Something about Spring Born practice."

I stayed quiet that time. I'd never seen Tucker like that—so tense, shutting me out. I instantly knew he was lying and it alarmed me. He'd never done that either.

After a few minutes of grasshoppers and fire cracklings, I said, standing up and brushing myself off, "Well, I should probably get to bed too. I—"

He had been picking at his food again when he looked up and cut me off, "Can I ask you something, Galayne?" His voice sounded quiet and gentle like usual.

It caught me off-guard, so I just said, "Yeah. Sure."

He put his plate off to the side, clasped his hands and looked down on them, "Now, I understand if you can't tell me. But being an inventor of sorts . . . I love to know how things work . . . and I can't help but wondering . . ."

I went and sat next to him. "Wondering what?"

He sighed and looked at me with hesitancy in his eyes. He bit his lip, and I began to get apprehensive for his next question, realizing what it might be. Suddenly he decided to get it out, "I was wondering where the *Doors* to *The Outside* are."

I must've had a great deal of shock on my face because he said quickly with a hint of apology, "It's okay, Galayne, you don't have to tell me."

I couldn't respond. I knew that's what he wanted to ask, but hearing it seemed to be a new step in the development of the fear I couldn't control.

"I'm sorry . . . it's just . . . I've been thinking about it a lot recently. I've wondered how no one else has ever seen them, and where they're hidden." His face filled with a happy sort of wonder as he stared off into space. His brown, puppy dog eyes filled with the stars above and were highlighted with the flickering flames.

He looked back at me and stifled his excitement, "Galayne, it's fine. I don't need to know. I—"

Suddenly my voice came from nowhere, breaking out of my tight throat, "No, it's okay. I'll show you."

"You will!?" He couldn't contain himself when I gave a small nod. Without a second to lose, he pulled a map from his satchel and a pang of sickness throbbed in my gut. *He's planned this.*

He kneeled on the stone path and unraveled it, spreading it out with his hands. He looked up expectantly as I went and knelt beside him. The voice curled right down from my mind and swirled around my stomach, *This is going too fast, think about it!* Before I gave myself the chance, I pointed out the three *Doors* I knew of. His eyes became distant and calculating which was concerning after the information I'd just shared.

He stayed in some far-off world when I stood up and broke his concentration, "And the reason no one ever finds them is because they move. At least every few months. But they're not scheduled to change for at least a few more weeks by Arnet's estimate."

His face contorted into some sort of amazed bafflement as he thought that over.

I stood there, exhausted. The secret was out. I reminded myself that it hadn't been mine to keep, but it didn't make me feel much better. I finally said, "Well, I'm going to bed now, I—"

He stood in a second, arms around me, "Thanks, Galayne," true appreciation in his voice.

I hugged him back, "You're welcome." And I meant it, but not entirely.

He stopped hugging me and rolled up the map, tucking it into his bag which he swung up onto his back. He grinned, his tired mood of earlier nowhere to be seen. The argument with Lily seemed to have slipped right from his mind. "Can you get to your room yourself?"

Of course I could, but since the ball, he'd asked every night. "I'm fine," I smiled gently, holding back my uneasiness.

"Okay," he said, somewhat distracted as he looked up at the sky.

I began to walk off and realized he didn't follow. I turned, "You comin'?"

He was still looking up at the stars when he broke his gaze to look at me long enough to say, "Yeah, I will in a second. Goodnight, Galayne." After I told him, I figured he would've wanted to ask me all sorts of questions, but he seemed content as he stared into the great above. I guessed his mind already teemed with possibilities and he didn't need any more information to come to conclusions.

Since that seemed to be the end of the conversation, I walked into the darkness, beyond the rim of light. After a few steps, I stopped again. Though I didn't know why, I inched around campfire's radius and stopped to observe him without fear of detection.

He stared at the moon for a while until he broke into a large grin, his eyes looking almost insane. After a moment, he hefted the pack on his back and I saw that he said something to himself, but I stood too far away to hear it. Then he walked in the direction of the castle, fading into the dark gardens.

I wish I could have known. I wish I would've read the warning signs in his behavior. His eyes, filled with that crazy determination, should have been enough. I should have seen it coming...

The next morning, I woke up before dawn and, not really wanting to try for the extra sleep I'd recently been allowed to have, I dressed.

I thought I'd go riding that day. The weather felt perfect, and it was as if the sun, the grassy plains, and the gushes of wind were calling me. Not to mention the strange new telepathic ability that had been slowly unfolding over the months was pretty strong by then. So when I say calling, I mean literally. It not only allowed me to enjoy nature on a new level, but it allowed me to feel certain emotions from my animal friends. And the emotion I detected constantly from Caspian, Elon, and Drayla, was longing. We hadn't had much time together since I was confined to the castle's walls. I was ready to be out of them again. I planned on asking for Arnet's permission to go for a ride, trying to further his trust.

While I double tied my laces, I made up my mind on something that had bothered me all night. Tossing and turning in bed, I thought about all that I had revealed to Tucker. After the nervousness of that, a new feeling of guilt mounded up in me. I couldn't tell just Tucker, I'd have to tell all of them. And after thinking that over a bit, I decided I'd tell Lily first. I mean, she would figure out I'd told Tucker sooner or later, and I wanted the information to come from me.

I grabbed my sword—which I had been trying my best to keep with me at all times since previous problems I'd faced because of its absence—and strode to Lily's room. I thought I would invite her to a walk around the castle. I used to do walks a lot with her, so I thought picking up the old habit might make her less mad at me for telling Tucker first. I mean, *if* she was mad. Because of the night before, I wasn't sure how she would respond. But I wanted to do it anyway; I felt that I needed to. I hadn't spent much one on one time with any of my friends lately, and I thought it was time to pick up my previous meetings with each of them.

I walked right into her room and made straight for the washstand. The sunlight had just started to shine in through her window, warm and gold. "Morning, Lily!" My back was to her as I filled her washbasin like I used to, but I could tell she hadn't stirred from her sitting position on the bed, her legs and nightgown pouring over the side. "I thought we could go for a walk this morning. I have something to tell you."

No response.

I put her washcloth to the side of the basin, saying with a small laugh, "If we hurry, we could maybe beat the others to breakfast, and finally get some bacon for once."

Silence.

I didn't notice though, and I turned to go to her wardrobe to pick an outfit for her, when I froze. I drained of my happy mood as I looked at her and whispered, "Lily?"

There she was, as lovely as ever even though she'd just wakened. But she wouldn't look at me, her face pale. She looked down on a piece of unfolded parchment, but I couldn't make out her expression as her beautiful locks fell in front of her face. She stayed still until a few moments later she raised her head, and my heart throbbed, and the air caught in my throat. Fear, shock, betrayal—all of these were magnified a hundred times over on her face, crushing her, stopping her breathing. She seemed out of our world and in another of complete sorrow. Large tears rimmed her once cheerful, blue eyes.

"Lily?" I choked out once more.

It was as if she was looking at me, but she wasn't. Distracted, she slowly turned away, the parchment slipping from her hands. It floated gracefully, doing delicate somersaults in the air until it landed softly on the stone floor. The sun licked the shiny black ink . . . right down to Tucker's signature.

FOR THE INTENDED

SHATTERED

I pounded down the castle hall, heart throbbing, eyes blurring with hot tears. Moments before, I'd snatched up the letter and tried to read it despite my panicked disbelief. I had tried to preserve their privacy by skipping over the intimate parts, while my eyes fell on other words like "I have to go," "my quest for you," and "*The Outside.*"

With a growl and the gritting of my teeth, and the panic and confusion turning into self-loathing and understanding, I didn't notice as the paper turned into a crinkled ball in my clenched grip. It returned to its place on the floor as I dashed from the room.

I made my way for the pastures. In all the chaos running through my body, the questioning emotions from Drayla and Caspian came. I'd never tried calling with my own feelings to something else before, and I wasn't sure how to do it, but I screamed in my mind, *Drayla! I need you!* Instantly, I felt as though something were swirling inside of me, and I lost my bearings for a second as I braced against a wall. I took a jagged gasp from the running and the attempt; it had taken more energy than I would've thought, but then again, it was my first try. I didn't know if my message had been received, though, until a faint affirmation came from Drayla. I took off again, shaking and cold, but still able to manage a sprint.

She was with Caspian, waiting at the gate, stamping her feet with impatience. The closer I got, the more I could feel the uncertainty rising up in both of them.

"What?! What is it?!" She asked as I immediately jumped on her back and flung open the gate.

"What's going on?!" Caspian added, "She hasn't told me a thing!" His mental presence was stronger, and I was sure it was because of our Nightlar Bond. I could feel his mind start to enter my own, but I shut it out abruptly.

"*Go!*" I yelled, and no one argued.

It'd been only a few seconds before I realized I was digging my heels into Drayla's side and jerking her reins in the direction of the nearest portal as she galloped along, and I had a brief moment to step back. I hadn't told them anything and the way I was treating Drayla was unacceptable. My anxious thoughts were rushing back into my mind, though, so when I tried to make up for it, all that happened was a loosened grip and, "Tucker's in trouble! We need to get to him before the *Door* closes behind him!"

Caspian looked up at me in disbelief as he skimmed along beside us, "You told him?!"

Drayla stayed silent, but I knew she disagreed with that decision.

"Yes, I told him!" I snapped, totally not myself. I wanted to say something else when a shout came up from the castle in the distance, and a new thought came. "Caspian, I need you to go tell Arnet! Let him know where I'm going!"

"But I—"

I turned for a second to pierce him with my fiery, green eyes, "*Now!*"

His eyes narrowed as his mouth opened without words, and then I heard a low growl before he wheeled around and shot off in the opposite direction. Drayla gave her all, even though I knew she was furious with my behavior. With everything going through my head, that seemed to be the least of my worries. I'd just apologize later.

FOR THE INTENDED

Despite the determination of before, on the journey to the woods I lost all my anger and heat and had to struggle to keep a hold of myself. I shook uncontrollably, wanting to just break down into a million pieces and sink beneath the ground; alone, forgotten, a big mound of nothing. My biggest fear had just come true—the fear that had been with me since before I even knew about the portals. I could've just lost my brother, and the pain brought up more hurt from my past, but my memories wouldn't say why. They were a murky cloud of doubt and despair.

When I broke from a deep trance, we were in the woods. Drayla maintained a gallop only occasionally, but most of the time was limited to a small canter, making me squirm with panic. *This isn't fast enough*, I thought. *He could be gone already!*

We were getting to the denser part of the forest when Drayla halted. "I can't get through; it's much too thick here." She began to walk to the right, "I'll go along the perimeter until—"

I slung off her back and dashed between the close trees as fast as I could, knowing the portal was somewhere near in all the mess. Somewhere in my desperation I heard her calling after me, but it sounded faint compared to my screaming thoughts of Tucker.

I tore past bushes, briars, and tripped on rocks. The darkness of the forest didn't help much. I got cut up and slapped by various branches as I went along and kept bruising myself on protruding roots. I knew I was only feet away when it happened; The burst of white light as Tucker left the world shot out in rays where it could—only a few trees away.

"Tucker!" I shrieked, and plunged through the underbrush into a small, open glen. There was an impenetrable—but normal looking—wall of trees in front of me, but no Tucker. I sunk to my knees in total defeat.

Drayla burst into the clearing, angry and seething, "I told you to wait!" She was bleeding on her left shoulder, probably from charging after me right into the branches, thinking I'd leave Edgeladine without her. She was about to go on some angry rant when she realized where we were, and who wasn't there, and her anger subsided with one long sigh. She walked up to me and nuzzled my arm apologetically, knowing what Tucker's absence meant. It meant that we couldn't just go in and get him. That would stress the portal, and anyone within a thirty-foot radius could be instantly vaporized. We had to wait for it to recharge, and if we waited too long, the portal could move, making it nearly impossible for Tucker ever to find one again.

   Somehow, Drayla had gotten me on her back, and we were walking up to the garden's entrance. I was constantly in and out of reality on the ride. It's funny when your worst fear happens—it's not like you'd expect. Once the emotions come and go, you're left with a sort of emptiness; a dreary bleakness of failure rimmed with only a trace of previous excitement and terror. My thoughts went like this: *Tucker... It's chilly... Tucker... The clouds are gray... I've lost him... The castle... It's all my fault.*

   Drayla clopped down the gray stones toward the dying campfire, past the shadowy trees and faded flowers. I saw people gathered around it; Robert, Arnet, Dare, Caspian, and a couple of guards discussing something hurriedly with tension.

   Drayla broke into the circle and everyone silenced instantly, eyes on me. I slid off, not able to make eye contact with anyone, and murmured, "He's gone."

   No one moved. No one spoke. But it wasn't necessary. Everyone felt the same as I did. Wait no, was that possible? I didn't think so. No one could miss Tucker the way I did. No one could feel the anger—the emptiness—that his absence brought. No one could feel the despair of knowing Tucker's disappearance from the world, was all on their shoulders.

   Arnet was about to say something when the person we were all dreading burst from a side door, calling over and over again with a crazed tone, "Tucker! Tucker?!" Lily's shock of earlier had disappeared and she'd entered the emotional tornado I'd just escaped. She was followed by three concerned maids, one of them Milly, trying to calm her down. They were saying comforting things, and trying to usher her back to the safeness of the castle; the place where she wouldn't be able to see that Tucker wasn't with me—the place where she wouldn't be able to realize that Tucker wasn't coming home.

She stood in the middle of all of us, turning frantically about until after about four full turns, she realized. Milly was in silent tears, and no one had the heart to move, to do anything. Lily faced me, and I stared at her as I watched her face morph into one of confusion, then shock, then a horrible face I can't describe. She lunged at me, pinning me to a tree. Perfect nails digging into my shoulders, she screamed, "Why did you tell him?!"

I couldn't move or breathe.

She looked ready to commit murder when several people tore her from me while she shrieked and clawed. I stayed frozen, my eyes wide as I watched them lead her away to her chamber. I whispered, "I'm sorry. I'm . . ."

As I neared my room I could hear Lily still going in the next room over. Since the ball, I had been moved next to Lily so I'd have a source of comfort. But once everyone realized I was half the cause of her tantrums, they immediately recommended we be separated. But I couldn't move for fear of the spies, and nobody even considered moving Lily. Not at that time.

I heard the maids pleading with her, but she was in a desperate state that I knew too well. I walked into my room and bolted the door, but it didn't help—the walls weren't thick enough. I heard Milly mumble something, but instead of making it better Lily yelled, "Get out!" Then she shrieked again more despairingly, "*Get out!*"

I heard the maids tumble out of her room while Milly said, "Bolt it!"

I heard the door shut abruptly while Lily threw things against it, the outside bolt sliding into place.

"There's no use," I heard Milly mutter sadly. "Poor dear." Then I heard them making their way down the hall until they were gone and all that was left was Lily's weeping.

I walked over to our adjoining wall and slid down against it, able to hear her clearly. I don't know how long I sat there, listening to her outbursts of sorrow for Tucker and rage directed at me, but the moon was high when I came out of a trance that had lasted hours.

Lily's dinner was in the middle of being delivered. I listened closely, noticing Lily was more controlled. By her voice, she was exhausted, but was collected enough to say please and thank you. The person who brought her food sounded as if they were about to go, when all of the sudden Lily's manners were gone as she asked abruptly, "What's that?"

"What? This?" I heard the girl say with a voice I'd never heard. She was probably new, a person Lily wouldn't know—a person Lily would have no cause to be upset over.

"Yes, that."

"It's a flower, miss. My Johnny gives one to me every morning. I always have one in my hair," she giggled, completely oblivious to Lily's painful thoughts.

In the tense silence that followed, I could practically see Lily's hand go up to brush the flower hairpin above her ear, the one that had never left its place since Tucker had put it there.

Then there was an explosive shriek, bringing a third, "*Get out!*"

The maid scrambled for the door which shut right after her.

Lily was throwing things, one after the other; Wood things, candles, and pillows which thumped on the walls, until she found it; the one vase the maids forgot or didn't have time to rid the room of.

I wasn't expecting it as glass shattered inches from my head on the other side of the wall. The barrier didn't matter; I felt as though I'd been hit by every single shard. Each piece signified defeat, despair, sorrow, emptiness, failure—all of those had pierced me right through, right to my inmost being...

FOR THE INTENDED

GOING HOME

It was a watch and wait game. No one could go after Tucker except me, and I didn't think Arnet would let me go. But either way I didn't ask. What was the point? I could be transported anywhere in *The Outside*, and I couldn't be certain it'd be by Tucker's drop-off point. Plus, as the due date for the portals to move neared, I doubted Arnet would even consider it.

So, we all watched, and waited, and listened, and lost hope each day. Every time we heard that someone was approaching the front gate, we'd all go running towards it, only to be dreadfully disappointed at the sight of some traveler.

The emptiness and failure didn't leave me, but the shakiness did. I became stronger and more in control of my thoughts, though the weight of Tucker's disappearance only grew. But thankfully that only increased my will to get him back.

Lily, after a few days, ran out of tears. She became dry and vacant. She talked to nobody and I heard she just sat on her bed without eating or drinking, staring at the stones in her wall. Of course, I never got to see her myself since I got banned from that section of the castle due to her previous explosion. Arnet thought the threat of spies had died down enough for me to move to one of the castle towers. Yeah, yeah, I know; "Once upon a time there was a fair princess high in her tower," but it wasn't like that at all. I moved to one of the shorter, older side towers of the castle as a precaution. It wasn't the main one in the center of the fortress, and it certainly wasn't the elegant place you hear about in some story books. Dark, hot in the day, cold at night, and far from most of the life in the castle, it seemed more like a prison. But given the circumstances, it was just what I needed. It gave me space, quiet, and time alone to formulate a plan to save Tucker.

I had just spent hours thinking about it one night, when a black blur swooped in through my window and landed softly on the floor.

"Hey, I see you've been . . ." Blue began with a smile, hands on hips, but after looking around the room his face cringed, "You know I was going to say 'upgraded,' but now . . ."

I smiled a little, "It's temporary."

He came and bounced into the spot next to me on the bed, "Oh, good. 'Cause I was like, what in the world did . . . you . . . Galayne?" He realized I wasn't listening to him.

My attention had drifted from him back to a list I'd made of things I could do to get Tucker.

1. *Wait.* (I hated that one.)
2. *Go after Tucker and don't tell the others.*
3. *Ask Arnet's permission and then go get him*

Before I'd realized I was writing a fourth option, it was already there.

4. *Lose him forever . . .* then some angry scribble marks.

Blue snatched the paper away, but I made no attempt to stop him. His eyes skimmed it over quickly and he stood, smile gone. "Galayne, where's Tucker?" He tried to keep his voice calm, but the brotherly alarm was rising.

I sighed, not wanting to say it again, but managed, "He's *Outside.*" I knew he'd be upset, but I never expected what came next.

He whirled on me, shouting, "What?! You *told him*?! You didn't tell *me*, but you told *Tucker*! What were you thinking?!" His blue eyes were clouding.

I gaped.

"You're always so hasty! Constantly running into things! You never think! You're just—"

I stood abruptly, putting my face inches from his, our eyes meeting in a fierce lock of blue and green.

He began to pace back and forth, breathing hard.

A new thought came to mind. "Wait a second... what do you mean 'didn't tell you'?! I tried! *You* wouldn't listen! *And you*..." I snarled, "Where were you? You disappeared for a week! You could have stopped Tucker before he got there!"

He stopped pacing, "*Well, I wouldn't have told him in the first place!*" He hissed back. "And I didn't leave by choice! But you can't seem to wrap your mind around that!"

"Okay, *fine*! But you could have at least told me where you went! You leave without warning, and I have no way of finding you! You—"

"Look, Galayne, it's fine!" He said loudly to overcome my words, trying to conceal how badly he didn't want to talk about life outside the castle. When I died down, he came over and said quietly, "It's fine. Fighting over it won't help. We just need to get him back." I didn't reply while I tried to forget my anger, so he said, "What's the plan?"

I could tell he was still upset, confused, and afraid just like the rest of us, but he always had the most amazing ability to cover it up. But he was angry... really angry; angry that I told Tucker about the portals and the fact that he wasn't the first to know. I remembered the time when I almost told him, around eleven years old. I remembered how telling him about *The Outside* wasn't like trying to tell the others, and I didn't even hesitate. But not long after I started, he interrupted me...

We were busy moving grain from the side of a barn, and were momentarily alone. Feeling like it was the right time, I began to tell him about the portals but he immediately cut me off.

"No, Galayne."

Surprised, I stopped lifting my sack. "What?"

"Don't tell me." He hefted his load to a hay bale, pausing to gather his strength.

I thought about it a second before asking, "Why?"

He smiled his famous smile, "It's better if I don't know." And then he went into the barn, leaving me very confused.

And that was it. He never asked me, and I never tried to tell him again. He should've let me tell him then. I'd had years to hoard over the secret and think about the effects of its reveal, and then *experience* the effects of its reveal. Blue had grown too mysterious . . . I wouldn't know how he'd handle the information . . . and I couldn't lose him too.

So, he wasn't the only one who was glad to move onto another topic. "Okay," I said plainly, and walked over and sat on my bed. I unrolled the map and began contemplating. Blue came and leaned against my bedpost, hovering over me, but after a few hours we momentarily forgot that we were mad at each other, and he eventually ended up sitting next to me, giving input where it was needed.

Hours later, he stood up and walked over to the window again. My eyes were saggy and sore, but I couldn't stop pouring over our sheets of ideas. We hadn't decided on any of the elaborate plans to get him back. Some were outrageously risky, like bringing the others out with me to search, or using my powers to search out Tucker's lifeform. By the way, my lifeform-finder power was still developing, so it could've proven fatal.

I suddenly realized the sun was rising, but I didn't have to see the sun or the brightening sky to know—I felt it. I wasn't outwardly angry anymore and said calmly, "You should go."

He nodded and leaped into a crouching position on the windowsill. I skimmed over the sheets again. It had been a few minutes, but he still hadn't left. He was watching the world waking up. I was beginning to wonder why he was still there, and was getting a little agitated because it was about to be dangerous for him to leave, when I realized what it was he wanted. I thought about it, and then decided, "I'm going. *Outside*. I'm gonna go get him."

He didn't move, "You gonna tell Arnet?" His voice was calm and distant.

I paused, "Yes." I couldn't afford to lose Arnet's trust again.

"Bringing anyone else?"

I didn't have to think on that one, "No." That had been the plan he'd suggested, and though I hadn't said it out loud, I had rejected it instantly.

He simply nodded but didn't take off. What was he waiting on?

I began to clean up all the papers and the quill and ink jar, when finally, he just asked, "Hey, Galayne?"

I turned, but he still wasn't looking at me—his gaze was fixed out that window. "Yeah?"

"If I asked where the portals are now . . . would you tell me?" His dark hair tossed gently in the morning breeze, and his feathers ruffled. For whatever reason, he looked seven years old again—crouching in the bushes to hide from monsters.

I took a deep breath . . . "No." It was plain and definite.

He scoffed, as if he'd expected as much. And then he took off, gliding away from my room and our previous relationship . . .

I took a nap all day long—frustrated, upset, and as agitated as ever. I packed everything I thought I'd need for the trip, but it wasn't much. I didn't want to appear different in *The Outside*, or people would start to ask questions. That's why swords, bows, daggers, armor, cloaks, horses, wolves, and overly tamed birds weren't allowed. Meaning, everything that could comfort me outside of Edgeladine wouldn't be there, including my animal friends. I put on the nearest thing to pants and a t-shirt I could find, and a pair of leather sandals. I put my hair in a ponytail down my back and slung something close enough to a backpack over my shoulder. After being around Edgeladine's finest fashion for so long, all I could think of was how ridiculous I looked.

I thought over Blue's question when I went down for dinner. I was early and glad of it because it turned out to be the opportune moment. There was Arnet, all alone, stirring the soup with a large scoop at the campfire in the gardens.

"Hello, Galayne," he said when he spotted me from the corner of his eye, "I thought you wouldn't be—" Then he saw what I was wearing and the determined look on my face. "Galayne?" he asked firmly.

I stopped right in front of him. "Arnet, I have to. The portal is moving in less than three weeks... I've got to get him before that happens."

He sighed and put the scoop back, closing the lid gently. He crossed his arms, but said quite coolly, "I agree."

My face must've revealed my surprise. I'd thought I could convince him it was right, but I never thought he'd agree with me so easily. But I could see his hesitancy, and I knew he hated the idea. I almost didn't like his compliancy... It reminded me of all the officials who would let me get away with things just because I was The Summer Born. Was he... scared that I would leave anyway? Or that I would be mad if he didn't let me go? I mean I would, but... I didn't want him to be afraid of me like so many other people were.

He woke me from my thoughts when he acknowledged my supplies and asked, "Is Winlit Cordial with you?"

I felt the large silver pendant dangling close to my chest where it always was. "Yes."

"Going alone?"

"Yes."

"Good. It seems you're ready. The only thing you must realize is that I'm not even sure if we have three weeks. I would set your trip to a limit of two weeks just to be safe."

My heart sunk. Would that be enough time?

FOR THE INTENDED

He turned me around and started stuffing muffins into my pack for dinner and a later snack, "I would hurry... before dark you will want to have reached the *Door*, and hopefully even before that." When all the muffins that could fit were in my pack, he turned me back around, put his hands on my shoulders and said, "Promise me you'll be back in two weeks—that you won't wait any longer than that."

Though I didn't like it, I said, "I will."

He nodded, but still eyed me as he went back to the soup, as if he were reconsidering the plan.

I decided that was all I needed, so I nodded and started to walk away quickly. I hadn't gotten far when a new thought came, "Oh, Arnet?"

He had started to ladle the soup into bowls, acting as if the previous conversation hadn't happened, "Yes?"

"Don't tell the others... at least not yet." I began to feel homesick before I even left. "And make sure Drayla stays here." She'd follow me. I was sure.

He nodded firmly, "I will."

That settled it. I was officially ready to leave. I'd packed everything I needed, been given needed instruction, and left needed instructions for those I was leaving behind. And even though I felt sick with worry, and already knew I'd miss my home, I had such determination that nothing could break. So, I began to march down the stone path to the end of the gardens and the front gate, sure that everything would be alright.

I'd only taken a few steps, and was really getting into my adventurous mood, when Arnet's voice came from behind, "Galayne?"

I turned, "Yeah?"

His face was dead serious, and his tone even more so, "If you don't find him before the two weeks are up... *leave him*."

I couldn't speak, so I turned and dashed. I ran all the way to the front gate and right through it. I pounded down the castle's hill and into the meadow, running on and on in the direction of the portal.

I made it there before dark with some time to spare. I guess Arnet didn't plan on me running most of the way. But I had shoved and kicked my way through the brush twenty minutes before sunset, and just stood in front of the *Door*, staring. I was breathing hard, but I didn't think it was from the run.

Tucker had gone through those gnarled, twisted branches, into the world beyond . . . I stared at the *Door* angrily—unjustly blaming it for all my current problems before I realized I'd wasted fifteen minutes doing so. It was time to get a move on.

"Okay, *Door*," I grumbled. I slung my pack off my back and grabbed a muffin from it, "I'm going to walk through you, and you are going to drop me off in the right place." I took a huge bite out of the tiny muffin and mumbled through it, "Got that?"

The door must've had a sense of humor because it glowed faintly around the edges, almost as if saying, "We'll see."

My mood soured even more. I hefted my pack, "Alright, I'm ready."

It glowed brighter with a whirring sound, the energy surging through it. I had waited six days since Tucker left, and that seemed to have been enough time for it to recharge.

I shoved the muffin in my mouth. I prepared myself to march through the *Door* when I almost choked. A surge of clouded memories and painful events I couldn't make out assaulted my mind.

The door's light temporarily faded.

I swallowed my muffin without thinking as I tried to regain myself. The past swirled in front of my eyes, but it was awful to once again realize it was indistinguishable. Just fragments of Christmas, brownish-blue eyes, and my mother. The portal pulsated, unsure as me if I wanted to leave or not.

Finally, after a few minutes of recovery, I stood straighter. I gripped my backpack's straps, forgetting the murky memories as best I could, but they still whirled about inside of me. I swallowed hard and whispered angrily, "Take me home."

FOR THE INTENDED

The portal suddenly burst with light, glowing brighter and brighter by the second, and the whirring became a constant, high-pitched buzz. The light slowly engulfed me, and when it did, I was transported back to my real homeland.

Haven Berg

Be sure to get all the books in the series!

For the Intended is available as paperback, hardcover, ebook, and audiobook on Amazon!

Want to Support FTI?

- Please consider leaving your honest review on Amazon. Haven loves to read them!

- If you would like, take a picture with this book and post it with **#fortheintended**

- If you want, leave your mark in the front of this book and pass it on!

- Post your fan art on social media with **#ftifanart**

- You can purchase FTI merchandise at **fortheintended.com/shop/**

- You can follow Haven **@havenillustrates** and visit her websites **fortheintended.com** and **havenillustrates.com**

FOR THE INTENDED

@havenillustrates

Haven Berg began writing *For the Intended* at twelve years old and published it seven years later at the age of nineteen. Creating the series became a coping mechanism, as Haven struggled with obsessive-compulsive disorder and anxiety throughout her school years. The main character in *For the Intended*, Galayne, experiences related challenges and strives to overcome them. Haven hopes that *For the Intended* will not only be a portal to a new world for all its readers but also help those struggling with mental health. She lives in North Georgia and looks forward to imagining new worlds for years to come.

havenillustrates.com

Made in the USA
Monee, IL
28 April 2026

49136207R00156